Ghost Times Two

Ghost Times Two

Carolyn Hart

BERKLEY PRIME CRIME
New York

BERKLEY PRIME CRIME
Published by Berkley
An imprint of Penguin Random House LLC
375 Hudson Street, New York, New York 10014

Copyright © 2016 by Carolyn Hart

Library of Congress Cataloging-in-Publication Data

Names: Hart, Carolyn G., author.
Title: Ghost times two / Carolyn Hart.
Description: First edition. | New York : Berkley Prime Crime, 2016. | Series: A Bailey Ruth ghost novel ; 4
Identifiers: LCCN 2016017638 (print) | LCCN 2016024238 (ebook) | ISBN 9780425283738 (hardcover) | ISBN 9780698411531 (ebook)
Subjects: LCSH: Women detectives—Fiction. | Mediums—Fiction. | Spirits—Fiction. | Murder—Investigation—Fiction. | BISAC: FICTION / Mystery & Detective / Women Sleuths. | GSAFD: Mystery fiction. | Ghost stories.
Classification: LCC PS3558.A676 G525 2016 (print) | LCC PS3558.A676 (ebook) | DDC 813/.54—dc23
LC record available at https://lccn.loc.gov/2016017638

First Edition: October 2016

Printed in the United States of America
1   3   5   7   9   10   8   6   4   2

Cover art by Emily Osborne
Cover design by Jason Gill
Book design by Laura K. Corless

To Jim and Susan Warram with great affection

Ghost Times Two

Chapter 1

A bright yellow sheet, eight inches wide, six and one-half inches deep, sprouted in my right hand. Excitement propelled me from a hammock strung between two thirty-foot-tall palms. I luxuriated in the warmth of soft white sand beneath my bare feet. Out in tranquil translucent water Bobby Mac completed a cast from the deck of the *Serendipity*, our cabin cruiser. Perfect beauty on a perfect day.

If that sounds idyllic, Heaven provides every pleasure. Whatever vista we most enjoy, there we are. Steep slopes with fresh snow, a bustling visit to a Heavenly Harrods (oh my, that royal blue body-sculpted sleeveless knit dress), reverie in dappled shade beneath live oak trees. Or perhaps it is conversation you enjoy; Dorothy Parker's wit is always pointed and poignant, Abigail Adams's pithy comments intrigue, Socrates provides gentle queries.

Eagerly I scanned the telegram: *Come soonest. Spectral scandal brewing. Wiggins*

I waggled the telegram to catch my husband's attention. Braced against the pull of a fish, Bobby Mac shouted, "Wiggins? Good for you. Have fun."

A summons from Wiggins. What could be more Heavenly?

Telegram in the age of digital connections? Heavenly? Dorothy Parker? Abigail Adams? Socrates? Wiggins? Perhaps I should explain. If we haven't met before, I am Bailey Ruth Raeburn, late of Adelaide, Oklahoma. Late as in *deceased*. Late as in *dearly departed*. Late ever since Bobby Mac and I went down to the depths when a storm struck the Gulf and sank the *Serendipity*. If contemplating spirits and Heaven makes you uneasy, it isn't my intention to distress you. Unequivocally real are a pump jack's rhythmic chug as it pulls oil to the surface, a moose on a hillside, bacteria in a petri dish. Equally real are gossamer thoughts, the caress of a breeze, the memory of a kiss. From there, the imaginative understand there are dimensions beyond the material world.

That's where I come in. Or from. I am pleased to inform you that I have the honor to serve as an emissary from Heaven's Department of Good Intentions, returning to earth to help someone in trouble.

Do I sense amusement? A dismissal of the possibility of Heaven? Pause, please. Recall an instant when joy suffused you. Perhaps you heard a haunting melody or someone you loved stepped into the room or dawn splashed the sky with red and orange. You've experienced moments of transcendent glory that can never be described or explained. For a quivering, unforgettable instant, you knew beauty in your soul. Well, my dears, that is Heaven.

As for the Department of Good Intentions, come with me.

Travel in Heaven is as quick as the thought. I wished to be at the Department of Good Intentions. I was there. I walked up a wide path toward a small redbrick country train station, circa 1910. Wiggins, who runs the department, was a stationmaster in life and chose a train station to dispatch Heavenly emissaries to earth.

A gentle breeze stirred my red curls. I knew my freckle-spattered face was alight with happiness. I looked my best in a brightly patterned sarong blouse and white Bermuda shorts. My pace slowed. Wiggins is a fine man, but rather formal. I learned his first name in my most recent visit to earth, but I would never presume to address him as Paul. Wiggins he is and Wiggins he remains, a man of his time in a high-collared white shirt, heavy gray flannel trousers supported by both suspenders and a wide black belt, sturdy black leather shoes. Arm garters puff his shirtsleeves between shoulder and elbow. He wears a stiff dark cap unless seated at his desk, where he dons a green eyeshade. Wiggins is always warm and welcoming, but he has a somewhat unrealistic view—at least to me—of the qualities he expects from the agents he dispatches. He envisions emissaries who excel in decorum and restraint and, of course, modesty in dress.

I do not excel in decorum, restraint, or modesty in dress. Oh fudge. To be absolutely honest—a Heavenly requisite—I have been known to belt out "Come On-a My House" in a loud soprano while tap-dancing in a décolleté spangle-spattered midthigh red chiffon cocktail dress. Heaven encourages us to be the best we ever were, and I am partial to a rollicking twenty-seven, which was a very good year for me. I'm a flaming redhead, narrow face with curious green eyes, freckles, and a willingness to smile.

I looked at my reflection in a crystal column. Were the cerise and crimson in my sarong blouse too much? Wiggins doesn't understand how the right outfit makes a woman feel on top of the world, which can be quite an aid in a tough situation on earth. I like dramatic colors. I adore short skirts. (Who doesn't have good legs at twenty-seven?) Shoes can be a glorious adventure. I looked down at red leather sandals adorned with delicate white shells.

. . . decorum, modesty, restraint . . .

With a sigh, I watched my image transform in the crystal. As with traveling from one point to another, a change in appearance occurs immediately. Instead of the brightly patterned sarong blouse and Annapolis white shorts (who's cuter than a sailor in bell-bottom whites?), a long, bilious green dress drooped over dull green moccasins. I shuddered. There was a limit. Modest white sandals replaced the moccasins.

I clutched the long skirt, held it aloft, couldn't resist a ruffled white petticoat, and rushed up the path and the steps to the station. I hurried through the waiting room. Travelers of all descriptions occupied the wooden benches: a bearded monk with a staff; a young woman in a WWI Red Cross nurse uniform; a Roman matron; a cowboy in a Stetson, white shirt, black vest, stiff denim trousers, and boots; a flapper in a beaded dress; a farmer in a heavy flannel shirt, coveralls, and earth-stained work boots; a broad-faced, heavy-set financier in a Savile Row suit and homburg, hands folded atop a malacca cane.

I passed through the door marked *Station Agent*. Wiggins sat at a sturdy golden oak desk that faced the platform. Through a broad window, he could see shining tracks that wound into the sky. A telegraph sounder rested to the left of a heavy manila folder.

At the sound of my steps, Wiggins swung around in his swivel chair, came to his feet. "Bailey Ruth." He removed his green eyeshade. He strode toward me, reddish hair thick and unruly, walrus mustache magnificent, broad face smiling, hands outstretched. "You came at once."

"Of course." I resisted the impulse to stand stiffly and salute. There is something about Wiggins . . .

He stopped and looked down at me.

♫

I saw the usual register of emotions he displayed upon my arrival, whether responding to a summons or volunteering my assistance, affection mixed with apprehension, admiration diluted by wariness.

He cleared his throat. "Harrumph."

Honestly, that's what Wiggins often says, *harrumph*.

I resisted the impulse to serenade him with "(Ghost) Riders in the Sky." Wiggins takes great pride in the Rescue Express and abhors the term *ghost*. Wiggins insists that those he dispatches are Heavenly emissaries. That's all very well and good, but I know a cabbage when I see a cabbage, a love song when the violins play, and cashmere when I touch it. A spirit returning to earth, even if well intentioned, is a ghost.

"Ghost," he blurted.

Startled, I blurted in return, "Ghost?" Was he reading my mind? That simply isn't done in Heaven. Private thoughts, though hopefully sacred and not profane, are private thoughts.

He began to pace, broad face furrowed in frustration. "Not acceptable. Irresponsible." A rueful smile tugged at his generous mouth. "I can't say I don't understand." He swung toward me. "That's why I sent for you."

This did not sound promising.

"True love," he said, his voice gentle, "never ends." A huge sigh. "You know how I feel about Precept Two."

I didn't see a connection between true love and Precept Two, but I certainly was well aware of his feelings about Precept Two. I hastened to reassure him, my voice earnest, one hand squarely above my heart. "Far be it from me to ever willingly"—strong emphasis on *willingly*—"consort with another departed spirit." I saw the modifier as my escape hatch. Of course, I wouldn't willingly collaborate with a departed spirit, but circumstances had been known to alter cases. In effect, a ghost will do what a ghost has to do. To underscore my total dedication to the Precepts, the rules for emissaries on a mission to earth, I stood straight and tall, recited the Precepts in my husky, carrying voice:

PRECEPTS FOR EARTHLY VISITATION

1. *Avoid public notice.*
2. *Do not consort with other departed spirits.*
3. *Work behind the scenes without making your presence known.*
4. *Become visible only when absolutely necessary.*
5. *Do not succumb to the temptation to confound those who appear to oppose you.*
6. *Make every effort not to alarm earthly creatures.*
7. *Information about Heaven is not yours to impart. Simply smile and say, "Time will tell."*
8. *Remember always that you are on the earth, not of the earth.*

I hoped my dramatic rendition and stalwart posture evoked an image of that hardy horseman galloping from Ghent to Aix. In the spirit of things, I swirled from the dull green dress to a cream turtleneck, tan jodhpurs, and glistening leather riding boots. What a relief.

Wiggins's mustache drooped. "I'm afraid"—his voice sounded as though it emanated from a deep well—"the Precepts—"

I could scarcely hear him.

His eyes stared as if into a gray distance. "—do not apply here. It grieves me to realize that my Precepts, so thoughtfully fashioned, so attuned to every temptation, are to no avail in this instance." Another heavy sigh. "That's why I summoned you."

I feared his admission was not a compliment. I decided to look on the bright side. Wiggins needed me. Yee-hah! "Wiggins"—I tried to keep the eagerness out of my voice—"I will do whatever the department commands."

He jammed a fist into the opposite palm. "That's the spirit."

For an instant, I was almost sure there was a twinkle in his spaniel brown eyes.

He strode decisively to the slotted rack on the wall near the ticket window, snatched a red ticket, gave it a stamp, and hurried toward me.

A clang of wheels against steel and a throaty whistle of a proud coal-puffing engine announced the imminent arrival of the Rescue Express, thundering down the line.

"Quick." He thrust the ticket at me. "Do what you can. He's an irrepressible young scamp. He simply must face up to Heaven. No matter how much—"

The scent of coal smoke. Whoo-whoo. I turned and dashed for the platform, thronged now with travelers.

Wiggins's voice carried over the rumbles and roars.

"—he loves her."

෭ඁ

Once I'd asked Wiggins why he didn't send me to Paris. He'd inquired, *How's your French?* I haven't given up hope that someday he may dispatch me to Greenwich Village (I've read about it and I can quote Dorothy Parker) or Vancouver (Bobby Mac and I holidayed there once) or even Tumbulgum (Wiggins left me blessedly unsupervised while dealing with a crisis in that tiny remote outpost in Australia). Until then, between us, I adore returning to Adelaide, where I grew up, fell in love, married, raised a family (daughter, Dil, and son, Rob), worked (English teacher until I flunked a football player and became secretary to the Chamber and oh, what I knew about everyone in town), and lived happily until our last voyage in the *Serendipity*. Adelaide is more prosperous than during my time, but it is still Adelaide, a beautiful small town in the rolling hills of south central Oklahoma. I know Adelaide inside and out and upside and down. I blinked against a glare from lake water as I swung off the caboose. A late-afternoon sun was bright as new copper in the western sky. I know the hot heavy heat of Oklahoma summers. The wise hunker down in air-conditioned offices, homes, or cars. They do not choose to stand in boiling heat on the old wooden pier in Adelaide's White Deer Park.

I shaded my eyes and saw the exception to the rule. At the end of the pier, a tall young man, his posture forlorn, stared toward shore. His droopy seersucker suit clung to him, damp with sweat.

He held up his right arm, looked down at a wristwatch, the age-old gesture of someone waiting. Why would anyone arrange a meeting on the pier with the temperature nudging a hundred?

A red Dodge squealed into the graveled lot near the pier, slid to a stop next to a very old yellow Thunderbird. The driver's door slammed. A small young woman bolted forward. Her high heels clattered on the steps to the pier. She hurried toward him on the wooden deck, almost running. I liked her rose linen suit, a three-button front jacket, and a short straight skirt with tiny bows embroidered above the side slits. Very high pink heels.

The Civilian Conservation Corps dammed a stream to form a lake in the '30s. (1930s.) The young men built a pier into the lake, used local stone to create an amphitheater on a natural slope. The outdoor venue provided a site for plays and concerts and on sunny days a fun place for children to clamber. *Last one up is a monkey's tail.* A carousel offered sweet tinny music. On the carousel, a majestic dark brown wooden buffalo, Oklahoma proud, was the prized perch. A muscular catfish, of course with whiskers, was next most popular.

I felt a catch at my heart as the young woman ran toward the end of the pier. How many times had Bobby Mac and I come to the park and walked hand in hand in the moonlight to the end of the pier? I remembered a spring evening in 1942. Bobby Mac was in uniform and I held tight to him. I was a high school senior, wildly in love. I wanted us to marry before he left, but Bobby Mac, cocky as always, said he'd come marching home as long as I was there waiting for him. He shipped out with the 45th Division to North Africa and on to Italy and Germany. He came home from the war as he'd promised. I was waiting as I'd promised. In June of '46 in a sunset ceremony at the amphitheater, I became Mrs. Robert MacNeil Raeburn. We've been hand in hand ever since.

I brought my attention back to the young couple at the end of the pier in the blazing summer heat.

She skidded to a stop, dropped her cotton handbag to the surface of the pier. She moved closer to him, trying to catch her breath. She spoke unevenly, "I'm sorry I'm late."

I dropped down beside them.

"Something came up at the office." Her voice was still breathless.

His lopsided, quick grin was engaging. "Goes with the territory. I'd have been glad to pick you up."

"Then my car would be at the office." She looked out across the lake, then back at him. "I love the smell of the water."

It takes only a heartbeat to sense whether there is a magical connection—or the beginning of one—between a man and a woman.

They faced each other, not touching, but he was intensely aware of her and she of him.

Tall and lanky, in his late twenties, he was fair skinned with big freckles, dark brown eyes, and features too uneven in a long face to qualify as handsome. Short-cut, straw-colored hair resisted taming, unruly sprigs hinting at clipped curls. His two-button blue and white striped seersucker suit was wilted, no surprise. Bony wrists jutted from the sleeves of a coat a shade short for him. The droop I'd seen when I arrived was gone. His expression was jaunty, eager. "I'm glad you're here."

"I love to come to the park." Her voice was unusually deep for a woman, especially such a small woman. Curly dark hair framed a heart-shaped face. She placed small hands on the railing, looked out at the sun-sheened water. "My uncle planned a treasure hunt here for my sixteenth birthday and he rigged the clues. I was the one who found the keys to a car. A car for me, a shabby, secondhand Dodge, but she was red and she was mine." A quick wry smile. "I'm still driving her. On a good day, her name's Dancing Queen. On a bad day, she's Witch of the West. But she's always Dancing Queen when we come to the park."

"And here"—he knocked on the wooden railing—"is where my dad proposed to my mom. And"—his voice was fairly deep, too, resonant, and now he boomed—"I have a proposal for you."

She swung a startled face toward him.

He stammered, "I mean, not that kind of proposal."

Her eyes widened for an instant, then she laughed, a lively, throaty, happy laugh. "Blaine, that sounds somewhat compromising."

His fair skin flushed bright red. "Be my partner," he blurted. "The office . . ." He was clearly struggling to get back on track, be dignified. "I've rented an old house two blocks off Main, not very big but the bottom floor living room can be the reception area and there's a study and a downstairs bedroom to convert to offices."

She listened gravely. Petite and slender, she was perhaps an inch or so over five feet in height. Her face was distinctive with deep-set gray eyes, high cheekbones, straight nose, and generous mouth. She gazed at him with a depth of intensity. There was intelligence here, quickness, and perception. And, at the moment, great focus.

His words rushed out. "I'm fixing the place up. I refinished a white desk and painted the bedroom walls pale green. You wear a lot of green. . . ." He trailed off.

"Partner?" She spoke steadily enough, but her eyes were luminous.

"Smith and Wynn, PC, attorneys-at-law." His sandy brows drew down. "I put my name first since I rented the place but—"

"Of course your name would be first. You've worked hard to build up a practice." She was emphatic. Her lips spread in a delighted smile. "You're asking me to go in with you?"

He gave a quick nod, then stared out at the water. "I know you're with an established firm. Lots of clients. A great future. I can't offer anything solid like that. I guess maybe I shouldn't even think about it."

He didn't see her face, a wash of excitement but something more, intense and emotional. Relief? Deliverance? An odd reaction.

He rubbed knuckles along his right jaw. "I don't guess you'd want to take that kind of chance since you already have a good job."

"Want to?" A huge breath. "Blaine, how wonderful. Yes, yes, yes. I can't tell you how—" She came to an abrupt stop.

I felt I could finish the sentence that she'd begun: . . . *awful it is where I am . . . much I want out of there . . .* Not . . . *how exciting to be on my own . . . how wonderful it will be to work with you . . .*

He was oblivious to that truncated sentence. He swung toward her, eager, excited, amazed. "You'll do it?" He reached down, and his large knobby hand closed over her small hand. "We can make a go of it." Now he was on top of the world, rushing to a future festooned with ribbons, heralded by trumpets. "You're first-rate. I've seen you in court." And his eyes told her that she was lovely and desirable.

"I'd love to be with you." It was her turn to flush, say hurriedly, "In an office."

"I know you'll have to think about it. There's no rush. That space is for you." *And so is my heart*, his eyes said.

"I'll give notice tomorrow."

Had he been less excited by her acceptance of the offer, he might have realized—and wondered at—her heartfelt relief at the prospect of exiting her current job. Instead he was triumphant, "Hey, that's great. That's wonderful. Megan, you're wonderful. We'll build a great firm, you and me. Together." Now his left hand caught her free hand. He pulled her near, looked down, slowly bent to kiss her.

Megan's large tote bag, bright cotton with peonies and violets and dandelions, rested on a wooden plank a few feet away. A slight movement caught my eye. My gaze settled on an outside pocket. A cell phone rose an inch or two, the screen flashed on. Music blasted, a high, sweet male voice and guitars.

Megan gasped and jumped. She flung a panicked look at her purse.

Blaine looked from her to the purse.

The forlorn song continued at a decibel level that made me wince.

Megan bolted toward the purse and blaring cell phone with an expression of fury. "Stop it. Stop it now." She reached down, grabbed the cotton handles. The cell phone, still playing, bounced from the pocket, landed on the pier. Megan's breaths came in quick spurts. She bent to grab the phone, lifted it, pressed down to turn it off. She straightened, phone firmly gripped in one hand, and looked frantically about, her face set in tight lines of irritation.

Blaine Smith watched with an odd look of confusion.

I imagined he was trying to make sense of what he'd hoped to be a sweetly romantic moment, standing at the end of the pier, partnership offered and accepted, a winsome face upturned, bending toward Megan, then the abrupt, stunning blare of music where there should be no music, and Megan stalking toward her purse with the intensity of a hunter sighting a marauding wolf.

"Megan—"

She stood a few feet away, still breathing quickly, cheeks flushed, the now mute cell phone clutched in one hand, her purse in the other. "Blaine—sorry—have to go—I'll give notice tomorrow—talk to you later." She whirled and clattered toward shore.

"I thought we'd have dinner—"

"I'll call you," she flung over her shoulder.

He stared after her, puzzled and disappointed.

She walked swiftly, head down, reached the path, strode to the parking area. She flung open the driver's door of her car, slid behind the wheel, plopped the purse onto the passenger seat. Her face set in grim lines, she turned on the motor. She backed up and glared again at her purse. "Jimmy, you are a louse."

No answer.

"How could you do that to me?"

No answer.

Megan drove at a furious pace, jolted to a stop at Reverie Lane, the main entrance to White Deer Park. I always loved the name. Reverie suggests tranquillity, a Zen delight in a moment fully realized whether in pleasure at the past or anticipation of the future.

The small bundle of fury crouched behind the wheel emanated no such tranquillity. She started to turn right, shook those dark curls vehemently, turned left.

I gave a small murmur, but she was too engrossed in her thoughts, thankfully, to hear me. I cautiously edged the tote bag nearer the center console to afford myself a small space on the seat.

As the Dodge picked up speed, Megan continued to speak. "I've reached the breaking point. This has to stop. Who knows if I'm ever alone?" She glowered at the passenger seat, twisted to look in back. "Jimmy, you know where I'm taking you. And I want you to *stay* there."

We rode in silence then turned onto a familiar road. We passed St. Mildred's and suddenly I, too, knew where we were going. We passed through open bronze gates to the lovely old cemetery adjacent to the church. It seemed an odd destination for an angry woman on a hot summer evening. Not that I don't enjoy the cemetery. Some graves date back to the early nineteen hundreds with dull gray granite stones tilted to one side. Mausoleums mark the final resting places for a family of means. Much more modest was the cheerful memorial our daughter, Dil, erected for Bobby Mac and me.

The Dodge picked up speed, rather too much for a cemetery. As the car curved around a hill, I knew Megan was heading for the more recent grave sites. I took an instant to visit the Prichard mausoleum, gleaming in the late slanting sun. The Prichard mausoleum was a favorite spot for Adelaideans down on their luck. At the head of Maurice Prichard's tomb a carved greyhound stares forever ahead. A carved Abyssinian cat curls atop Hannah's tomb. Legend has it that stroking the greyhound and the Abyssinian with proper reverence, noble dog, regal cat, will right foundering lives in a flash and good fortune is sure to follow.

I ducked inside, respectfully patted the greyhound's head, slid my hand across the back of the stone cat.

Tires screeched outside.

I popped into the sunshine.

In a plume of dust, the Dodge pulled up to a gentle slope with shining urns and bright granite stones. Several Bradford pear trees, their leaves deep green, offered a smidgeon of shade.

Megan jumped out, slammed the car door, marched, I can only describe her progress as a march—shoulders forward, hands clenched—up a slight incline to a grave site. She looked over her shoulder at the car. "Get out, Jimmy. I know you were on the pier and rode here with me even if you wouldn't say a word. You're always where I am, and right now I'm where you should be." She pointed at the headstone. Her curly black hair quivered with fury.

I dropped down beside her. I was reminded of a small black cat who came to our house as a stray. In peril or anger, her fur increased her stature from the size of folded socks to a ferocious miniature hedgehog.

"Jimmy, you've got to stop." Her deep voice seemed too large for her height, possibly five-two. She stood taller on those pink stiletto heels.

"Jimmy, please!"

She stared straight at a white headstone.

JAMES NICHOLAS TAYLOR
July 4, 1990–July 4, 2014
To the next great adventure . . .

"Jimmy, how could you do it?" She stood with her hands on her hips, glaring at the stone.

"You can do better than that dweeb." The voice was undeniably male and young, a warm tenor with charm.

No one stood near us. A male voice, the girl in the pink suit, and, unknown to her, me. No one else. I looked at the stone. James Taylor. Jimmy?

"Blaine is not a dweeb." Her deep voice was adamant.

"Blaine is a pain. In the rain. Or sun. Or whatever."

She stamped a foot. "You made me look like an idiot. I freaked out. I couldn't believe that song started. I knew it was you."

"Yeah, well, kind of rude to act nuts." His voice exuded hurt. "That was our song."

"He starts to kiss me and all of a sudden my cell phone blares Sam Smith singing 'Stay with Me.'" A pause. "Jimmy, how'd you do that?"

"Oh," he said, sounding pleased with himself, "I planned it. If you'd turned on iTunes that's what you would have got. I had the song ready to play. See"—and now his voice drooped—"I figured he'd want to kiss you and when he tried . . ."

"Oh, Jimmy, what am I going to do about you?"

"I have your best interests at heart."

"You sound like my friend Janey. *Megan, don't you think you could do better? After all, he isn't very handsome.*" Clearly she was quoting.

"There's an astute woman. I heard the rest of it, too." His voice oozed satisfaction. "*Jimmy was sooo good-looking.*" Clearly he was also quoting.

She gave a reluctant laugh. "Self-esteem chugging right along? Okay, you were the handsomest guy in the room."

"She said I looked like Ansel Elgort."

"You did." She sighed. "But you're gone. At least you're supposed to be gone. Why are you still here?"

"I can't go yet. The thing about it is, I don't want you to marry a guy with a chin that juts. By the time he's fifty, he'll be a clone to George on Mount Rushmore."

"Blaine has a perfectly decent chin." Her voice was hot.

"He's a suit."

"Of course he's a suit. He's a lawyer."

"Most lawyers swank around in dressy casual. What's with him and a suit? Does he think he's Clarence Darrow? Besides, his suits never fit him, the sleeves are too short, and the pants too long. The next thing you know he'll drape his Phi Beta Kappa key on a watch chain."

"Jealous," she taunted.

"There's more to life than grades. I had a great future at the *Gazette*."

"A great future . . ." Her voice trailed off.

The leaves in a nearby cottonwood rustled in the hot late-afternoon breeze. A scent of new-mown grass mingled with the sweetness of honeysuckle. A mourning dove's haunting cry sounded once, twice, again.

Abruptly, she whirled. Head down, she hurried toward the little red car.

Again a male voice called after her, "Hey, Megan, don't go away mad."

Chapter 2

Megan again drove fast, small hands clamped on the steering wheel.

I nodded approval at pink nail polish that matched her suit. An eye for detail distinguishes those who dress well. Her suit made me feel festive. I know what I'm wearing even when I'm not visible. I changed to an adorable rosebud print silk polyester dress, the rosebud pattern enhanced by a deeper rose band a few inches above the short hemline. The finishing touch was rose high-heel pumps with ankle straps.

Megan stared straight ahead. "I'll be graceful, say all the right things, such a splendid experience to be at Layton, Graham, Morse and Morse, but here's a chance to go out on my own." Her smile was huge. "The icing on the cake is being with Blaine! Maybe Jimmy will leave me alone. Maybe I'll stop hearing his voice. Maybe I can leave Layton, Graham, Morse and Morse behind forever. Or stop feeling like I'm in a twilight zone instead of a law firm. Or am I nuts about all of that, too? Mr. Layton and Doug never talk to each other. They pass in the hall and don't say a word. Sure, they have their own clients, but it's something more than that. Ginny and Carl are really nice but I never work with them. And ever since last winter, they treat Mr. Layton politely but look at him with about as much warmth as two boa constrictors. And maybe Sharon's having a midlife crisis even if she is only in her thirties. Sometimes when she comes out of Doug's office, she looks drained and sad. I mean, the man can make anyone mad, but sad? She needs some of Geraldine's spunk. But if she had Geraldine's sex appeal maybe she wouldn't mope around. And if Nancy tells me again how she lusts for a Porsche like Doug's I'll lose my control and tell her wanting what we can never afford is terminally stupid. Even sweet Lou, who never says an unkind word about anyone, has eyes like ice when she looks at Doug. And poor Anita! I hate to leave Anita. I've covered for her as much as I can, but if I don't get out of there I'll go crazy. Or maybe I'm already crazy. Maybe I'm imagining the gloom I sense around me. I didn't used to talk to myself. Now I can match Hamlet for soliloquies. Maybe that's why I keep imagining Jimmy. Maybe I shouldn't go with Blaine. He doesn't need a nutty partner." Her voice held despair.

"Of course you should go with Blaine." I spoke with the authority of a lifetime lived. Carpe diem is trite because it's true.

"No, she shouldn't." The young male voice was equally adamant.

Megan jammed on the brakes, swerved to the shoulder of the road. Her head jerked toward the passenger seat.

I wasn't buckled. Not that I am one to flout rules. I do my best with the Precepts, but even a most abstracted driver might wonder if the belt in an apparently vacant seat slid into its slot and clicked. So I was riding untethered. The abrupt halt flung me forward along with Megan's tote bag.

"Ouch." Fortunately, in my invisible state I am not subject to injury although I'd come up hard against the dashboard. I grabbed the bag from the floor, returned it to the seat, squeezed in next to it.

Megan stared at her striped tote, apparently rising of its own accord to nestle beside the console. Her dark curls windblown, her smoky gray eyes strained, Megan had the look of a stricken creature. "Jimmy, it's bad enough when it's you, but it's weird if you sound like a woman. You say I should go with Blaine, then you say I shouldn't. And keep your hands off my tote."

"Oh heavens." I'd blown my cover. Metaphorically speaking. "Megan, I'm not Jimmy."

"She sure isn't." The tenor from the backseat sounded bemused. "Who the hell are you?"

I was chiding. "Hell is not to be lightly invoked." However, this wasn't the moment for an exposition on Heavenly attitudes. "Suffice to say——"

Megan turned the motor off, stared at the empty passenger seat, flung a harried glance at the equally untenanted backseat. "I . . . have . . . lost . . . my . . . mind." The halting words signaled defeat. She lifted a trembling hand to her cheek. "Jimmy's dead. I keep hearing him. Weird things happen, the music in my iPhone, my favorite chocolate on my pillow——"

I spoke to the backseat. "Jimmy, that is truly sweet."

"Hey, thanks. She loves Dove chocolate bars. I figured the corner drugstore wouldn't mind if I filched a few. I drank their mud for coffee and paid a buck and a half a cup. And last night I swept out the storeroom, saved somebody a job this morning. But who the hell are you and where are you?"

"I'm Bailey Ruth Raeburn and I'm here for Megan."

Megan scrunched farther down in the seat, gazed in the direction of my voice. "I'll go home, call a doctor. Or go to the emergency room. What will I say? I'm hearing voices and will you please—"

I reached out, patted her arm.

She went rigid.

"You poor child." I looked at the backseat. Now I spoke with the authority honed by teaching English to high school football players. "James, return to the cemetery. Immediately."

"Aw . . ." He sounded very young.

"It is imperative I have a moment alone with Megan."

A masculine sigh. "You sound like my Aunt Harriet. Aunt Harriet could have been a Marine DI. Maybe she was. I'll have to ask some—"

"James, now."

Megan closed her eyes, muttered, "If I hear two voices, why not three? We can play bridge. That would be fun. A deck of cards, me holding mine and three bunches of cards floating in the air. Would they float? Maybe they'd hover. Maybe the get-back-to-the-cemetery voice is my feeble mind's last desperate ploy to get rid of Jimmy. Maybe if I think really, really hard, there aren't any voices, I didn't feel a touch on my arm, maybe—"

"Megan"—I hoped my cheery tone was reassuring—"all is well. I'm sure Jimmy has departed for the moment." Now to business. I asked sharply, "You've heard Jimmy speak, have you seen him?"

Her eyes flared. "Is that the next stage? Voices in my head first,

22

then visions? Progressing from minor hallucinations to full-fledged over the edge? I haven't seen him. Is that a good sign? Maybe I'm just slightly hysterical and this new voice I'm imagining is going to turn the tide, right the ship. Now I'm not only nuts, I'm trite. Mrs. Carey, she was my high school English teacher, had a thing about triteness. Swim like a duck, bring it on, I'm just saying, in for a penny . . ." Megan's voice trailed off. She pressed against the driver's door, watched colors swirling in the passenger seat.

I took a moment to smooth the skirt of my dress. Perhaps the deep rose wasn't best for a redhead. Something cool. Oh, perfect! A pale blue sleeveless scoop-necked midcalf linen dress enhanced by an enchanting lace hem. I flipped down the visor, looked in the mirror. Too plain? I nodded approval at a necklace with chunky white stones on a silk cord and a gold medallion drop. I smoothed back a red curl to admire golden wire hoop earrings. Feeling at my best, I turned to Megan. "Good for Mrs. Carey. I asked about seeing Jimmy because it's best if he doesn't know he can appear."

She sagged against the seat. "Why did I do this to myself? Voices were bad enough, but imagining a gorgeous redhead—"

I gave her an appreciative smile.

"—is completely nuts. Redheads are always trouble. There was Gussie Hodges in third grade. She persuaded me to tell Mrs. Bacon she smelled like breakfast, and I had to write *Rude girls are an abomination* on the blackboard one hundred times. I'd better check in at the ER. Do they take people who are seeing things?"

I reached out and took her hand.

She shuddered and pressed as far back against the driver's door as possible.

"Breathe deeply, Megan. Everything is all ri—"

"Oh sure. Right as rain. Steady as she goes. Hunky-dory. Easy as pie. Where do you suppose that one came from? Pies are hell to make and my crust always tastes like foam."

"I'm here to help." Succinctly, I described the Department of Good Intentions. "It's time for Jimmy to come to Heaven. I will persuade him."

Megan's quick breaths slowly eased. She looked at me with a probing gaze. "Let me see if I get this right. You're a ghost—"

"Emissary." In case Wiggins was nearby.

"—and you're here to corral Jimmy. Do you think you can?" She gave a violent head shake. "I'm going from bad to worse. I hear Jimmy and now to yank him out of my head I've invented this redhead from Heaven—"

"Redhead from Heaven," I murmured. How nice. It would have been a lovely title for a movie starring Myrna Loy.

"I said it. I don't need an imaginary ghost to repeat what I said."

I opened the passenger door.

She gripped the steering wheel so tightly her fingers turned white as her eyes followed the opening door.

I yanked the door shut with a decisive slam. "I am here."

She loosened her grip on the wheel, sagged against the seat. "Please go away. Go to the cemetery and talk to Jimmy. You have a lot in common."

"Jimmy," I replied with certainty, "will be at your house."

"Apartment," she corrected.

"Shall we go and see?"

"Damn. Damn. Damn." She reached out, turned the key. The car jolted forward. To hush the seat belt signal, I pushed the connector into its slot. "We drove for years without seat belts," I remarked conversationally.

Megan stared straight ahead. Her profile was appealing, springy dark hair, fine features, firmly set small chin. I admire determination.

"You're driving rather fast."

"You concentrate on Jimmy, I'll take care of my driving."

"So you're a lawyer."

No reply. The Dodge swerved out of the cemetery, picked up speed.

"Are you excited about joining Blaine?" And what is it that you hate about your current job? Was *hate* too strong a word? Somehow I didn't think so.

"I'll meditate. Push out extraneous thoughts, become one with the universe."

"If you keep going this fast, you may become one with the universe before—"

A siren wailed.

Megan looked in the rearview mirror, checked the speedometer. "Uh-oh." She gradually slowed.

I twisted to see. Flashing red lights atop a cruiser came nearer and nearer.

Megan eased the Dodge off the road onto the shoulder, rolled down the window.

The cruiser pulled up behind. The driver's door opened.

It was dusk now, the soft shadowy beginning of sunset. The road from the cemetery into Adelaide wasn't well traveled. There was a sense of summery peace, birds settling into trees, their chitter intense. I've often wondered at the content of that loud prelude to darkness. Perhaps mama birds murmuring, *Good night, sleep tight.* Or strutting males focused on what mattered. *Did you see that hot chick by the pond this morning?*

The officer came nearer. Now it was my turn. "Uh-oh," I murmured. I swirled away.

Megan was absorbed in opening her purse. She fished for her billfold, lowered the window, and turned to look up into the face of a young officer I knew well. She offered her license. "I'm sorry, Officer. I was so involved in conversation I wasn't paying attention to my speed."

Johnny Cain was classically handsome, thick brown hair, strong features. Even better, he was kind and brave. I will always remember when he faced death for the woman he loved.

I popped out to look over Johnny's shoulder, scanned the license, noted the address on Magnolia, apartment 6, returned to the passenger seat.

"Seventy-four miles an hour in a fifty-five-mile-an-hour zone." His familiar voice was disapproving. He held a tablet, glanced down, likely checking the car license for violations.

"I've never had a ticket. Truly, we were just so excited—"

"We?" He bent to look inside the car, scanned the backseat.

Megan looked around, stiffened. She stared at the empty passenger seat. "She—" Megan hunched in the driver's seat, abruptly lurched out a hand and grabbed.

An interesting aspect of being an emissary is physicality. When I appear, I am there. Or here, if you prefer, all five feet five inches of me with curly red hair, green eyes, freckles, and my twenty-seven-year-old svelte self. When I swirl away, I am not visible and

I can pass through any physical substance but I am still, so to speak, here. Megan's lunge and grasp caught my arm in a tight vise. I used my free hand to touch a finger firmly on her lips.

To her credit, she understood.

Her grip eased. Numbly, she turned to Johnny. "I . . . I mean . . ."

I leaned close, whispered in her ear. "Working on a script."

". . . I've been working on a script. Sometimes I get carried away. I didn't mean to speed." Her voice trembled.

Johnny Cain's eyes squinted in remembrance. "I might not have understood, but we had an incident at the inn recently. A bunch of writers." His voice was bemused. "I interviewed some of them."

The encounters had obviously made an impression on Johnny.

His voice had an uneasy tone. "They talk about characters in books like they're real."

Megan looked at him gratefully. "Thank you for understanding. I—we—it was a conversation and I was thinking and I just didn't know how fast I was going." There was a depth of sincerity in the last statement.

Johnny nodded. "Try to keep your mind on your driving. No ticket. This time." He turned away.

Megan remained stationary, hands gripping the wheel.

The cruiser pulled onto the road, reached the crest of a hill, was out of sight.

"You can drive on now." I remained unseen.

"Will you go away?"

"For the moment." Not only would Wiggins frown upon continued interaction, Megan needed a respite from emotion. I knew where to find her.

⌒

To think is to be, and I arrived on Main Street a few doors down from Lulu's Cafe, fabulous for comfort food in my day and still in business. Lulu's is where townsfolk meet and greet, a long counter with red leather stools facing a mirror, a few tables in the center, and four booths against the opposite wall. I stepped into a nearby doorway, made sure no one was watching, and appeared. I opened a summery blue cotton handbag, smiled. The change purse held quite enough for my needs.

In Lulu's, I sat at the counter, ordered iced tea and a chicken-fried steak with mashed potatoes and green beans. As I ate, I pondered. How could I persuade Jimmy to depart the earth? My English teacher persona might hie him briefly back to the cemetery, but prying him away from Megan required insight I didn't at the moment have. I knew he had been young and had a great future at the *Gazette*.

The *Gazette*!

⌒

I was familiar with the *Gazette* newsroom, a cluster of unimaginative gray metal desks with computer monitors, the city editor's desk in the center of the room. I popped from desk to desk and was unable to access any monitor. Passwords are a hindrance to everyone but cyber vandals, who gleefully bypass them in a twinkle. I tried *twinkle* as a password on the lifestyle editor's computer. No luck.

I yearned for the old days, everything on paper and easy to find in filing cabinets. Instead, the information I needed was somewhere in the electronic netherworld. None of the reporters had helpfully written down a password.

In an instant I was in Police Chief Sam Cobb's office on the second floor of City Hall. I'd had occasion to assist Sam in solving several crimes, and we had forged a bond. He considered a voice in space an interesting exercise in contemplation. I was sure he wouldn't mind my using his computer to assist my investigation, though my search had nothing to do with crime.

I looked about the office fondly, a long room with dingy beige walls. Several maps of Adelaide were interspersed with Matisse prints. I admired a new print, Modigliani's famed *Woman with Red Hair*. Was it possible? I shook my head. My red hair was red and hers . . . Well, there are many shades of red hair. Nonetheless, I felt the addition was perhaps a toast to our friendship.

I settled behind the chief's battered oak desk, pulled out the center drawer, smiled. A small note card held a list of words, all scratched out but the last. Mayor Neva Lumpkin, no friend of Sam's, insisted all city employees change passwords weekly.

I glanced at the list, turned to the keyboard, entered *Shi7eld*. Voila! In an instant, I'd accessed the *Gazette* news story of July 5, 2014.

STAFFER DIES IN RIVER ACCIDENT

General reporter Jimmy (James Nicholas) Taylor, 24, drowned Friday on the Snake River, Snake, Oregon, when his kayak capsized in the Wild Sheep Rapids.

A sheriff's deputy said Taylor suffered a fatal head wound. When the craft overturned, Taylor's helmet was lost and his head struck a granite boulder.

Taylor joined the *Gazette* two years ago. He covered City Hall, the county commissioners, Chamber of Commerce, local civic clubs, and general news. Taylor uncovered abuse at a local nursing home and received an award from the Oklahoma Press Association for investigative reporting.

City editor Ralph Logan described Taylor as a throwback to the days when reporters were brash, cocky, irreverent, and incorruptible. "Jimmy was a smart mouth, equal parts Don Quixote, D'Artangan, and (James) Dean. He was a crooked politician's worst nightmare. He listened when people talked and learned more than anyone ever realized. Hell of a guy."

Taylor was a native of Adelaide. He was a journalism graduate of the University of Oklahoma. He worked for the *Norman Transcript* before returning to Adelaide to join the *Gazette*.

Services are pending.

An adjoining photo showed Jimmy at his desk in the newsroom, looking with a mischievous grin toward the cameraman. He wore a paper pirate's hat.

Oh my, yes, he was handsome, thick tangly dark hair, high smooth forehead, bright dark brown eyes, strong nose, full lips, firm chin. Very young but a promise of resoluteness and humor and intelligence.

I clicked several times, found the funeral home page. Among the condolences:

> *You drove too fast, climbed cliffs without a harness, skied off trail, barely got out of Old Man Harkin's pasture when the bull charged, but you kept your promise and never told anyone about the night I cried.—Bud*

A swell dancer, a sweet guy. Love you—Allie

Remember the night we put the barber pole on top of the church steeple? And left a vial of Viagra on the principal's desk? And showed up at the sorority skit in tutus?—You know who

You volunteered at the old folks' home and you listened when my mom told you they'd hurt her. You sneaked in and hid a videocam in her room. If it hadn't been for you, no one would have helped her.—Violet's daughter

No one cared about the old guy who lived under that bridge until you wrote your story. I got help. I've been clean and working at Major Market for nine months.—Chuck

Dude, you ran fastest, climbed highest, dared the most. Always in your dust—Harry

⌒

Megan's living room was shabby but spotless, a cheerful plaid sofa, two wicker chairs, and a worn Persian rug. Framed prints by Rothko, Klee, and Martin brightened pale gray walls. A calico cat curled on the sofa.

Actually the calico was elevated above the sofa.

I strolled across the room, looked down at the cat, obviously quite comfortable on a lap. I judged distances, reached out, firmly gripped Jimmy's arm.

"Hey." His voice was halfway between a shout and a yelp. He tried to yank away.

I hung on with the determination of a sweepstakes winner clutching the winning ticket in a heavy wind.

The startled cat launched herself into the air.

Rapid footsteps sounded. Megan burst into the living room. She was slim and lovely in a white cotton top and navy Bermudas.

"Let go." He wriggled and I held on.

"Jimmy." She looked wildly around the room.

He broke off. "I was just petting the cat."

The cat stared balefully toward the sofa.

"You're upsetting Sweetie. I thought you went back to the cemetery."

I felt his shoulder sag. He leaned back against the sofa, his resistance gone. "It's nicer here." His voice was small.

Megan flung herself into a wicker chair, pressed fingertips against her temples. "I will not imagine Jimmy's here. Sweetie had a nightmare. I didn't hear Jimmy's voice. It's all in my head."

I increased the pressure on Jimmy's arm. "Jimmy, despite the barber pole on the steeple and your proclivity for living dangerously, you tried to help people. Please look at Megan."

"Now she's back, too." Megan's hands fell slackly in her lap. She slumped against the cushion, clearly miserable and more than a little bit scared.

"Hey, Megan." He was contrite. "I don't want to upset you."

"Of course you don't." I made my voice admiring. "You want to help. Here's what you can do. Megan won't mind if you're with her at the office—"

Megan's eyes were wide and staring. I hoped her inner monologue wasn't tending toward hysteria.

"—in the daytime. Will that be all right, Megan?"

She managed a pathetic smile. "That would be dandy. At the office."

"And"—I was feeling generous—"you can accompany her until seven p.m. Then, as a gentleman, you will agree to respect her privacy until the next day."

Megan hunched her narrow shoulders. "Am I bargaining with myself? I will only be nuts in daylight hours?"

"You can see," I was chiding, "that she desperately needs some time alone."

"I wasn't going to bother her. I've stayed here most nights. Me and the cat on the sofa."

"Take in a movie. See what some of your old friends are doing. Without," I added hastily, "making yourself known."

"Okay." He was forlorn.

I released my hold on his arm, shook my fingers, which were a bit numb, and moved to a chair near Megan, looked toward the sofa. "You can catch up with her at the office."

"How come you're special? Do you get to stay?"

"Only for a few minutes. I need to confer with Megan and then I, too, will leave."

Her head swung back and forth from the sofa to the chair where I'd settled. "When you two get it all worked out, can I be the first to know?"

Suddenly a burst of male laughter gurgled. "Hey, Megan, you haven't lost your spirit."

I laughed.

Megan pressed her eyes together for an instant, opened them to stare stonily at the—to her—empty chair. "Hilarious."

"Begone, James." If I sounded Shakespearean, I simply couldn't resist.

"On my way. Tomorrow I'll be at the office."

Megan looked startled, lifted a hand to her head.

As he departed, I was sure Jimmy had gently stroked a shining swath of dark curls.

Silence.

I was sure Jimmy had left. I became visible. I opted for casual comfort, a keyhole tie sweater in a pale green, white slacks, and lime leather flats. "He's gone."

Smoky gray eyes studied me. "How do you know?"

"Jimmy doesn't want you to be unhappy."

A tiny smile curved her lips. "Jimmy really is—" A pause. "—was kind, a real softy beneath his brash poke-it-and-see-if-it-bites exterior. I know he wanted me to be happy. With him. He doesn't want me to be happy with Blaine."

"That's why I'm here." She needed reassurance. "I meant what I said. I'll leave in a moment. But first, let me congratulate you. Smith and Wynn, attorneys-at-law."

It was like watching lowering purple clouds transform to blue skies. For an instant, I saw Megan as she should be, eyes shining, her face eager.

Her voice was soft. "It will be wonderful. I can get up in the mornings and be excited again, instead of dreading each day. Although I really should turn Blaine down."

"You want the job. You want to be happy. Why should you turn him down?"

"Money." She spoke as if the word were heavy as a boulder.

I was surprised and disappointed. I thought it very likely she'd earn more in an established firm, but I wouldn't have pegged her as a woman who put money above everything.

"I see."

"Do you? You reek with disapproval. I owe forty-eight thousand four hundred and six dollars and thirty-three cents. That's my debt out of law school. That's why I was ecstatic when I got the job with Layton, Graham, Morse and Morse, the best law firm in Adelaide. Brewster Layton was a good friend of my uncle's. I interviewed with Brewster and he hired me on the spot, an associate at seventy-two thousand a year. I can't tell you how happy I was." There was no trace of happiness in her grim expression.

"What went wrong?"

"Mr. Layton—I'm supposed to call him Brewster—I always admired him. He's tall and thin and scholarly-looking with a goatee, a widower. He's had a sad life. His wife died from cancer a couple of years ago and then his daughter was diagnosed with congestive heart failure. Julie died this spring. He's been pretty withdrawn ever since I came to work. I thought he was the lead partner. That's what I always understood. But he almost never comes out of his office. When he does, he looks like the Hounds of Hell—"

She gave me a quick look.

I nodded, quite familiar in myth and poetry with the supernatural beasts with glowing red eyes and matted black fur.

"—are after him. I thought I'd be working for him. Instead I work for Doug Graham." There was no pleasure in her voice.

"And?" I prompted.

"A big guy. Maybe six foot three. Thick blond hair, blue eyes, good-looking. Played football. Makes a room seem small. Big laugh, big smile, but his eyes aren't smiling. He can definitely turn on the charm. He massages clients with phone calls, e-mail updates, texts over the weekend. But I do most of the work while he's out on the golf course. A bully in depositions. He's made a lot of money. He lives in one of those fancy houses with copper spires, brick, stone, stucco, and anything else the architect can think to throw in. When I took the job, I didn't know I'd end up as his minion. *Megan, I need an extra woman at dinner, show up at seven, Megan, drop off the car for an oil change, Megan, take a run up to Victoria's Secret and get a red teddy in a small.* You get the picture. And I thought I was trapped."

"A red—oh, my dear." I was appalled.

She shot me another quick glance and this time she was amused. "My honor is unsullied, if that's your concern. I don't know who the teddy was for. He has an ex-wife, and I doubt it was for her. But he's everything my uncle taught me to despise in a certain kind of lawyer, more interested in big fees than honest work, padding his hours, always ready to cut corners."

"Why have you stayed?"

"How do you think it looks for someone fresh out of law school to join a firm and leave in a few months? It looks unsteady, unreliable. Worse, it looks like there's something wrong with me. Doug Graham's a big deal in Adelaide, bonhomie all around town, has clients stacked up in the waiting room. I can't go around saying he's a jerk and maybe half-crooked. It's a shame, because Mr. Layton and Ginny and Carl Morse are good, honest lawyers. Besides, I can't prove anything on Doug. He's too smart for that. But there have been little things, and I really don't trust him. I thought I'd stick it out for a year, then look for a job. I had top grades. I could have gone with one of the big firms in Oklahoma City or Tulsa but I wanted to come home. Jimmy and I had been dating off and on, and I didn't know, hadn't thought it through. We had a wonderful spring semester together in Italy, at the campus in Arezzo. We'd dance in the moonlight to the mandolins. But we're—we were so different. My friends said he was a wild man. I knew they were right. He was—maybe he still is—wild and crazy. Always up for a dare, skiing, rock climbing, river rafting. When I got the call, I wasn't surprised, Jimmy gone in the rapids. But I was here and I thought I was stuck, but now"—suddenly she looked young and happy and eager—"now I can leave the firm. I'll give notice tomorrow. I have to finish up anything I was working on, but I can do that in a month. Of course, I'll probably be in debt forever. There won't be much money, just Blaine and me. But I can be happy again. And"—she reached out, touched my arm—"you're here to take care of Jimmy. Everything's going to be wonderful. Tomorrow I give notice. Tomorrow everything gets better." She looked at me intently. "What's your plan for Jimmy?"

"I'll have more to report tomorrow." It's lonely when you are on the field of battle and have no clue, no map, no weapon, no strategy. "Tomorrow," I said profoundly if ambiguously, "is a new day. Sleep well." I disappeared.

I hoped Wiggins was pleased. . . . Oh, likely not pleased that I'd appeared, but perhaps he understood I meant well and had successfully encouraged Megan. I felt that I'd bought a bit of time. She didn't expect a solution to Jimmy's presence before tomorrow.

I took the opportunity to make brief visits to places dear to me. Besides, it distracted me from the worry that was like a burr in a sock. How in the world was I going to persuade Jimmy to say good-bye?

I dropped in on my daughter, Dil. She was studying her checkbook at the kitchen table. She called out to her husband in the living room, "What do I do when the statement shows three thousand less than I have in the register?" A long-suffering voice replied gloomily, "I suggest a calculator, aspirin, and prayer." "You sound like my dad. He always told Mom, *Please don't subtract.*" Dil's nose wrinkled. "That's funny. It's like Mom's here. I can smell gardenia. She loved gardenias. Once when she'd really screwed up the checkbook, she distracted Dad by doing a cancan through the kitchen."

As Mama always told me, "If you make a man laugh, all will be well."

Laughter and chatter rose on the summer night air on the terrace by a swimming pool. Shaded lamps illuminated small groups. My son, Rob, slipped his arm around his wife, looked down with a happy face. "Everyone's having fun, aren't they?" "We give great parties," she replied, not smugly but confidently. "Just like your folks did." I blew her an unseen kiss.

I wafted here and there in Adelaide, ending up in a comfortable room at Rose Bower, the mansion owned by the college and used to house important guests. I knew I could always count on finding an unoccupied room.

I selected a stately room with a canopied bed and a chaise longue. I appeared in a short white nightie. Soon I was comfortably settled in bed, lights off, but my gaze wide and staring. I could avoid the truth no longer. I hadn't an inkling how to propel Jimmy Heavenward.

Chapter 3

Not even country smoked ham, fried eggs, and grits at Lulu's improved my mood. I gave a worried glance at the mirror. I looked fine, red curls fresh, green eyes clear, freckled face youthful. Twenty-seven is such a good year. But the Count of Monte Cristo had nothing on me when it came to feeling trapped. I couldn't bribe Jimmy. I couldn't coerce Jimmy. I took a last sip of coffee.

In her small modest apartment, Megan no doubt was eager to start her day, confident she would soon be free of a disappointing job and free also of Jimmy's attentions. I glanced at the clock on the wall. A quarter to nine. Jimmy was probably at the law firm ensconced in her office.

Ready or not, it behooved me to be on hand. Perhaps inspiration would strike en route. I paid for breakfast, walked unobtrusively to the ladies' room. Inside, I took a last admiring glance at a sedate but stylish short-sleeve navy matte jersey dress with a V-neck, natural waist, and slightly flared skirt. I fluffed my hair and disappeared.

༄

The law firm of Layton, Graham, Morse and Morse occupied the first floor of a redbrick building on the corner of Third and Comanche.

The waiting area was well-appointed, two brown leather sofas and several deep, comfortable easy chairs. An elderly woman in a violet print dress was bolt upright in an easy chair, fingers gripping the straps to her leather purse. A walker sat squarely in front of her. A slender young man in a yellow polo, jeans, and sneakers, his hands laced behind him, stared out a window, his back to the room. A dark red Persian rug added a dash of elegance.

The receptionist, a motherly woman in her late sixties with Mary Worth white hair, a plump face, bright blue eyes, and a rosebud mouth, sat behind a metal desk. A nameplate identified her as Louise Raymond. She took a dainty bite of a buttery croissant as she stared at her computer screen, flicked a crumb from a ruffled white blouse.

I strolled down a long hallway. Bronze nameplates were on each door. I passed the offices of Carl Morse and Virginia Morse. Megan's name was on the third door. Three desks sat in open alcoves on the other side of the hall. Another desk was tucked in an alcove between Megan's office and a conference room. Desks in the alcoves were occupied. I noted nameplates. Sharon King was likely in her midthirties, light brown hair, delicate features. Wide-set, dark brown eyes were her most striking feature. She was conservatively dressed, a striped long-sleeve blouse, a midcalf skirt, modest white pumps. Anita Davis looked thrown together, an untidy mane of chestnut curls, no makeup, a baggy brown knit blouse with a snag on one shoulder. At the third desk, Geraldine Jackson was at the other extreme, masses of dyed blonde hair, lots of eye makeup, blazing lip gloss, huge hoop earrings, a carnelian necklace. A too-tight red and white striped rayon blouse emphasized voluptuous curves. Her white linen trousers were stylish. She was the kind of woman Bobby Mac described as a pistol. In the alcove across the hall, a sharp-featured young woman with jagged bangs and short black hair hummed as she separated stapled sheets of paper in different stacks. Her lacy white blouse was demure. Her nameplate was larger: *Nancy Murray, Paralegal.*

At the end of the corridor on the left, gold letters on a mahogany nameplate read: *Doug Graham.* A corner office.

I passed through the closed door of Graham's office. I looked about and raised an eyebrow. Perhaps a little grandiose for a small-town lawyer? I circled around an eighteenth-century baroque desk with cabriole legs, which had likely belonged to a nobleman or a prince of the church. Walnut parquetry veneer decorated the serpentine front. The green leather desk pad was embossed with a gold design. I moved behind the desk and noted the central frieze drawer and two drawers on either side with ornate cast-bronze foliate handles.

Opposite the desk was a Victorian red-buttoned soft leather sofa. A silver tea tray sat on a rosewood-inlaid coffee table. In one corner of the spacious room, a six-foot palm flourished in a ceramic pottery stand. Matching Windsor chairs sat at angles to the desk. Gold damask drapes framed three windows. One wall was dominated by an oil painting, clearly an original, of a horse galloping on a trail, bunched muscles straining.

I wondered who decorated the office. Was it the product of a middle-aged lawyer's perusal of *Architectural Digest*, his wife—or ex-wife's—fancy, or a cynical interior decorator? All the surface of the desk lacked was a Borgia ring on one corner. There were no papers or folders scattered about. Burnished oak in- and out-boxes held some papers. A heavy silver frame on one corner of the desk contained the photograph of a striking woman, smooth golden hair that drooped artfully to one side, a cool, straight gaze from quizzical blue eyes, chiseled features, lips curved in a slightly mocking smile. I recognized a particular kind of woman: wealthy, privileged, comfortably superior, always expecting deference.

I opened the center drawer. Heavy silver letter opener, tin of breath mints, calculator, assorted pens, small leather address book. A plush red velvet ring case nestled at one side. I picked up the case, lifted the lid. In a shaft of summer sunlight through the east window, a huge multifaceted diamond glittered bright as a piercing reflection from a snowcap. Magnificent. Breathtaking. To whom did it belong? I supposed the answer was easy. The ring was in Doug Graham's desk drawer. I slowly closed the lid, replaced the velvet case. For whom was the ring intended?

I carried a memory of the stone's beauty with me as I passed through the door into the hall. The opposite office belonged to Brewster Layton. It figured that the law firm's partners occupied the largest offices. I passed through the door and was surprised. The contrast was dramatic. There were no expensive furnishings here. A maple desk, an undistinguished couch upholstered in a subdued green and black plaid, two serviceable wooden chairs with blue vinyl seats.

The door opened.

I recognized Brewster Layton from Megan's description, perhaps a little over six feet tall, close-cropped gray hair, sharp features, a neatly trimmed goatee. He closed the door, leaned back against the panel as if gathering strength. Knowing himself to be unobserved, there was no effort to school his expression. Megan felt like he was pursued by the Hounds of Hell. That suggested hot pursuit by horrors. To me, he looked like a very angry man, a man consumed by a cold, hard rage, a man pushed beyond endurance.

The telephone rang.

He took a breath, crossed the room, picked up the receiver. "Brewster Layton." His voice was level, uninflected. "I'll be right there." He hung up, reformed his face, looked tired but contained, businesslike.

I followed him into the hall and to the reception area.

The receptionist smiled at the elderly woman. "Here's Mr. Layton."

The woman gripped the handles of her walker and eased to her feet. "Brewster, I've been looking at the cards. They couldn't have spoken more clearly. Trouble. Rash. The number twenty-nine." A portentous pause and meaningful stare. "Janet turns twenty-nine next week! I want to redo that codicil to my will. . . ."

They were in the hall, she pushing her walker, he at her elbow. His deep voice was soothing. "Winnie, perhaps we should consider the tax aspects—"

The untidy secretary was holding letters and large envelopes in one hand. "Looks like Mrs. Kellogg's redoing her will again."

The receptionist's smile was kindly. "That woman finds all kinds of trouble in her cards. She's lucky Mr. Layton takes good care of her. He'll spend an hour and she'll come out and the will won't be changed but she'll be much happier."

Anita Davis stared down the hall, her plump face resentful. "She doesn't know trouble. She looks at cards and thinks she knows trouble."

The receptionist said diffidently, "A bad night?"

Anita pressed her lips together, nodded. Her face was slack with misery.

"I'm sorry." The older woman's voice was kind.

"Thanks, Lou." Anita took a steadying breath. "I'd better sort the mail." She moved down the hallway, slow steps suggesting fatigue.

The front door opened. Megan hurried inside. She was lovely in a lemon cotton piqué knit dress. A white knit shoulder bag swung as she walked. Her young face radiated happiness. "Hi, Lou. I'm running late this morning." Likely as a young law associate she was usually at her desk by eight a.m. I wondered if she'd taken time this morning to drive by the frame house Blaine Smith had re-modeled for offices. Her eyes were shining. "Has Mr. Graham arrived yet?"

"He just went to his office." The receptionist looked toward the young man at the window. "Keith Porter's waiting to see him."

Megan nodded. "Please let me know when Mr. Graham is free."

The receptionist smiled. "I will."

Megan walked briskly down the hall. She called out pleasant good-mornings. Sharon gave her an abstracted nod. Geraldine lifted a beringed hand in a salute. Nancy chirped, "I'll have that deed ready this afternoon."

Megan stopped at Anita Davis's desk. "Hey, Anita, how's Bridget feeling?"

Anita looked up. Tears welled in her eyes.

Megan bent forward, said softly, "Do you need to go home?"

"I better not. Mr. Graham called there yesterday. I answered because I thought it might be the doctor. He wanted to know what I was doing at home. I told him I'd gone out to run an errand for you and it was near so I just dropped by for a minute. He said he'd talk to me today. He hung up on me." Her voice was high and scared.

Megan looked somber. "I'll talk to him."

Anita's eyes flared. "That might make it worse. I'll promise I won't ever do it again. I'll promise anything. I'll work late for a month. But I can't lose the insurance. It covers this doctor. I've checked it out. If I quit, if we tried to make it on what I've saved, that government insurance won't cover this specialist, and he's her only hope."

Megan said swiftly, "The doctor's been encouraging, hasn't he?"

Anita's face brightened. "He thinks a new drug can make a difference. He's working on getting Bridget enrolled in a study."

"That's wonderful." Megan gave her an enthusiastic smile, turned away. In three quick strides, she was in her office. Nothing sumptuous here. A plain maple desk, the usual computer screen, bookcases along one wall, a single window. She gazed about, and her face was utterly open, a woman saying farewell and not with regret. She was smiling as she settled behind her desk. She reached for the mouse. Next to it lay a Dove bar, dark chocolate with raspberry filling. Her smile was tremulous. "Jimmy . . ."

"Top of the morning to you." Jimmy's voice came from the corner of her desk, and I imagined he was sitting on an edge.

A sharp rap and her office door opened. A big blond man stood in the threshold. He stepped inside, looked around. "Thought I heard somebody."

He was handsome, strong features, full lips, but his blue eyes had a depth of coldness. Standing in the hall behind him, scowling, clearly impatient, was the slender young man who had stared out the window in the waiting room. Slightly overlong fine brown hair framed a slender face now tight with anger, jaws tensed, chin jutting.

"Good morning, Mr. Graham." Megan ignored his comment. Obviously, she was alone in her office. She nodded at the young man, her eyes registering a quick understanding that he was primed for a quarrel, but her voice was pleasant. "Hello, Keith."

Keith managed a nod. "H'lo."

Graham was brusque. "I'll buzz in a minute. As soon as I'm free." No *Good morning*. No *How are you?* Curt. Peremptory. He turned away, not bothering to close the door or look toward the young man, who followed him. Keith Porter's voice was clear for a moment, "Look, you got to—" The sound of a closing door cut off his words.

"Somebody sure needs to kick his ass." Jimmy's tone was dark.

"Hush." Megan glared at the corner of her desk.

Sharon King stood in the open doorway. The slender secretary stared around the small room, her expression puzzled. She held an orange folder in one hand. "I heard a man's voice." Her voice was soft, pleasant. She was attractive in a subdued way, and she looked intelligent.

Megan looked about. "Not in here."

Sharon King was firm. "A man said somebody needed to kick his ass. I thought it was Keith Porter. He's in a fighting mood today." Again she surveyed the office, empty except for Megan.

Megan was decisive. "Mr. Graham just went down the hall. Keith Porter was right behind him. Do you have something for me?"

Sharon was instantly secretarial. "Mr. Graham wants you to review this file and send a letter to the client." She walked toward Megan's desk.

I moved fast. I reached the desk, that particular corner first, grabbed, found Jimmy's elbow, tugged.

"Hey." A baritone yelp.

I reached up, placed my fingers across his lips.

Megan stared toward the doorway. "Yes?" she called out, as if Jimmy's voice came from that direction.

Sharon was rigid in the middle of the room, her gaze focused a few feet to her right.

I wondered what she would think if she could see Jimmy standing there. I imagined he was tousle haired, incredibly handsome, likely in a well-fitting (yes, I keep up with the style for young men) polo shirt, shorts, and espadrilles. Probably, as was also the fashion for his age, slightly unshaven. A stubble of beard is alluring to women. Another time, I would ponder that fact. Was the attraction the unmistakable masculinity of bristly cheeks? The hint of a bad-boy aura? Or the suggestion of careless comfort? I recalled— But I must focus on the moment.

Megan rose, moved past the secretary, poked her head out into the hall, then returned, shrugging. "I don't see anyone in the hall. Thank you, Sharon. I'll be talking to Mr. Graham in a few minutes."

Sharon nodded, her face still puzzled as she walked toward the door.

Megan closed the door after Sharon, stared coldly toward the desk. "Jimmy, don't say anything else unless we're alone."

"It's that woman's fault."

"Woman?" Megan's gaze flickered around the small office.

"You know, the one who wants me to go up the stairs."

Megan's shoulders sagged. "Here I go again. One imaginary person apparently isn't sufficient. No. I have two imaginary—" She broke off, stared in the direction of Jimmy's voice. "Stairs?"

"You don't see them? Over there by the window. Wherever I go, there they are, these gleaming white steps in a kind of golden haze going up and up."

Megan's eyes widened. She spoke barely above a whisper. "Stairs to . . ."

"Up." He was abrupt. "Megan, you can do better than this Blaine guy."

I spoke out. "Jimmy, you always looked for adventure. I'll help you help Megan to make the right choice, then you can take the stairs to the greatest adventure of all." It always worked for me when I could persuade an adversary that really we were on the same side.

I felt an approving pat on my shoulder. Dear Heaven, Wiggins was here. But apparently he understood and approved my approach with Jimmy. I felt a breath on my cheek. "Off again to Tumbulgum. Make every effort to resolve his presence as soon as possible." His murmur was too low for Jimmy and Megan to hear.

Megan was staring at the window. "If I see stairs, I'll know my mind's out of control."

As clearly as if a tattoo sounded, I knew Wiggins had departed. The dear man would surely be hurt if he knew I hoped his visit to Tumbulgum was prolonged. Tumbulgum, Australia, in July was certainly a good twenty degrees cooler than Adelaide. Dislodging Jimmy was not going to be a lark and would likely require time.

The buzzer on the desk sounded, several quick short burrs.

Megan said forcefully, "Jimmy, do not say another word. I don't care what happens. Do not speak." She grabbed a file folder, walked to the door. She stepped into the hall. She was just outside Doug Graham's office when the door was yanked open. Megan drew back.

Keith Porter stood in the doorway, his face flushed. He blinked rapidly, and I had a feeling he was trying not to cry. He half turned to look toward Graham. "Why won't you listen to me? Mom and Dad didn't want you to treat me like this. You don't have any right to—"

Heavy steps sounded. The lawyer was in the doorway. "The matter is closed. I told you a year and I meant a year. It won't do any good to throw a tantrum. If you keep it up, I'll make it a year and a half."

The back of Keith's neck reddened. "Someday somebody's going to—"

Graham ignored him, turned away, slammed the door shut.

A deep, boisterous, king-of-the-mountain shout boomed from the reception area. "Where's that lucky son of a gun?" A big man burst through the doorway, strode forward, making the wide hallway seem small. He was well over six foot five, a Stetson pushed back on a shock of iron gray hair, a seamed face, broad shoulders, slim waist. His blue Tommy Bahama polo pulled out over a slight paunch. His Levi's were well worn, but his Tony Lama red leather boots gleamed with polish. "Yo, Doug. Come out, come out, wherever you are." He planted himself solidly in the middle of the hallway, boomed, "Listen up, ladies. Have you heard—"

White-haired Lou, her round placid face anxious, hovered nervously in the doorway to the waiting room. She turned over her plump well-cared-for hands as if to say, *I couldn't stop him, he barged right in.*

Sharon's slender fingers rested on her keyboard. She half turned to look at the newcomer. Anita was slumped in her chair. She ignored the gathering in the hall, scrubbed at her splotchy face. Geraldine twirled a yellow curl on one finger. Her eyes held a look of appraisal, a woman sizing up a man and liking what she saw. Nancy Murray leaned forward to watch, dark eyes bright with interest.

Megan glanced from Keith Porter, glowering outside Graham's office, to the big man standing with his arms akimbo.

Brewster Layton's office door opened. His small gray-haired client peeked out, her eyes darting up and down the hallway. Layton came up behind her. He nodded toward the big man. "Morning, Jack."

The visitor clapped his hands together. "Good to see you, Brewster. Did you know what your partner's up to?" He gave Brewster no chance to reply and bulled past Keith Porter to Graham's office, pounded, flung open the door. "Come on out, Doug."

Graham moved into the open doorway. "Hey, Jack, tamp it down. You aren't on a rig. Look what you've done." The lawyer gestured at the watching faces. "Nobody's working. I'll add a surcharge to your bill to make up for the loss."

The big man shoved his cowboy hat farther back on his head. "Don't try to calf rope me, Doug. I want to see the ring."

Graham's blond brows lifted in surprise.

A guffaw. "Did you think you could keep that rock a secret? Not in Adelaide. Don't try to pretend. I know all, just like a palm reader in a tent. Maisie's planning a big midsummer bash with a fortune-teller and some feng shui guy out of L.A. and a swami—I asked her if that was pickled or smoked—so everybody can get a heads-up on next year. But I'm one up on the local gossips. Maisie was at Jory's Jewelry store yesterday. That woman spends more money on little old trinkets there than I put into a new well." He spoke with a rueful tone, but the message was clear: *My wife buys expensive jewelry, and I can afford any damn thing she wants.* "Maisie always gets the goods on who's bought what, and she tells me you slapped down a hundred grand yesterday for a diamond engagement ring. Just last week you shrugged off my questions, said Lisbeth Carew was a friend and a client and the fact you've spent time at her ranch in Wyoming was all business. I guess we know what kind of business now. I guess you got around to talking about something besides cattle sales and drilling rigs. It figures you'd shell out a bundle for a ring for the richest widow in Pontotoc County. Probably the richest and most gorgeous widow in all seventy-seven counties. And as everyone knows, Lisbeth Carew is the marrying kind. No sneak-around affairs for her. A fine woman despite all that money. So I'm here to celebrate with you, and the more the merrier, right?" His head swung. He nodded respectfully at Layton's client. "Morning, Winnie." In a small town, well-to-do people know each other. He gazed at the watching women, ignored the combative young man with a sullen face and hunched shoulders. "Hey, where's Ginny and Carl Morse? I want everybody in on the act."

Doug's gaze was cold, but he kept his voice pleasant. "Carl and Ginny took a villa outside of Florence for a month." He gestured toward his office. "Come on in."

The oilman rocked back on the heels of his boots, looked as immovable as a recalcitrant bull. "I'll bet Ginny's bought out the jewelry shops in Florence. Bet she's a regular at Walter's Gold and Silver. That's where Maisie always shops. From what I hear about your ring, Ginny'd want one pronto. But we have a right nice audience without them. I know everybody wants to see that hunk of stone. Right?"

White-haired Lou's blue eyes were eager and excited. Megan's expression was studiously courteous. Anita hunched in her chair as if she scarcely heard the hullabaloo. Sharon's face was stiff, as if she found the entire scene distasteful. Geraldine gave a whoop, pushed back her chair, bounced to her feet. "This I got to see." Nancy gave an excited giggle. Keith Porter, hands jammed in his jeans, glared at Doug Graham. Brewster Layton's brows drew down in a tight frown. Beside him, leaning on her walker, his client, Winifred Kellogg, watched intently, bright dark eyes skittering from Doug to Jack to Brewster.

The big man savored the moment. "Ladies love romance, right?"

Geraldine bolted up the hallway, stood a little too near the oilman. "I'll bet you're exaggerating, Mr. Sherman. But I'm here and ready to clap." She lifted her hands high above her head in a flamenco dancer pose, which drew her blouse even tighter across her chest.

Sherman gave an appreciative whistle.

Geraldine dropped her arms, grinned. "If you need someone to model the ring, I really like jewelry." She fluttered her right hand with rings on three fingers.

Sherman took two big steps to tower over Keith Porter. "And you, young fella. You can see how a man with means snags a rich widow." He swung around, faced Doug. "Bring Out The Ring." His tone added the capitals. "Come on, man, haul that ring out here, share the glitter."

Doug's expression was strained. "A time and a pl—"

"Want me to twist your arm? Remember the last time we arm-wrestled? Cost you a thousand. Now I want to see the stone. I hear it's as big a chunk of ice as Jory Jewelry's ever had in the store. I'm here, and here I stay until you haul that sucker out." He glanced down at a massive watch. "I got to hustle out to the rig, but I'm not leaving—"

Doug pushed his office door wide, stood aside. "Come on in, Jack. I'll—"

The jovial oilman passed him with a punch on a shoulder that slightly staggered Graham. Jack Sherman's big voice was clearly heard. "Where's the ring? In your desk?" Heavy steps across the room, a squeak as a drawer slid out. "Red velvet!" A whistle. "Man, you know how to celebrate a conquest." Sherman elbowed past Doug to the hallway. He held up the large ring case, which looked small in his callused palm.

Doug's voice was clipped. "That's enough, Jack." He thrust out his hand. "You've had your fun."

Jack flipped open the ring case, whistled. The diamond flashed its brilliance in the stark light from overhead fluorescents. The oilman bellowed, "Ladies, you can tell your grandchildren you saw the ring that Doug Graham will be sliding on the finger of Lisbeth Carew."

Geraldine reached out and grabbed the velvet case. "That's the biggest diamond I've ever seen." She lifted out the ring, slipped it on her left ring finger, held her hand high.

Sherman clapped appreciatively. "Sparkles real pretty."

Geraldine preened, made a pirouette.

Doug took a step forward and there was no good humor in his face.

Geraldine proclaimed dramatically, "This ring should have my name on it," but she was pulling off the ring, replacing it in the box. She pressed the box to her heart for a moment, then, clearly reluctant, handed it to the oilman. "That is one big ring."

Sherman's laughter boomed. "Doug, the lady put her finger on it. And in it." Geraldine's face was a mixture of cupidity and jealousy. Megan gave the ring a brief glance, one eyebrow slightly raised. Sharon's gaze locked on the vivid, sparkling stone. Anita blinked, perhaps trying to merge this odd moment into the welter of fear in her mind. Lou made a soft cooing sound. "Oh, so lovely. So beautiful. That's the biggest diamond I've ever seen. The little stones around the setting are amazing." Nancy's eyes were wide, her lips slightly parted. Winifred touched a cameo pinned to her blouse. Small pearl earrings were her only other jewelry. Her expression suggested she thought the stone and its setting gaudy and vulgar.

Sherman stopped in front of Keith Porter. "Ever seen anything like this, son?"

Keith stared down at the glittering diamond.

The big man threw back his big head, delighted to stretch out the moment. "Don't ever say Jack Sherman didn't give you a glimpse of life among the one percent in Adelaide, Oklahoma." He turned back to the cluster of women. "Ladies, you're among the first to know that Doug is landing in a big patch of clover. When he marries Lisbeth Carew, he won't need clients." Sherman snapped the ring case shut. "On your toes, Doug." He tossed the ring case in a smooth underhand throw to Doug. "Better put it in the bank 'til you need it."

The lawyer moved fast, caught the red plush velvet case in his right hand, held it tightly. "Maybe I should." He tried to sound good-humored, but he was obviously angry.

"You got to promise to send a selfie of you and Lisbeth when you give it to her. I hear she's due back from Lucerne next week. Now, I got to get out to the rig." Sherman clumped heavily up the hall.

Keith Porter scowled at Graham. "I'll be back in touch. Like tomorrow." He turned, walked away. He reached the door to the reception area as it was closing, gave one last angry look over his shoulder, stepped through, and pulled the door shut. Hard. There was silence in the hallway.

Doug Graham looked at his partner. "I'm sorry the noise interrupted your meeting with Winifred. I know you'll both dismiss Jack's performance from your minds and not mention it to anyone."

Brewster raised an eyebrow. "I don't discuss private matters."

Winifred gave Doug a chilly glance. Her tone was clipped. "I wouldn't dream of speaking of the matter. It is of no interest to me." She turned and stepped into Brewster's office. He followed and the door closed.

Graham's face was touched with red. He knew a put-down when he heard it. He turned toward the others in the hallway. "The show's over." His tone was brusque. "Like everything else in a law office, anything discussed in the hallway this morning is confidential. I expect everyone"—he looked at each in turn—"to dismiss this from your mind." In other words, no gossip, no description of the scene, keep your mouths shut. He looked at Megan, jerked his head toward his office.

Megan, green folder beneath one arm, followed him.

As if that had been a director's cue, Lou hurried toward the waiting room, murmuring, "I believe I heard the phone." Anita sagged back into her chair and plucked at the wad of tissues in her lap. Sharon sat immobile with one hand on her mouse, staring at the computer screen. Nancy immediately hurried to her desk, but a pink flush of excitement still stained her cheeks. Geraldine tugged her sweater down a little on her hips, strolled toward her cubicle, looked amused.

In Graham's office, he was already seated behind his desk, half turned toward his computer screen. As Megan crossed the room, he waved a hand at one of the wing chairs. He didn't bother to speak or look her way.

Megan sat down, settled the folder in her lap. She said nothing, waited with a pleasant expression.

He swiveled in his chair, punched the intercom. "Sharon, I want Anita here. ASAP."

Megan reached forward to place the folder on his desk.

He glanced down, frowned. "That brief in the Adams case won't do. I told you to cite the Carson case."

Her voice was even, but firm. "The Carson case was overruled in a new opinion."

"I've told you before. That's up to the plaintiff's lawyers to find." He leaned back in his large leather chair, amused. He waved a big hand. "I'll take care of it."

"Mr. Graham, I'm giving notice this morning. I've been offered another position. I'll be leaving September first."

He was silent for a moment, his face unreadable. Big blond brows lifted. "Who's the lucky firm?"

"It's a new firm. I'm joining Blaine Smith." Although she tried to be impassive, her eyes shone and her voice was buoyant.

Behind her the knob to the door twisted and the door began to open.

She didn't announce the firm of Smith and Wynn. I suspected she intended to insist to Blaine that she be an associate, not a full partner, until she could build a practice.

"Let me be the first to congratulate you." There was no warmth in his voice, instead an edge of derisiveness.

Her eyes glinted, but she merely nodded. "Thank you." She rose, ready to depart.

"Of course, that means we'll have to let go of Anita." His voice was smooth as honey.

Megan stopped, gazed at him steadily. "Let Anita go?"

He was calm. His voice held a regretful tone. "Always sorry to trim staff, but we won't need her if you leave."

Megan stared at him. "She was here when I came."

"Was she?" He raised an eyebrow. "Times change. Oil boom, now a bust. We can get along with Sharon and Nancy."

Behind her the hall door was open perhaps an inch, then another.

Megan took a step nearer his desk. She spoke quickly, forcefully. "Anita has to have her job."

The hall door stopped.

I moved to the hallway.

Anita bent forward, listening. Her face was slack, the hand on the knob began to tremble.

Megan's voice was low, but clearly audible. "You know how difficult it is with insurance now. Different policies cover different things and some won't allow a choice of doctors. Anita has found a doctor who has a plan for Bridget."

Anita gripped the knob, held tight for support.

"Anita's an excellent secretary." Megan was emphatic.

Through the slight opening, I watched Doug Graham lean back in his huge expensive leather chair, lace his fingers behind his head. His broad face was bland. "She used to be. Seems distracted these days. But maybe you can help her find a job. I suppose your new firm might need a secretary."

"It would not," Megan spoke stiffly, "be the right time for her to make a change. You know her daughter—"

"I don't inquire about the personal affairs of my employees. It's up to you. If you leave, we won't need her services. If you stay, she has a job. So"—and now his cold smile was challenging—"shall I accept your resignation?"

Megan spaced the words. "If I leave, you'll fire Anita?"

Anita leaned against the wall, still clinging to the knob. She struggled to breathe.

I wished I could wrap my arms around her.

"It will be a shame." Graham's smooth voice was mocking. "Would you like to tell her?"

One silent moment, another. Megan's back was rigid. Abruptly, her voice expressionless, she spoke. "I withdraw my resignation." Megan turned to walk toward the door.

Anita drew a gulping breath, let go of the knob, stumbled away. She hurried blindly toward her alcove.

The door to Graham's office was pulled back. Megan stepped into the doorway.

Graham called out, his voice lazy with an underlying taunt. "About the Adams case. On second thought, you make the change in the brief."

Megan stopped, almost turned, then, her face set and hard, she strode up the hallway. She was obviously angry, holding herself in check.

At her desk in the opposite alcove, Sharon King looked up. She glanced from Megan's set face to Graham's partially open door. The secretary's gaze was intense. Perhaps, as all employees do, she was wondering how to deal with a superior who was obviously not in a pleasant mood.

Megan was a few feet short of her office when she saw Anita huddled in her desk chair. Megan swerved to the alcove, came around the desk, put a hand on a shaking shoulder.

Anita looked up, her lips quivering. Tears streamed down her face. "I heard what he said." Her anguished whisper was low enough that only Megan could hear. "Bridget . . . I don't know what I'll do." She held a gold-framed photograph of a young girl, perhaps twelve or thirteen, with springy brown curls and a laughing face.

Megan plucked tissues from a box on the corner, tucked them into Anita's free hand. "It's all right."

"All right?" Anita's voice was thin, scratchy. "The doctor—"

Megan gripped her arm. "It will be all right."

Her eyes wild and desperate, she stared at Megan. She held the picture in one hand, scrubbed at her face with tissues in the other.

"I'm sorry you overheard my talk with Mr. Graham, but you will not lose your job." Megan also spoke softly, but her tone was decisive. "I'm not leaving. It was a possibility, that's all. You are not to worry."

"But you told him—"

Megan's face was composed, her voice firm. "I changed my mind. Everything will be as it has been. I promise you that."

The intercom buzzed. Sharon King's voice was disinterested, matter-of-fact. "Mr. Graham no longer needs to see you, Anita."

Anita stared up at Megan, her face splotchy. "If he fires me—"

"That isn't going to happen. I'm here. And I'm staying." Megan glanced at her watch. "I'd better get to work. Print out the petition in the Branson case for me."

Megan stepped into her office, closed the door. She walked purposefully to her desk.

"Megan, you got to—"

She cut Jimmy off. "Not now." She slipped into her chair, bent to her right to open the bottom drawer.

"That guy's rotten." Jimmy was angry. "You can't stay here. You can't let him treat you like that."

She picked up her purse, yanked out her cell. "Oh, right. I walk out. He fires Anita. He knows about Bridget. He knows she only has a slim chance to live." Her voice trembled. "So yes, I want to go with Blaine. I want out of here more than I've ever wanted anything. Bridget's eleven years old. Will she get another year? I don't know, but I have to do anything I can to give her a chance. If the new drug works, if she gets better, maybe Anita can leave. Until that happens, Graham's won."

Jimmy exploded. "There has to be something we can do." I knew he was standing nearby, handsome face furrowed, hands clenched.

I tried to help. "Maybe Megan can check out insurance policies. Maybe Blaine could offer a policy that would cover Bridget's doctor."

A slight ping sounded from the cell she held in her hand. "Hush. Both of you." She looked at the screen and a new illuminated text.

I peered over her shoulder, knew Jimmy was right beside me.

Champagne on ice. Have grill and steaks. Six o'clock?

Chapter 4

"I'm sorry, babe." Jimmy's voice was soft.

She blinked away tears. "Isn't this what you want?" Her voice was shaky. "Smith and Wynn knocked off the map? When I tell Blaine, he'll think . . . I don't know what he'll think. I can't tell him why."

"Of course you can," I said emphatically. "He's a decent man. Anyone can tell that."

Megan looked in the direction of my voice. "He's a very decent man. If I tell him what happened, he'll be furious. He'll want to confront Doug. I don't need anyone, not even Blaine, to fight a battle for me. Bridget's battle is the one that has to be fought. I'm the one on the front line. Even if Blaine could offer the kind of insurance we get here, it isn't worth a hassle. Anita can't take a chance on derailing her coverage. You know how it goes—sure, there's insurance available but it's likely to cost more, have higher deductibles, and the idea you can keep your doctor or hospital is a joke for every-body except the people in Washington."

She pressed her lips together, texted: Hold champagne. Will explain. White Deer pier six o'clock. She clicked off the cell, dropped it in her purse. At her desk, she drew out the bottom right drawer, dropped her purse into the drawer, slid the drawer shut. Slipping into her chair, she punched the intercom. "If anyone"—a slight pause—"calls for me, I'm not available. Offer to take a message. You don't know when I'll be in the office." She clicked off the intercom.

A muffled peal sounded from the closed drawer holding her purse.

Megan rubbed knuckles hard against one cheek. When the ringtone—the cheerful sound of marimbas—ended, she picked up a pen, reached for a folder.

"Babe—"

"Go away, Jimmy." Her voice was tired. "I'm working." She flipped open the folder, began to read a record of a deposition.

I spoke quickly. "Megan needs some time alone, Jimmy. What do you like to do on a summer day?"

A considering pause. "Spoon chocolate ice cream out of a straw-berry soda. Flop in a hammock. Fish. Tube on the river."

Big black truck inner tubes offered a silky wet journey, fairly cooling when the temperature nudged a hundred. I squeezed my eyes in thought. Perhaps there was something similar. "Megan, does Graham's fancy house run to a swimming pool?"

She looked up, her expression wary. "Yes. Why?"

"Obviously, he's single since he's getting ready to marry a rich widow, so no one should be at the house."

"Like they say, the rich get richer. He came out on top in the divorce. He has the fancy home with spires and turrets and a swimming pool. His ex-wife Rhoda lives in a 1950s brick house in the old part of town. She's a bookkeeper for a construction company. Two kids, both in college. Last I heard one was a camp counselor in Missouri and the other one's waiting tables in Colorado. There won't be any family at Graham's house. Maybe a housekeeper." Megan shrugged. "For that matter, maybe a chorus line for all I know. He thinks he's irresistible to women."

"Is that why they divorced? Did he have interests outside the home?" That's small-town parlance for *extramarital affairs.*

Megan wasn't interested. "I never heard that. The divorce was pretty quiet."

I focused on the main point. "Housekeepers keep houses. They don't lounge in a pool. Jimmy, meet me at Doug Graham's pool." In case Jimmy was unaware of the ease of transport for spirits, I added, "Think *Doug Graham house* and you'll be there." And I was.

Graham's turreted, copper-spired, stone and brick house was on the curve of a heavily wooded street. A stone deer was forever alert in the center of a huge front yard. Stone walls provided privacy from neighbors. Over a wall, the roof of a large home to the east was more than a football field away.

I hovered over the house, looked down on a back terrace and pool with a cabana to one side. Sparkling water splashed over boulders at one end, creating a faux fall. Beyond the pool was a stretch of a golf course fairway. Several tall sycamores separated the pool and patio from a three-car garage. Summer sounds included a not-too-distant lawn mower, a burst of Latin music likely from a yard worker's truck, and the steady clack of a hedge clipper.

A geyser of water exploded from the deep end.

The watery plume reminded me of long ago and Rob cannon-balling off the *Serendipity* into the Gulf. What makes cannon-balling into water irresistible to young men? The curtain of water rising and falling? The satisfying smack on impact?

I remained invisible. Should Wiggins in faraway Tumbulgum be aware of my status, he would be pleased I was not seen. Nevertheless, I always like to be appropriately costumed. I changed into a moderately cut blue floral swim dress with a full skirt. White hibiscus on top melded into a blue background with clever dark vertical streaks on the skirt. Had I been visible, I was confident I would have looked my best.

I picked up a plastic float and slipped into sun-warmed water. I stretched out on the float, used my hands to propel the float to the deep end.

An inner tube moved through the air and plopped into the pool. Jimmy jumped next to it, then pushed the tube down into the water as he settled in the center.

"Pretty nice." He didn't sound happy.

I heard sadness in his voice as he remembered wonderful hazy days of summer when he was alive, pools and rivers, mountains, cars, a beautiful girl.

"Tell me about Megan."

His voice lifted as he recalled school days and picnics and occasional snowfalls and sledding down Adelaide hills. "She moved here in junior high . . . Some of the girls made fun of her because she was skinny and wore big glasses and didn't have the right kind of shoes, whatever they were back then. And she came into town and everybody already knew each other at school so she was on the outside. Sometimes she didn't have anyone to sit with at lunch, so one day I stopped by the table and asked if she'd explain a poem to me for English. Girls liked me."

There was no particular pride in his voice. He was simply stating a fact. Handsome Jimmy, always desirable, a magnet to admiring girls.

"First thing you know, we had a whole table full and some of the nicer girls found out Megan was funny and quick and always kind."

"That was sweet of you."

A robust laugh. "Sweet old Jimmy? Not. You want the truth? The first time I looked at her, pigtailed, skinny, intense, always striving to be the best, I was sunk."

"Why?"

"She's Megan." He spoke with finality.

I heard caring and kindness and a tinge of awe in his voice. I liked him very much.

"I followed her to OU and I was always there when she needed me. Everything changed the semester we spent in Tuscany. The university has a campus there. Pretty amazing place. When we danced under the stars, I'd tell her"—his voice was suddenly soft—"*Mi cara ti amo.* And *Il mio cuore ti appartiene.* And *Vi soro pio bella che la luna e stelle.* We came back to school and suddenly it was the two of us."

The water rippled and warmth touched us. I didn't know Italian, but I didn't need a translator to tell me they were words of love. I felt surrounded by remembered happiness.

"The happy summer. The best summer. I even thought about being a lawyer because of her." A hoot of laughter. "I knew that wasn't for me. Maybe a trial lawyer. But you have to wear a suit in court and say, *Yes, Your Honor* and *No, Your Honor,* and I'd come into some pompous jackass's court and end up in jail for contempt. Megan always knew what she wanted to be. Her parents died when she was twelve, and that's when she came to Adelaide. She lived with her uncle. He was a judge, very respected. He died when she was in law school, so she doesn't have any family. Maybe that's why she's so thoughtful about other people. She started a drive in high school to raise money for a teacher whose house burned down. She tutored me in English and never told anybody and helped me graduate. At least"—he sounded embarrassed—"she thought she did. Actually, I was good with words. I never tried to make grades. But I'm not good enough with words to explain how I feel about Megan." A pause. *"I never saw so sweet a face / As that I stood before. / My heart has left its dwelling-place / And can return no more."*

"'First Love' by John Clare. The last verse." Astonishment lifted my voice.

"Not what you expected from me? Like they say, sometimes the cover doesn't tell what's in the package. I was always a fool for the romantic poets." He slapped his hand on the water, making a splash. "That's . . . that was a deep dark secret to everyone in the newsroom. I would have gotten cute e-mails every day. Like . . . *and such are daffodils / With the green world they live in . . .* The subject line would be something like: *Daffodilling this morning, bud?"*

"Keats," I murmured automatically.

"How'd you know?" Now he was surprised.

"At one point I taught high school English." Touching so many bases, Beowulf, Shakespeare, Keats, Shelley, Dickens, Twain, e. e. cummings, Millay . . .

"You sound like a lot more fun than my high school English teacher."

I laughed, remembering one rowdy class that loved to chant: *Mrs. Raeburn has a crush on Charles Darnay.* I won't say there wasn't some truth to their claim.

"Now you're a ghost—"

"Emissary."

"Whatever. You're here to kick my butt up the stairs." Robust splashes and the inner tube moved toward the swirling water near the boulders.

I followed, propelling the float with matched strokes.

The inner tube moved with the current created by the falling water. "Hey, fun."

I positioned my float in the current and fetched up beside the inner tube. "Speaking of the stairs—"

"Do you see them?"

I looked toward the evergreens. Despite the intense summer sunlight, the curving stairway glowed silver and gold and white. "Don't you think they look welcoming?"

"Maybe. I can't go yet. Megan's in big trouble. I didn't want her to work with Blaine Smith, but I don't want her stopped by a big blowhard bully. Maybe I'll leave an anonymous message for the guy who took my place on the *Gazette*, how a local lawyer would let a kid die to get his way. Hey, that's an idea. Lawyers hate bad publicity—"

"Graham would be smooth as honey and say he can't imagine why a young lawyer would spread that kind of story about him although her work had been in question."

"Oh."

I made the likely outcome perfectly clear. "He'd assume Megan leaked the story. He thinks only he and she heard their conversation. He'd get back at her. Actually, the conversation was overheard. Anita was at the door. She listened, but she'd be the last to tell anyone. Graham holds all the cards. Sometimes we have to recognize we're caught up in something we can't control. All Megan can control is her actions. If she stays, Anita stays."

"Graham's a son of a bitch to treat Megan like that." Jimmy's voice was loud. "Somebody—"

I have excellent peripheral vision. I caught a flicker of movement among honeysuckle vines in the arbor near a cluster of outdoor tables and chairs of white wrought iron.

"—may kill him one of these days."

I looked toward the arbor.

A slender young man about twenty in a tee and shorts and grass-stained athletic shoes stared at the pool. A pair of clippers dangled from his right hand. Slowly his eyes, huge in a darkly handsome face, traveled up and down the pool.

Jimmy's voice was gruff. "If I were here, I'd punch Graham out. I'd flatten him."

To anyone listening, the voice clearly came from the pool, the brusque threat and the soft lap of water against the tiled sides.

The yard worker bent forward, stared, perhaps seeking a swimmer submerged for a moment. Then his gaze swept the terrace.

70

Of course, he saw no one.

"Jimmy . . ."

His voice overrode my whisper. He sounded steely, dangerous. "I'm going to stop Doug Graham. I'll do whatever it takes. I've got some ideas."

The yard worker moved backward. Fast. His eyes looked wild and frantic. "Shh." My warning was too late.

With a panicked bleat, the yard worker dropped the clippers, turned, ran. His thudding steps grew fainter and he was out of sight behind the Bradford pears.

"He heard you threaten—" I broke off.

The inner tube, no longer low in the water, floated empty. Jimmy was gone.

I didn't call out for Jimmy. I had no doubt that I was alone. I was very much afraid he was out to make trouble for Megan's nemesis. Jimmy was angry, young, and rash. I had to find him, stop him.

I started at the law office, changing my apparel en route, a short-sleeve pink silk sweater, beige silk crepe trousers, pink sandals.

Megan's fingers flew over the keyboard. I had no sense of Jimmy's presence. There was no telltale impression on her sofa. I doubted he could be in Megan's presence for long without speaking.

With a feeling of panic—Jimmy likely acted on impulse and didn't think through the possibility of unintended consequences—I moved to Doug's office. In a quick glance, I felt relief. There was no vandalism. Not that Jimmy was likely to resort to petty destruction. But he was both angry and frustrated.

Speaking of angry . . .

Doug's big face was hard and set. His hand moved in savage

jerks as he wrote on a legal pad. He stopped, read, ripped off the page, crumpled and threw the sheet into the wastebasket to join a growing mound.

I looked over his shoulder.

He started fresh. No salutation. *I never promised anything. If you make any claims, I'll deny everything. You—* He stopped, shook his head, tore off the sheet, threw it away. He started again. *Let's talk again. We can work this out.* He looked satisfied. This sheet was carefully removed, folded, tucked in his shirt pocket.

I glanced longingly at the wastebasket. If Jimmy were here, he'd be pawing through it. I considered trying to filch some sheets but moving crumpled wads through the air and out the door without being noticed would be impossible. I would return tonight. The sheets might make interesting reading. Possibly there might be information that could be used to force—

I forbore to complete the thought. Wiggins would be appalled if an emissary used blackmail, no matter how well deserved. I dearly hoped Wiggins was not in an ESP mode in Tumbulgum.

I felt a tap on my shoulder and the tickle of Wiggins's mustache near my ear.

A breath of a whisper. "City Hall roof."

Wiggins and I had conferred there several times in the past. The asphalt roof would be radiating heat. Quickly, I whispered, as lightly as he, "Cemetery? Jimmy's plot?"

"Excellent idea." His whispered tone was approving.

In an instant, I was at the cemetery. Instead of hurrying to the shade of a Bradford pear, I stopped in front of Jimmy's grave. "Jimmy?"

No reply.

"You've lost track of him?" Wiggins was beside me.

That seemed rather unfair. "You're the man in charge. Surely you know where he is." I felt a surge of relief. Wiggins could set me on Jimmy's trail.

Wiggins made a harrumphing sound. "James has yet to climb the stairs. Until he's welcomed, the connection is faint, and if the heart and mind are closed, the matter is fraught with challenges."

I was stunned. I expected Wiggins to be omnipotent.

"I will find him, of course." He wasn't quite defensive.

"You always know where I am." I tried not to sound accusatory.

"You are an emissary. Of course I know where you are." A sigh. "And I am painfully aware of your continuing struggle with the Precepts. I understand your intentions are of the best, an effort to reassure Megan, poor child, and to persuade James to find his way home to Heaven. It's unfortunate you've had no success."

I heard the rumble of wheels on the tracks. The Rescue Express was coming near, too-roo, too-roo, too-roo.

"Wiggins, we have to think of Bridget." I'd seen her photograph on Anita's desk.

"Sweet child." His tone was soft. "Painfully thin now. Too weak to run and play. Megan will make it possible for her to get the best treatment."

"Jimmy—James—may make things harder for Megan. Let me see if I can find him, persuade him not to interfere."

Coal smoke tickled my nose. The rumble of wheels on the rails made it difficult to hear. But over the trombone wail of the whistle came a reluctant shout. "Twenty-four hours. Do your best. Try . . . Precepts . . ."

Silence.

Wiggins was gone. The air was sweet with the scent of fresh-cut grass. The only sound was the distant roar of a jet overhead.

Twenty-four hours.

I gazed around the quiet cemetery, tried one more time. "Jimmy?"

Had he returned to Doug Graham's house?

I arrived on the terrace. The inner tube, high on the water, drifted near the center of the pool. I stepped into the cabana. Mmm, nice. Comfortable easy chair, divan, one bamboo wall, a braided rug on the floor. Doors on one side revealed two small dressing areas, each with a bench and shower. A door near a wet bar opened to reveal a bright bedroom with a king-size bed. Fresh flowers sat in a bowl on a glass coffee table in front of a white wicker divan. If I wrote tabloid copy, the headline was obvious: "Love Nest."

On the steps to the cabana, I shaded my eyes and followed a path that wound past the Bradford pears. The garage was built of fancy stone that matched the house's front facade. I passed through a closed door. Three empty bays.

The flagstone walk from the garage split into a walk that paralleled the drive, the other passed under a honeysuckle arbor to the terrace. I entered the house from the terrace, stopped next to a pool table to listen. A grandfather clock near a doorway ticked, but I heard nothing else. The house appeared to be empty. I made a cursory check of the lower floor, pausing in the doorway of a study to breathe a sigh of relief. Everything was tidy. "Jimmy?" I lifted my voice.

I strolled disconsolately through a hallway to the terrace room. I was out of ideas. Time was fleeting. The tick of the grandfather clock was an urgent reminder. I had twenty-four hours to convince Jimmy to climb the golden stairs. I'd not planned to be on the pier at White Deer Park at six o'clock. Megan deserved that moment alone with Blaine.

But that's where I could be sure to find Jimmy.

༄

When it's hotter than . . . Actually, not a good comparison. Adelaide's summer is slap-in-your-face hot but steaming with sweat is as lively a reminder of life as any I know. I was tempted to plunge into the lake, but duty called. I did change to a gossamer-thin aqua cotton top and shorts with an adorable print of dolphins at play and aqua sandals.

Megan's red Dodge slewed into the parking lot, jolted to a stop. She burst out of the car, turned, stopped.

I watched heartbreak happen.

Vigor drained away. Sadness and disappointment drew the youth from her face. She lifted a hand to shade her eyes. The pier stretched empty into the water, silent.

She looked at her watch.

The quarter hour chimed from the bells at St. Mildred's. I'd arrived precisely at six. The pier had been empty then as well.

She crossed dusty ground cracked from lack of rainfall and climbed to the pier. Her slow steps on the weathered planks sounded forlorn, defeated. She reached the end, looked out at water glittering in the late-afternoon sunlight.

A screech of tires.

She turned, eyes wide. Recognition was followed by relief mixed with apprehension.

An old yellow Thunderbird with back fins stopped next to her

Dodge. The door opened, and Blaine Smith was out of the car and striding toward the pier, one long arm lifted in greeting.

Megan hurried to meet him. She was grave and somber, her eyes filled with sadness.

They faced each other in the middle of the pier, a small young woman struggling to retain her composure and a big man whose face twisted in concern at her obvious distress.

"Sorry I'm late." The sun turned his wiry straw-colored hair the color of summer wheat. His suit today was a worn green cotton, again with sleeves that didn't quite cover his large bony wrists. His open face reflected thankfulness she was here with an undercurrent of inquiry. He gazed at her searchingly.

She managed a laugh that held a hint of tears. "I was late, too. Lawyers always run behind. One more call, one more e-mail, one more text." A quick breath. "Thank you for coming. I was afraid—" She broke off.

"I wouldn't come? I'll always come. If you want me."

Megan tried to steel her face, but her lips quivered. "There's no good way to tell you. I can't come with you. I wish I could find a way to explain. I wanted to be in your firm"—now her voice was shaking—"more than I've ever wanted anything in my life."

"If that's what you want, then why not?" He reached down, took her small hands in his large ones, held tight. "We'll grow the best firm Adelaide ever saw." His deep lawyer's voice was hopeful.

"I can't." She tried to pull free of his grasp.

Blaine held tight. "Why?"

Her heart-shaped face held misery. "I can't tell you. I spoke to Mr. Graham. I can't quit." She pulled away.

Blaine shoved his hands in the pockets of his suit, hunched his shoulders. "I know you've got a lot of student debt. I guess if he offered a lot more money, you'd be a fool to quit."

She looked at him in dismay. "Do you think I'd promise to come with you, then be swayed by more money?"

"Money's—"

"It's not money." She bit her lip. "There's nothing more to say. I wish it could have happened." She started to pass him.

He reached out, gripped her arm. "He can't hold you if you want to leave."

"I'm afraid he can." Her voice was thin. "There's a reason I have agreed to stay. It isn't about me, Blaine. It would cause great distress for someone else. I wish it didn't have to be this way. But I have no choice." That said, she seemed to find strength. "So, that's that. One of these days, you'll find a good associate and I hope"— her eyes glistened with tears—"that champagne will be wonderful." She pulled away, turned, and ran.

He stared after her, puzzled, disappointed.

She reached her car, yanked open the door, slipped inside. The Dodge revved, backed up, jolted forward.

He stood, hot, sweaty, head lowered, on the pier. Slowly his expression changed. "*It isn't about me.* What the hell is it about?"

"Graham's bullying her. That jerk—"

I moved to my right, hand outswept. I found Jimmy, clapped my fingers over his lips, hissed, "Hush. Carousel." My hiss held an echo of English Teacher Bailey Ruth Raeburn in a Jack Palance mood.

Blaine jerked to look at the shore. Not a single figure was visible, only a gaggle of geese, aloof, imperious, regal. His head swung out to survey the lake. No boat. No windsurfer. No one.

I gave a yank on Jimmy's arm, tugged in the direction of the carousel. He resisted, then moved with me. At the carousel, I led us to the gondola in front of the buffalo. On the pier, Blaine Smith was on his hands and knees, despite his suit, looking over the edge and underneath, seeking the source of the male voice.

"Jimmy, I know you don't want to see Megan upset, but—"

"I told you he was a jerk."

"Graham?"

"Oh yeah. But that Blaine guy, too. How can he think Megan could be bought off?"

"What were you going to tell him?"

"I guess . . . I don't know." He spoke in a mumble.

"That's the problem. There's no way to explain what happened without causing a terrible problem for Anita and her little girl. And Jimmy, the job isn't Megan's only difficulty. You are making her miserable."

His silence emanated resistance.

I reached over, patted his arm. "You mean well, but sometimes meaning well isn't enough."

"You're just trying to get me to climb up those stairs."

The stairs hovered near the carousel, the golden light inviting, the white steps shining.

"You're ready now to climb the steps. Do you know how I can be sure?"

"What makes you think so?" His tone was truculent.

"You truly love Megan. I know that's so because you spoke up on the pier. You want Blaine to know that Megan's good and kind and doing something for someone else, no matter the cost to herself."

"She ought to tell him." A huff. "But he should know she's doing the right thing without being told."

"Why didn't she tell Blaine?"

"Because she's Megan." His voice was soft. "If she told him, it would be like she wanted him to help, but there isn't anything he can do that wouldn't endanger the kid." A sigh. "The thing is, he's nuts about her. I get it. I am, too. He'd understand and keep quiet for the kid's sake. She should have told him."

I touched my fingers to my lips, wafted an unseen kiss in his direction. "So I know you're ready to climb—" I broke off.

I was alone.

✍

It's hard for me to remain quiet. Or sit still. Bobby Mac always said any physicist who wanted to understand perpetual motion should spend a day with me. Of course, I see myself as calm, cool, collected. He simply grins and says all good marriages are based on delusions.

Megan sat on her small plaid sofa in the small living room, Sweetie snuggled next to her. A throaty purr was the only sound in the silent room. Megan had changed into a charming white T-shirt with a daisy print, yellow chambray shorts, and white sandals. She held a tablet.

I looked over her shoulder. Hmm. A book by Ann Ross. I read over her shoulder and stifled a gurgle of laughter. I tamped it down soon enough that Megan, after one hunted look over her shoulder and a skittering gaze around the room, simply shook her head and focused again on the book.

She read determinedly, trying, I felt sure, to hold at bay the negative, sad feelings within. She'd gone from a pinnacle of hap-piness this morning to a dreary acceptance of the pain that right choices sometimes require.

I wished I could swirl present and offer admiration and support and encouragement, tell her she would get past this rough patch. I would suggest she write Blaine a thoughtful note, not revealing the reason for her decision, but carefully explaining that her deci-sion was required to prevent difficulty for another person, that the reason must remain confidential, and hopefully within a year cir-cumstances would change. She could close by assuring him that she held him in the highest regard and always would. Such a note would reassure him that something beyond Megan's control caused her to refuse his offer.

But if I appeared, she would certainly ask how I planned to remove Jimmy from her presence. I didn't want to add to her distress by admitting I had no idea where he was or what he was going to do or whether I'd made any progress in luring him to the stairway.

Which led me to depart again for the cemetery. "Jimmy?" My call was soft, quiet. No reply. Where was he? I couldn't aimlessly roam Adelaide, calling out for Jimmy. Of course, he might well be here or at Megan's apartment and staying mum, hoping I'd give up my efforts to direct him Heavenward.

Sighing, I returned to Megan's apartment. I was tired of remain-ing silent. Perhaps she and I could have a nice chat. I'd admit I wasn't making any progress in persuading Jimmy to—

The living room lights shone. The book was lying on the sofa, facedown, but Megan wasn't there. The calico cat watched me with cool blue eyes. There was no movement, no sound. The apartment had an aura of emptiness. I darted to the bedroom, even checked the bath. I returned to the living room and looked desperately about. Her purse no longer rested on the small table in the entryway and a brass bowl was empty of car keys.

I glanced at the clock. A few minutes after nine. Perhaps she was restless and went for a drive. Perhaps she wanted an ice cream cone. Perhaps she would soon return. And perhaps I should pay attention to the quiver of panic that vibrated inside me. I sensed darkness and evil and danger.

Outside, I checked her parking slot on the east side of the building. The Dodge wasn't there. I had no idea how long she'd been gone. The Dodge . . . that was my best hope. . . .

Chapter 5

I landed beside Megan's old Dodge, illuminated in the soft glow
from lanterns spaced along the top of a brick wall to my left.
Her empty car, the lights off, was parked behind a silver Porsche,
also empty, in the driveway to Doug Graham's mansion. I stood
with one hand on the hood, listening. I heard the metallic chatter
of a faraway television set. A few feet away a wrought iron gate in
the wall was partially ajar. She certainly was not here in this silent
drive. The garage doors were down. Had Megan gone through the
gate?

On the other side of the gate, I paused to get my bearings. A
sidewalk to my left ran parallel to the house. Ahead was a broad
terrace that overlooked the darkened pool and cabana and the sycamores that bordered the golf course.

Light flooded through uncurtained French windows to illuminate orange and blue striped cushions on lawn furniture, several
glass-topped tables, and a hammock on an iron stand. More light

spilled out through an open door midway between the windows. The sound of a television was louder.

I hurried across the terrace, reached the open door, stared in shock. The room was tasteful, masculine, a collection of golf prints hanging on one wall, famous holes at Pebble Beach, St Andrews, Torrey Pines. Bookcases lined two walls. The furniture was comfortable, a chintz-covered sofa, several leather easy chairs. On one wall hung a huge TV screen. A ballplayer swung at a pitch. Cheers rose, the distant revelry an unsettling contrast to the grim scene in the spacious room.

Megan Wynn stood near an end table by a sofa. Blood stained her shirt. She scrubbed at stained hands with crumpled sheets of newspaper. Her face slack with shock, her lips trembling, she wiped and wiped and wiped and wiped at her hands.

On the floor a few feet away lay a large man's crumpled body. The body was near a leather chair that faced the television screen, now vivid with a car ad, an expensive sedan careening in a semi-circle on desert sand.

I reached the body, bent to look. The back of Doug Graham's head was disfigured by a gaping wound. Blood drenched the shoulder of a light blue polo shirt. I looked at the leather chair, saw bloodstains. A half-finished drink sat on the table beside the chair.

Megan's face was drained of color.

"I told you not to go inside." Jimmy's voice was uneven.

"What happened?" My voice was scarcely recognizable.

"My hands." Her voice held horror. Blood still streaked her palms and fingers. Breathing in quick, sharp gasps, she grabbed another folded newspaper from the end table, shook free several sheets, scrubbed again at her hands. She dropped the crumpled sheets to a floor now littered with bloodied pages. She reached down to open her purse, grimaced at her still-sticky hands.

Water gushed in an adjoining half bath. A wet hand towel came rushing through the air.

"Here." Jimmy's voice was shaky as he thrust the towel at Megan.

Megan grabbed the cloth and swiped until her hands were clean, the cloth stained with blood.

"You have to get out of here." Jimmy sounded young and panicked.

She dropped the hand towel on the floor by the crumpled pieces of newspaper.

I looked from the refuse on the floor to Doug's body. "What happened?"

She gazed frantically around the room, apparently empty except for her and the dead man. She held up a trembling hand. "All right, you two, I don't know if you're here or not. But I can't deal with either of you now. I have to call the police." She opened her purse and yanked out her cell, then stopped and lifted her head.

I heard the unmistakable sound, too, as the distant wail of sirens rose over the blare from the television.

Megan listened, the phone still clutched in her hand.

Louder, stronger, the sirens came nearer and nearer, reached a crescendo, their warning wail urgent, imminent.

I never doubted the sirens were destined for this house.

Megan's eyes widened. She looked around the spacious den. The television screen was bright and vivid, an outfielder running to catch a ball. Doug Graham's body rested awkwardly on one side, smaller in death than in life. Blood still trickled from the back of his head. He was freshly dead. Very freshly dead. Crumpled newspaper sheets and the blood-soiled hand towel lay in a mound on the floor by her feet.

The squall of sirens rose, louder, nearer.

Jimmy talked fast. "Run out the back door. Hurry."

Megan was abrupt. "My car's in the driveway. It would be hard to explain why my car was here and I wasn't." She whirled away, headed out onto the terrace.

I was crisp. "Keep quiet, Jimmy." I followed Megan outside.

She walked swiftly across the terrace and through the gate onto the driveway.

Three patrol cars, sirens shrieking, red lights whirling on the roofs, squealed to a stop behind Megan's Dodge. The sirens cut off.

Megan stood in the glare of the cruiser headlights, a small figure, summery in a tee and shorts and sandals, but her face was drawn, her eyes stricken. Blood splotched her white T-shirt.

Red lights atop the cruisers continued to flash, ominous, threatening. Doors opened and the drive was suddenly filled with uniformed police. Two patrol officers advanced, the female officer in the lead. Stocky with short-cropped gray hair, the officer's sharp gaze scoured Megan, her face, her posture, the position of her hands. The officer's gaze lingered on Megan's blood-streaked shirt, then lifted to stare at her warily. The taller officer moved his head back and forth, checking the surroundings for any hint of threat. He held a flashlight in one hand, kept the other on his holster. The beam swept either side of the drive, illuminating the shadows. Officers from the other cars fanned out, flashlights making the yard bright.

The lead officer was brusque. "Homicide reported. Where's the body?"

I noted her name tag. *Officer J. Roberts.*

Megan blinked in surprise, surprise and apprehension. "In the house. I found him just a moment ago."

"Anyone else on the premises?"

"I don't know. I just arrived. I saw no one."

"Lead the way." Roberts never took her cold gaze off Megan.

Megan stared at the officer's stolid face. "How did you know?"

There was a spark of interest in Roberts's cold eyes. "Know?"

"That Mr. Graham had been killed."

"Nine-one-one call. Didn't you make that call?"

Megan's eyes narrowed. A 911 call. Who called? Why was the call placed when she was in the house? Was the intent to put her at the scene of a murder? Megan's hands clenched.

The stocky officer's gaze noted those tight fists.

Megan saw Roberts's stare. Slowly her hands relaxed. She spoke in a measured tone. "I didn't call nine-one-one. I didn't have time. I'd just arrived and found the body. I was getting ready to call when I heard sirens."

Roberts was brusque. "Name?"

"Megan Wynn." A pause. "Attorney-at-law. An associate in the firm of Layton, Graham, Morse and Morse."

Roberts's expression didn't change. "Show us the body."

"Mr. Graham is in his den." Megan glanced from Roberts to a surrounding ring of officers. "We go through the gate and cross the terrace to the back door." She turned and walked through the open gate. Roberts and the tall, thin officer—Officer L. Burke—followed.

The clap of shoes on cement was the only sound as Megan led the way to the side door.

When Megan reached for the doorknob, Roberts intervened. "I'll get it." She pulled out vinyl gloves, slipped them on, delicately turned the knob.

Megan stepped inside, gazed at the body slumped on the floor, a sick, shocked look on his face. "I found him dead." She remained rooted only a foot from the doorway.

Roberts spoke to Burke. "Stay with her." She gestured to several officers behind him. "Check out the house."

Two officers moved cautiously across the spacious den, reached a door, stood to one side after flinging it open. "Police. Come out with your hands up. Police." In a moment, they stepped through the door. Their voices faded as they moved farther away. It would be a large house to search.

Roberts surveyed the room from the doorway, noted the body. I suspected she was looking for a weapon. I stiffened. Where were the crumpled newspapers? And the bloodied hand towel? I checked a wastebasket near the sofa. Empty. The bathroom wastebasket held a few crumpled tissues. I looked at the ceramic holder on the wall by the lavatory. One hand towel, obviously clean, hung on one side. I moved the single towel to the center of the bar. I rather thought I knew what had happened. Should I warn Megan?

She stood stiffly by the terrace door. Officer Burke watched her.

I saw no way to speak to Megan, even in the softest whisper, and escape Burke's notice.

Officer Roberts stood a few feet away from the body, talking rapidly into her lapel mic. "One-eight-seven at 93 Tudor Lane. Need medical examiner. Forensic van." As she listened, she looked at

Megan. "We have one person on the scene . . . no weapon . . . right. Scene secure until ME arrives." She clicked off the mic. She returned to look down at Megan, the officer's pale brown eyes cool and suspicious. "Name again." She pulled a small notebook and a pen from one pocket.

"Megan Wynn."

"Address."

"Three-eighteen Magnolia, apartment 6."

"Can you identify the deceased?"

Megan said quietly, "Douglas Graham. A partner at Layton, Graham, Morse and Morse."

"What happened?"

Megan stiffened slightly. "What do you mean?"

"How was the victim killed?" Roberts's gaze locked on Megan's face.

Megan frowned. "I don't know. I came in from the terrace and I saw him. He was sitting in that chair." One small hand waved toward the brown leather chair that faced the screen on the wall. "He was slumped to one side. I saw blood."

"How'd he end up on the floor?" The tone was accusatory.

Megan's words came in uneven spurts. "I could tell he was horribly hurt." Her eyes held horror. "I ran across the room. I had to try and help him. I picked up his arm to check for a pulse. I couldn't find any. I let go of his wrist. Maybe I jerked him. I don't know. His body started to slip sideways. I reached out and grabbed him, tried to keep him from falling, but I couldn't hold on." She glanced down at her shirt. "It was terrible. There was blood on my hands. I used newspapers to try and wipe it off." A pause. "And a hand towel from the adjoining bathroom."

Roberts stared at her, then turned and once again surveyed the room from the doorway. "Crumpled newspapers?"

"Yes. Several sheets."

Roberts faced Megan. "Where'd you put the newspapers and hand towel?"

Megan frowned. "I dropped everything on the floor near the sofa."

Roberts's gaze was probing, skeptical. "Let me see if I have it right. You got here, walked in. You claim the victim was dead."

Megan's face tightened. "He was dead when I came." She enunciated each word with force.

"Right. You claim he was sitting in the brown leather chair and you pulled him over to the floor and that's how blood got on your clothes and hands."

"That is what happened."

Roberts's gaze was accusatory. "Why were you here?"

"Mr. Graham texted me a few minutes before nine——"

Roberts held out her hand. "Let me see."

Megan considered the request. She was under no compulsion to turn over the phone. However, the text would be found—message sent—in his phone. She reached into her purse, pulled out the cell phone, handed it to the officer.

Roberts clicked, glanced, read the text message.

I hovered near her shoulder.

Imperative you come to my house now re matter discussed this morning. Will otherwise pursue termination. Park in driveway. Enter at gate, cross terrace, come in back door to den.

Roberts copied the text, handed back the cell. "Your termination?"

Megan looked surprised. "My . . . No. It was another matter entirely."

"You weren't about to be fired?"

Megan was firm, confident. "No."

"Whose termination did he want to talk about?"

Megan was silent for a long moment, finally spoke slowly, "I decline to answer that question." She wasn't combative, but she was definite.

Roberts spoke in a level, expressionless voice. "We'll have quite a few questions. You are the only person found at the scene of a homicide. You claim the victim was dead when you arrived. You claim you didn't call nine-one-one. We need to know when you arrived, what you saw, what information you are willing"—slight emphasis—"to provide. Burke, escort Ms. Wynn out to the patrol car. Interview her. Note any question she refuses to answer."

As Megan and Burke reached the drive, a crime van pulled up, followed by a red sports car and a dark green SUV. Two crime techs swung out of the van. Each carried a black case. They walked briskly toward the gate. A slender young man in a T-shirt, shorts, and espadrilles popped out of the sports car. I recognized Jacob Brandt, the brash medical examiner. As soon as he officially declared Graham dead, the painstaking investigation would begin, photos, measurements, sketches. Adelaide police Detective Sergeant Hal Price slammed the SUV door. He was as tall, blond, muscular, and handsome as I remembered from earlier adventures. Hal strode swiftly past the parked van and patrol cars, nodded to Officer Burke.

Burke led Megan to the second cruiser and opened the rear door.

Megan glanced inside, saw the metal grillwork that separated the backseat from the front. "I prefer to stand on the drive."

Burke's face furrowed. He resembled an unhappy bloodhound.

Megan's voice was pleasant, but firm. "I'd rather be out in the night air. How can I help you?" She was somber, but self-possessed and confident.

After a hesitation, Burke pulled out a notebook. "What time did you arrive?"

"A few minutes after nine."

"Did you see anyone near the house?"

"No."

"Did you hear any sounds? Voices, door slamming, footsteps?"

"Nothing besides the television."

"Did you see any vehicles?"

There was an instant of hesitation, then she said without expression, "As I turned into the street, a car pulled away from the front of the house."

He looked eager. "Make, model?"

She turned her hands palm upward. "I'm not knowledgeable about cars. The car was driving away. I saw taillights receding." She pointed to the east. "The lights were red." Her tone was bland.

I looked at her sharply. I had the sense she could have said more, had no intention of doing so.

"What happened then?"

"I pulled into the driveway, parked behind the Porsche. That's Mr. Graham's car. I went through the gate and crossed the terrace. The door to the den was open. I heard the sounds of a baseball game. I thought he wouldn't hear me so I called out as I pulled the handle. As I opened the door, I saw him."

"Were you surprised the door was open?"

"I assumed the door would be open since Mr. Graham directed me to enter that way."

"Had you been here before?"

"I have been at his house several times for dinner parties."

"You opened the door. What happened next?"

"I called out his name." A quick, strained breath. "Then I saw him. He was slumped to one side in that leather chair, his head tilted sideways. His arm was hanging down. I saw blood on the back of his head and his shoulder. He wasn't moving but I knew I had to see if he was alive. I hurried across the room and picked up his hand. I couldn't find a pulse. When I let go of his wrist, he started to fall. I tried to stop his fall, but he was too heavy. My hands were bloody and there was blood on my shirt. I went across the room to a stack of newspapers on an end table. I grabbed some and used them to wipe my hands off. My hands were still sticky. It was awful." Horror bubbled in her voice.

Burke was writing fast.

"I used a damp hand towel from the bathroom and that helped. But there's still blood on my shirt."

"Did you see a weapon?"

"No."

"Do you have or have you ever had possession of a gun?"

"No." Her face was pale and empty, her eyes dark with worry. And fear.

"What were your relations with Mr. Graham?"

"I am an associate at the law firm—"

I leaned close to her ear. "I'll be back," I whispered.

Her face didn't change. My presence or absence appeared to

matter not at all to her. I felt rather sure Jimmy was near, aching to talk to Megan, frightened for her. I knew he meant well when he removed the news sheets she'd used to wipe her hands but I hoped he refrained from tampering with any other evidence. I wished I had some means of finding him, but there was no time for that now.

As I arrived in the den, Jacob Brandt faced Detective Sergeant Price. "He was shot from about a foot away. The bullet smashed the back of his head. I'd say he was killed instantly. The slug may be pretty battered, but I'll dig it out for you. For the rest, Caucasian male approximately forty to fifty years old, estimated height six foot three or four, weight around two forty. No scrapes on his hands. I'd say the bullet caught him by surprise."

Hal Price, handsome and trim in a blue polo, khakis, and loafers, eyed the body. "Time of death?"

Brandt rolled his eyes. "We're not on TV. Within the hour, give or take thirty minutes. No rigor yet." He started for the door. "I got a hot date at home. I'll do the autopsy tomorrow. I don't expect any surprises. Somebody came up behind him, pulled out a gun, plugged him without warning. Might have been small caliber. A .38 or .45 would have blown off half his head." He picked up a small black bag, strode toward the door, his expression smooth and untroubled. His job was done for the night. Death had been officially declared, the investigation could begin.

As the ME reached the hall, Hal nodded at the crime techs, a fortyish woman with a blonde ponytail and a slender young man with a military crew. "Check for prints on the desk and chairs first." Hal looked at Officer Roberts. "What's the demeanor of the witness?"

Roberts was thoughtful. "She acts shocked at the crime. She claims he was dead when she got here. She claims she didn't make the call to nine-one-one. She has an explanation for everything, including bloodstains on her clothing. She said she used some newspaper sheets and a hand towel from the half bath to clean up her hands, then dropped the sheets and towel on the floor. There are no bloodied newspaper sheets or a messed-up hand towel in this room or in the bath."

Hal looked interested. "What was she doing here?"

"She received a text from Graham that told her to come here." Roberts flipped open her notebook, read the text to Hal. "She clammed up when I asked her to explain what Graham meant by *Will otherwise pursue termination.* Sounds to me like he intended to fire her. She claims not. Burke's interviewing her now. Name's Megan Wynn. She also claims she was going to call nine-one-one when she heard sirens. According to dispatch, a nine-one-one call from the landline in this house came in at 9:04 p.m."

Hal held up a hand. "What was the delivery time on the text she received?"

Roberts didn't have to look at her notes. "Text received at 9:01 p.m." A sardonic look. "Maybe she thought if she received a text before the nine-one-one call was made that would prove she wasn't here. She could have shot him, used his cell to text her cell, then called nine-one-one. We'll check his cell for fingerprints. She says she heard the sirens and walked out on the drive and stood there waiting for us."

"Where's the gun?"

"We haven't found a gun yet. Definitely there's no gun in the room where he died." Roberts squinted in thought. "Maybe she knows the house inside out. She's a looker. Maybe she and the guy had something going on. We got here about six minutes after the nine-one-one. She had plenty of time to get rid of a weapon before we arrived."

Roberts's cell rang. She answered the call, listened, looked at Hal. "Wynn's asking to be driven to her apartment to change out of the bloody shirt, said she'll turn it over to us."

Hal was quick. "When Burke finishes interviewing her, he can follow her home, take the shirt, tell her we'll be in touch tomorrow."

Roberts replied to Burke, and then picked up where she'd left off. "She had time to hide the gun in the house or maybe she ran out to the end of the lot and threw the gun into the woods by the golf course or maybe she had a hole already dug out there and the gun's buried with leaves sprinkled on top of it. We can use a metal detector out there if we don't have any luck in the house."

"Why hide the gun?"

Roberts had an answer. "Create confusion. Same with the nine-one-one call. For her, the more confusion the better."

Hal was equable. "You think she's the perp."

"Seven-to-one odds."

"Why not admit to the nine-one-one? And why tell you about wiping blood off her hands yet you didn't find any newspaper sheets or a hand towel?"

Roberts was laconic. "Smoke and mirrors."

Hal persisted. "She could have walked out, not made a call."

"There was that text on his cell and hers."

Quick steps sounded and a hulking officer with a receding hair-line and large paunch stood in the doorway. "No sign of a break-in. No one found in the house. No apparent damage or disarray. Hurley canvassed the neighbors. Nobody heard or saw anything unusual. Neighbor across the street saw the Dodge arrive around the time Wynn claims. Another car was here a little earlier and some guy went up on the front porch, rang the bell, but nobody answered."

I hovered for a moment for a last glimpse. Except for the blood-ied chair and the body, the room appeared absolutely normal, a man's comfortable enclave, a half-finished drink on the table next to his chair, the baseball game on the big wall screen. I pictured Doug Graham in his last moments. If he was aware of his would-be killer's presence, it was no cause for alarm. I rather thought he was not aware of a guest. I glanced toward the door to the terrace. It was perhaps two feet behind the chair. Someone who knew him well, knew where he would likely be on a summer evening, may have silently crossed the terrace, eased the door open, crept up behind him, gun in hand. The banter of baseball announcers or the louder background of commercials would mask any sound. The intruder slipped across the den, came up behind the chair, lifted the gun, fired. Then the TV was muted, his cell phone eased from his pocket, the text sent to Megan, the call made to 911, the tele-vision turned back on. Before Megan arrived, before the police came, sirens wailing, the murderer hurried out into the night, unseen.

I believed in Megan's innocence. I had no proof. I felt somber as I rose through the house and out into the star-spangled night.

Lights flooded the pool area. Two patrol officers stood at the cabana door. "Police." The voice was loud, stern. A rattling knock. "Open the door." In the drive, officers spoke in muted tones, a police radio crackled, an occasional car door slammed, a distant owl whooed. A stocky officer knocked again on the cabana door. He turned the knob and at the same instant moved to one side, shielded from the interior. No movement. No sound. The light of the officers' flashlights illuminated the entry. The officer in the lead turned on lights. Doors banged and in a moment, the officers came out.

I understood that it was necessary to be sure, that they had to check out the entire house and grounds, but a murderer wasn't waiting for them with a welcome sign. Doug Graham's clever killer had moved fast, and there would not be any trace of his or her presence now.

I hovered near the far end of the yard, beyond the pool, peering at the darkness of the golf course. The golf cart path was dimly visible in the lights from the pool. No one moved on the path.

I was sure Megan Wynn hadn't hurried into the thick cluster of trees to bury a murder weapon, but I rather suspected a murderer walked this way. I didn't think a murderer parked in Doug Graham's driveway. Why drive through a neighborhood if you are on a mission to commit murder? The golf course was right behind the Graham house. Tomorrow I would look, but I didn't doubt there was access from a nearby street to a golf cart path. Anyone intent on remaining unseen would find it easy to park in a quiet spot, perhaps pull off into the woods, go to the cart path, follow the path to the fairway behind Graham's home.

Doug Graham had been enjoying a ball game with a drink. I didn't think he expected a guest. That was another good reason for his murderer to avoid the driveway. Doug Graham might have heard a car arrive or seen headlights flash. Instead, he had no warn-ing before his life ended in a burst of pain.

One telling fact might ultimately lead to the murderer's iden-tity. Only someone who knew Graham well could be aware of the confrontation this morning between Graham and Megan.

I had a swift memory of Anita leaning against the wall outside his office door, listening.

Chapter 6

Megan's Dodge was no longer parked behind the silver Porsche. Tires squealed. A shabby green Plymouth slammed to a stop behind a patrol car. A thin fiftyish woman with straggly brown hair bolted out of the driver's seat, rushed up the drive. The lights illuminated a sharp, bony, intelligent face. Her gaze flicked all around, not missing the crime scene van.

A tall, dark-haired officer stepped in her path. "Sorry, ma'am, crime scene."

"That's why I'm here, sonny. Who's in charge?" She stood with arms akimbo and a take-no-prisoners attitude.

The officer's bulldog face stiffened. "Detective Sergeant Price."

"Tell him Joan Crandall's here for the *Gazette*." She didn't wait for a response. "He doesn't want the lead story to announce the Adelaide Police Department refused to speak to the press about the murder of a leading citizen." A hard stare.

"That's telling him, Joanie." Jimmy Taylor's young voice sounded pumped up.

I was perhaps twenty feet above the driveway. Jimmy's voice was nearby. If not an answer to a prayer, Jimmy's arrival solved one problem for me. I spoke before I thought, "Jimmy, where have you been?" then held my breath. The last thing I wanted was for him to flit away and do Heaven knew what on his own.

"I could ask the same about you." His tone was combative. "You're supposed to be looking after Megan, but I'm the one who thought ahead and got rid of those crumpled-up newspaper sheets and the hand towel."

"Where did you take them?"

"Someplace nobody will ever find."

"Okay." There was no point in revealing that Megan had told the police about the crumpled newspapers and the towel. He was exuding pride at his cleverness. "Then you left?"

"Sure did." He was still pleased. "I went to the *Gazette*. Whoever took my place kept my Rolodex. Yeah, I could have kept all the numbers in my cell but I liked having them handy on my desk, too. Anyway, I got Joan's cell, used the landline, told her we had a tip Doug Graham had been killed, hung up before she could ask who was calling. Joan never heard a siren she wouldn't follow. I knew she'd come. Nobody's savvier about Adelaide and its upper crust and, for that matter, its crummy crust, than Joan. She'll be on this story like a cat on fresh liver. I don't trust cops. They like everything nice and easy. Man shot. Woman found at scene. Threat in text message."

I reassured him. "I'll make sure the police investigate everyone around Doug Graham."

"You'll make sure— Oh, you have some kind of direct line to the cops? They listen to voices in the air?"

"I have a contact." I wouldn't, of course, reveal that Chief Cobb and I had an understanding. Of sorts. Sam was quite open to information received in an unorthodox fashion.

"Yeah." Jimmy didn't sound convinced. "Good luck this time. They've got everything but a gun with Megan's fingerprints on it. I'm counting on Joan. She'll turn over every rock— Oh hey, look. I told you. That cop's taking Joan inside. I'm all ears."

He was gone.

I wondered how he'd feel when he discovered Megan had described cleaning her hands to both Roberts and Burke, and the missing news sheets and towel had fueled suspicion of her.

Likely I could set everything right tomorrow.

For now, I hoped to reassure Megan.

∽

Megan's purse was again on the side table in the entry of her apartment. The book she'd been reading was lying on the coffee table. Sweetie was burrowed into a corner of the sofa. The living room lights blazed. Through the open door to the bedroom, I heard the rush of a shower.

I glanced at the clock. Twenty past ten. I strolled into the small kitchen, opened the refrigerator. Several cheeses, longhorn, cheddar, Gouda. I shook my head. I opened the freezer door and smiled. I didn't think Megan would begrudge a snack. I found a bowl, a spoon, and soon I was seated at the small white wooden table with a bowl of vanilla—two scoops—and a chocolate chip cookie from a cookie jar on the kitchen counter.

I took another spoonful of ice cream—

"I'm glad you found the ice cream." Megan walked across the room, sat across from me. Damp hair curled around her heart-shaped face. She wore a fresh blouse and shorts.

"I didn't think you'd mind."

"Certainly I don't mind." Her reply was courteous. "But I rather prefer, if you're going to be here"—she stared at the spoon level in the air—"that you are here." Emphasis on *here*.

I chose a lacy hand-stitched short-sleeve pale lime pullover with a delicate central panel and white linen trousers. To be festive, I added high white heels.

She watched me without evincing pleasure in my arrival. "You have a lot of clothes. Do you just reach into an invisible closet and pick out a gorgeous outfit?" She sagged back against her chair. "Did tonight really happen? Did I go to Doug Graham's house and find him dead and get blood on my blouse? It seemed real enough at the time. And that cop followed me home and waited in the living room while I changed into a clean top. I watched him put my blouse— and it was a good blouse, I bought it up in the city at Macy's—into a plastic bag. Bye-bye, blouse. Bye-bye, police." A sigh. "But it isn't going to be bye-bye, police. I won't tell them what he meant by termination and they're going to be sure he was threatening to fire me. I never thought how hard it is to prove a negative. No, he wasn't going to fire me, but I can't prove that. I can hear it now, the Miranda warning. It never occurred to me in criminal law class that the Miranda warning would ever be directed at me."

I took a last spoonful of ice cream. Very satisfying. "We just have to make sure the police find the murderer."

"Oh sure. Wave a wand—" She looked at me intently. "Oh hey,

can you get the inside scoop? I mean, you're dead. You better be dead or I am absolutely loony, but maybe I'm loony anyway. I know Jimmy's dead. Why don't I see him? Never mind. Please scratch the thought. That would be the toothpick that toppled this over-burdened camel. Jimmy was— Anyway, you have a lock on the hereafter. Can you go ask Doug Graham who killed him?"

It was not a question I'd heard before. Could I—

A harrumph. Wiggins's mustache tickled my cheek as he whispered, "Roof."

"Excuse me," I blurted. "I'll be right back." I hoped.

I disappeared. The night breeze on the roof was warm but summer cheerful with a grassy scent from a recent mowing. "Wiggins?" I spoke cheerily.

"I fail to see progress with James." Wiggins sounded stern. If he was attired in his usual thick white shirt and heavy flannel trousers, he was likely also decidedly uncomfortable. I decided to attribute the dour note in his voice to the heat.

"Once a newshound, always a newshound." My reply was insouciant. I hoped putting a good face on Jimmy's decision to stick close to Joan Crandall would pacify Wiggins.

A sigh. "I know you've done your best—"

"Wiggins, all is not lost. In fact, I am confident Jim—James will rise to the occasion soon."

No chuckle from Wiggins.

A rumble coming nearer and nearer and the clack of wheels announced the arrival of the Rescue Express. I had perhaps a moment or two to change Wiggins's mind.

"Wiggins"—my tone was urgent—"Jim—James will never desert his post. As long as Megan is in peril"—if my language appears a bit florid, trust me. I know my audience, I could not overdo the Victorian prose—"James will hew to the course, carry the flag, lead the charge."

Coal smoke wafted through the night air. Wheels clacked. Whooo-whooo.

"I can do no less than he." My husky voice rose, a noble proclamation. "Wiggins, freeing Megan of Jim—James's presence will avail her nothing"—I am steeped in Trollope—"if she is unjustly accused, imprisoned, her career destroyed."

"Oh my."

I heard distress in his kind voice. I pressed on, wondered why this idea hadn't occurred to me before. I could take a quick trip on the Express, discover the identity of Doug Graham's murderer, be back in a flash. Megan's worries would be at an end. "If I popped up to Heaven and asked Doug Graham who killed him—"

A sharp intake of breath. "Bailey Ruth." Wiggins was scandalized. "That would never, never, never do. Such an inquiry would trumpet a serious lapse in emissary decorum."

I wasn't quite sure what Wiggins meant, but clearly I'd punched the wrong button. "I certainly wouldn't want to do that."

"The Precepts. Two, Three, Four." A swallow. "Seven."

I quickly reviewed the Precepts in my mind: Two, "Do not consort with other departed spirits." Three, "Work behind the scenes without making your presence known." Four, "Become visible only when absolutely necessary." Seven, "Information about Heaven is not yours to impart. Simply smile and say, 'Time will tell.'"

"Perhaps it is my shame that I have overlooked your frequent deviations from the Precepts on previous missions." Wiggins's voice had the lugubrious quality of an echo from a cavern. "I understood you needed to appear to Jimmy but I didn't intend carte blanche."

The Rescue Express engine roared, but English teacher moxie gave me volume.

"Of course"—I was fervent, which is easy when shouting—"it is always my intention to be faithful to the Precepts. I value the Precepts. I take the Precepts to my heart. Especially Precept Six, 'Make every effort not to alarm earthly creatures.' Think of poor Megan, unnerved by unintentionally disturbing manifestations. I thought it only kind"—Wiggins has a heart as big as a galaxy and I was shameless in giving it a tug—"to appear and reassure her. Surely, Wiggins, you agree"—I increased the decibel level—"that in person I am not the least bit frightening. As for Precept Seven, I absolutely understand. An emissary would be remiss to share information known only in Heaven."

An exasperated sigh. "You are too clever for me, Bailey Ruth. Words, words, words, and when you are done, I find myself bewildered and confused."

"You are always attentive to creatures in need, and believe me"—this was utterly genuine—"Megan is a creature in need. I will save her, dispatch Jim—James to Heaven, and do so with élan and"—great emphasis—"circumspection."

Whoo-whoo.

"You have a plan?"

I heard an edge of desperation. The poor dear man obviously needed a boost, one of my specialties.

"Do I have a plan?" I shouted. "Wiggins, I have a great big supersized extravaganza of a plan."

"Put your plan into action. Immediately."

The clatter of wheels receded. The wail of the whistle fainter. The scent of coal smoke was a memory.

Immediately? Of course. As soon as I reassured Megan.

Her expression somber, she sat on the plaid sofa, feet tucked beneath her, a legal pad on her lap, a pen gripped tightly in her hand, the calico cat pressed against her thigh. Megan wrote, paused, wrote, paused.

I peered over the back of the sofa to look at the legal pad.

Did Doug Graham text me? Or was he already dead? Most likely he was dead and the murderer used his cell to text me.

How did the murderer know Doug threatened to fire Anita if I left?
    A. Doug told the murderer about his conversation with me.
    B. Doug told someone else who told the murderer.
    C. Anita shot him.

Why did the murderer send the text to bring me to the house, then call 911 to report a crime? N.B. No proof as yet that the text and 911 call made by same person, but it is likely and also likely that person is the murderer.

Otherwise have to assume yet a third person found him dead, placed the text, made the call, left before I arrived.

If Anita shot Doug, would she deliberately involve me by sending the text? Wouldn't she be afraid I would tell the police what Doug threatened, thereby revealing that she had a powerful motive to want him dead?

A. If she shot him, she did so to protect Bridget. She would be sorry to make me a suspect but she would do whatever she had to do to remain free.
B. Find out if the police have Doug's phone and whether there are other texts near the time—

"Excellent idea."

She jumped, looked behind her.

I didn't appear. I hoped Wiggins appreciated my restraint. "It's a good idea to write everything down while it is fresh—"

"I don't think," she said, cutting in sharply, "that I am in any danger of forgetting what happened this evening. Speaking of, where have you been?"

"A conference with my supervisor." I was airy. "And now—"

"Did you find out who shot Doug?"

By this time, I was in front of her. I reached out, tapped her arm. She jerked around. "Why can't you stay in one place?"

My, she was touchy. "That's not my job."

"What is your— Never mind. Who killed Doug?"

"The answer is rather complex." I didn't think it fruitful to discuss the Precepts. "I'm not authorized to visit Heaven, discover the murderer's identity, and return to share that information. You started to inquire about my job. I actually have two jobs, persuade Ja—Jimmy to climb the golden stairs, and solve the murder of Doug Graham."

She stared a trifle balefully toward the sound of my voice. "So far, it's two outs and no score."

A baseball fan! "My favorite team's the Cubs. But the Astros are wonderful. I love Jose Altuve."

"You seem to be able to go anywhere you wish. Why not the ballpark?"

I was tempted. "Duty requires my presence here."

She massaged one temple. "I hope you do not literally mean *here*. Can't you go somewhere else? Solve Doug's murder."

I almost murmured *O ye of little faith* but I knew she'd had a traumatic day. "That's exactly what I intend to do."

Without warning, she leaned across the coffee table, poked in my general direction. "Okay. You're here. When you aren't, I hope you'll find some answers."

I was ready to leave, but not without a parting shot. "It's late, but he's young. Don't you think you better call Blaine Smith, find out what he knows?"

Her eyes widened. "You don't miss much, do you?"

"You were much too smooth about the car that pulled away from the Graham house."

"I have no comment about that car. I saw taillights. I'd like to talk to Blaine but not when I'm a murder suspect. It will be much wiser if I make no calls tonight. To anyone. If"—a quick breath—"if I'm arrested, the police could access all my calls."

"I'll make sure you aren't arrested." I spoke with confidence. "Leave everything to me. Tomorrow follow your normal schedule. Of course, you'll want to start the day by informing Mr. Layton."

"And wait for the police to arrive. But I feel better even if I keep hearing voices and touching— I don't think I want to pursue that thought. But having you around helps in a weird way. Today was so awful I lost perspective. I need to remember I didn't have any motive to murder him. You don't murder someone because you want to quit a job. Surely the police will see that."

"Of course they will." I didn't add that police want facts. I hoped to offer them a few pointers. I'd promised Wiggins a plan. If I didn't exactly have a plan, I had a campaign. When outnumbered (in this instance in a deep evidentiary hole), I look for inspiration to Hannibal, who defeated the much larger Roman army with a series of clever tactical moves. I intended to make my first move at the law offices of Layton, Graham, Morse and Morse.

⁖

The offices blazed with lights. A vacuum cleaner hummed. A washroom door was open. A mop and bucket sat in the hallway. Office cleaning crews work at night. It was still short of midnight. This crew likely attended to several buildings in the downtown area. Two women, one built like an NFL lineman and the other thin as a whippet, worked in the reception area to a nasal serenade about mama in jail and the dog's real sad blasting from a portable boom box. A broom-shaped emblem above the left shirt pocket on their gray uniforms read: *CLEAN SWEEP.*

The skinny blonde mopped the parquet flooring in the waiting room, chattering nonstop. ". . . and I told him he better put his shoes under my bed *every* night . . ."

The big woman nodded approval as she raked a duster up and down the waiting room window shutters.

The blonde stopped midstream, yelled, "Bucky, you missed the wastebaskets in here."

A cattle prod couldn't have moved me any faster. I was in Doug Graham's office just as the door swung in and a beefy hand flicked the switch. Bucky turned and bellowed, "In a minute. Starting at this end."

Earlier today an obviously angry Doug Graham started messages, stopped, tossed unsatisfactory versions into his wastebasket. I wanted those discarded notes.

Bucky ambled across the floor, a thirty-gallon plastic green trash bag in one hand. He hummed a tuneless accompaniment to the now faintly heard country music song.

I knelt by the wastebasket. I didn't have time for subtlety. Gray trousers and scuffed sneakers were in my peripheral vision. I tipped over the wastebasket. Papers spilled onto the floor. I glanced up at a face slack with stupefaction.

"Yeah?" His voice was uncertain.

I'd be uncertain as well if I thought I was talking to a self-tipping wastebasket. I ignored him and pawed through the mound of discarded envelopes, printed sheets, torn scraps from a legal pad. An unfortunate—for Bucky—by-product of my search was the unmistakable movement of the papers strewn on the floor. I easily picked out the material I wanted. I plucked five wadded balls from the heap of papers.

"Hey."

I glanced up.

Bucky's watery brown eyes were huge pools of disbelief. He stared at the crushed wads hovering in the air a few inches above the floor. He blinked, looked again. The paper balls remained in the air. He dropped the plastic bag, lurched around, and hurtled—as much as a five-eight man weighing about two forty can hurtle—to the doorway and into the hall, yelling, "Betty, Mag, something screwy's going . . ."

I stood up, opened a wadded ball, read. I kept the wrinkled sheet in my left hand, opened another. Variations on a theme. No salutation on any sheet. *Things don't have to change— Do you expect me to pass up*— I spread open the third crumpled wad, recognized the missive he'd begun as I read over his shoulder. *I never promised anything. If you make claims, I'll deny everything*— *Let me explain*— *Scandal won't help anybo*—

He'd tucked a final version in his shirt pocket. I remembered that it was bland. *Let's talk again. We can work this out.*

Had that talk occurred shortly before nine o'clock at his home?

It was one possibility, but not the only possibility. Doug Graham in his last day had exhibited the kind of controlling self-absorption that might have earned him not only dislike, but deadly hatred. Anita Davis came to mind. And the young man who slammed out of his office, stormed angrily up the hall, Keith Porter. I'd like to know the whereabouts of Anita Davis and Keith Porter at nine o'clock tonight. And Graham's ex-wife, Rhoda. I had a quick memory as well of somber-faced Brewster Layton. Layton had the aura of a man keeping anger tightly leashed. And was there more than bumptious male exuberance behind the loud oilman's visit?

Bucky's distant yell increased in volume. "I swear there was balls of paper up in the air. You got to come see."

A woman's reply wasn't audible, but the tone was dismissive.

"I ain't going down there by myself."

I pictured him glaring defiantly.

A labored sigh, slow heavy steps. "Gonna take up my time." The woman's deep voice held equal parts resentment and irritation.

Quickly I moved behind the desk, pulled open the center drawer. I pushed the red velvet ring case to one side, dropped in the wadded-up balls of legal paper, shoved the drawer shut.

Bucky reached the doorway, warily edged inside. He stopped, stared. "Where'd they go?" He took another step forward, gazing at the tipped-over trash can and the welter of papers. "They was right there. Right there." He jabbed a finger. "About five inches off the floor."

The big woman folded her arms, glared at him. She reminded me of Marjorie Main as Ma Kettle but there wasn't a smile. "You been drinking again? I thought I smelled vodka. People who think you can't smell vodka don't have a nose that works. But I got eyes that see and I don't see any balls of paper dancing around. You must have stumbled and knocked over the wastebasket and your eyes played tricks. Get yourself busy now. We got to do three more offices tonight." She turned and clumped into the hall.

As the sound of her heavy steps faded, he reached down to pick up the plastic bag, never taking his eyes away from the trash can and the papers. He cautiously moved forward until he stood over the tipped wastebasket and the strewn papers.

The papers lay there. Unmoving.

He hunched his shoulders defensively.

I had some idea of his internal monologue. *Those balls of paper was up in the air. . . .* Narrowed eyes. *I don't see no balls of paper. . . .* His head jerked convulsively back and forth as he surveyed the office. "Sometimes there's rats. Offices can have rats." His voice was shaky. "A big rat could tip over a wastebasket." His voice gained assurance. "That's what it had to be. I'll tell her it was a rat." His head jerked about again. "I don't like rats." With a frenzied breath, Bucky bent down, scooped up the trash, righted the wastebasket, and was out in the hall, the door closing behind him.

I took a deep breath. I was certain Bucky would not return to the office. The papers would be safe in Doug Graham's desk until tomorrow. All was well—

A harrumph.

When caught in flagrante delicto, it is important to remain calm and upbeat. "Wiggins, I know you are pleased." My voice rose in a trill of delight. "So perspicacious of you to instruct me to follow a plan. That's why I hastened here and I was in time to save important evidence from destruction."

"That poor man may have some difficulty in recovering from the appearance of floating paper balls."

"By the time he tells this tale, he'll have seen a glimpse of gray fur, heard claws on the wood floor."

"A rat?"

"Possibly as good an explanation as any?"

A rumble of laughter.

I sighed in relief. Fortunately, Wiggins, despite his focus on crossing i's and dotting t's, possesses a robust sense of humor.

"Ah, Bailey Ruth, always an inventive answer. But delivered with such charm and grace."

I soaked in approval.

"Obviously the product of much experience."

Ouch.

"Nonetheless, tonight you have aided the police investigation by preserving evidence. If a rat is blamed for the antics of the wastebasket, no harm done. I am pleased you are making progress toward the solution of the crime. That's also true of James."

James? Of course, Jimmy.

"James has attached himself"—Wiggins's tone was approving—"to *Gazette* reporter Joan Crandall. I know he has been elusive tonight, but it came to me that James, first and foremost, reveled in being a reporter. Therefore, I sought him at the *Gazette*. And there I found him." Wiggins was obviously pleased at the success of his search. "It's unfortunate that Precept Seven precludes informing him of the great newsroom in the sky. When he climbs the golden stairs, he can rub elbows with Webb Miller and Edward R. Murrow and Ernie Pyle and Dickey Chapelle and Maggie Higgins. At the moment, he has the newsroom to himself. He's excited about some material he's found. Every so often he looks around and yells, 'Hey, Bailey Ruth.' He's looked for you at Megan's apartment and Graham's house and even the cemetery. He seems quite anxious to confer with you. Ms. Crandall has completed her work for the night, but James remains at the *Gazette.*"

Chapter 7

The *Gazette* newsroom was dim except for the glow of computer monitors. A wedge of light spilled out from the break room. Several sheets of computer paper were spread on the top of a long narrow table. A can of Pepsi suspended in the air tilted.

I won't say Jimmy guzzled, but he drank the soda with a loud gurgle. He gave a satisfied sigh and the can rested on the tabletop.

I pulled out the chair on the other side of the table, gratefully sank into it. I would never admit that jousting with Wiggins stresses me, but whenever he appears I'm always afraid my departure on the Rescue Express is imminent.

"Where've you been?" Jimmy's tone was accusatory. "Seems like you're never around when you can be helpful."

"Here and there. I understand you want to see me."

"Yeah, I'd like to *see* you. Talking to a voice is kind of nuts. But you have a nice voice, husky, kind of sexy. Anyway"—he lifted the Pepsi, took another deep drink—"glad you showed up."

I glanced at the pop machine and was suddenly parched. If Jimmy weren't here, I'd appear with a purse and, presto, I'd have a Dr Pepper. Perhaps he'd figured out how to finagle a can out of the machine. "How'd you get that soda?"

"It wasn't easy. I always kept a stash of quarters in my desk. These cheapskates dump pennies in their center drawers. I had to go downstairs and filch some quarters out of a canister for pet rescue." He sounded sheepish. "I used to always put in a dollar when I walked past, so I figured it was okay."

I wanted that Dr Pepper. If I appeared, purse in hand, I didn't doubt Jimmy would get the point and demand to know how he could appear. Perhaps that will excuse my guile. "Jimmy, do me a favor and get these addresses for me." I took a sheet of his paper, retrieved the pencil from his hand, wrote down: Rhoda Graham, Brewster Layton, Anita Davis, Sharon King, Geraldine Jackson, Nancy Murray, Louise Raymond, Keith Porter, Jack Sherman.

He glanced at the list. "You can scratch Sherman. I was nosing around the newsroom. Bunch of photos of the Graham house but some great shots of a rig fire. Sherman's out there, dirty, sweaty, right on top of the action. The caption read: 'Adelaide oilman Jack Sherman predicts fire will be contained by Friday morning. An explosion rocked the Singing Jenny well at shortly after 5 p.m.' So Sherman wasn't creeping across Graham's patio at nine." Jimmy gurgled another sip. "Yeah. Tastes pretty good. They turn off the air at night to save money, so no wonder you're thirsty. I'll make a deal. I think I'm onto something big. First, I thought I'd write everything down"—he pointed at the paper on the table—"and put it on Joan's desk. But Joan won't run with a story until she's checked out the facts up and down and back and forth. I want the cops to get this pronto. If I call Crime Stoppers, that would go up through channels. I want this to get to somebody with clout. I'll get the addresses if you agree to pass on what I've found out."

"It's a deal."

As soon as he stepped out of the break room, I materialized with a purse, strode to the pop machine, dropped in three quarters. I disappeared, punched, and waited for the can to plunk. I was back at the table, sipping the Dr Pepper when Jimmy came in, a sheet of paper in hand.

"Here's—" He stopped, stared. "How'd you get the pop?"

I started to reply that I had rapport with machines, but he might have wanted another soda. "I gave it a thump and one came out." That was almost true. "I suppose it's malfunctioning."

He walked to the machine, punched for a Pepsi, kicked the side. Rattle, bump, thump.

He reached down, retrieved the can. "Thanks."

"You're welcome." Either Heaven has a sense of humor or understood the importance of keeping Jimmy unseen. I had no doubt that if he became visible, Megan's emotions would experience even more turmoil.

The chair opposite me squeaked as he sat. A paper was shoved across the table.

I picked up the sheet, scanned it. Jimmy had found all the addresses for me. "Perfect."

His chair hitched closer to the table. "Okay, listen. You might want to make notes so you'll have it straight for the cops."

Notes are nice. I encouraged students to become proficient note-takers. Unfortunately, the *Gazette* was built in the era of hermetically sealed windows. "I see that you have notes."

119

"I'm leaving them for Joan."

"That's fine. I won't need notes. I wouldn't be able to get any papers outside until someone opened a door in the morning. But I have a very good memory."

There was a skeptical silence.

"I required all of my students to memorize 'Thanatopsis.' I would not ask of my students more than I could achieve." I cleared my throat. *"To him who in the love of Nature holds / Communion with her invisible forms, she speaks / A various—"*

"So you're the reason I had to memorize that da—" A pause. "But I get your point." He picked up his notes. "I checked out the *Gazette* file on Doug Graham, found out a bunch. He belonged to every civic club in town. He hosted a golf tournament every year to raise money for sick kids. That makes him sound like a winner, but he had a six handicap and always ended up paired with some mover and shaker, so it looks like he was hustling clients to me. I got the public records on his divorce. Split what they had. Funny thing is, he got a lot richer the very next year. He bought his big house about six months after the divorce. Plus, he doesn't pay child support. They're both over eighteen. I'd guess the kids sided with mom so he blew them off. Might be something there. Then I ran across this story." He pushed a printout across the table.

I noted the date: October 21, 2014

FANCY MEETING YOU HERE

Lifestyle editor Estelle Luke

Adelaide law partners Doug Graham and Brewster Layton met with a bang Monday morning.

Literally.

At the corner of Country Club Drive and Reverie Lane, a four-way stop, the partners' cars collided at shortly after 7 a.m. Both men were headed for the offices of Layton, Graham, Morse and Morse, but neither was on his usual route.

An inset photograph pictured the middle of an intersection and a silver Porsche rammed into the right front of a black Toyota SUV. Hefty Doug Graham, a rueful expression on his broad face, stared at his car. Hands thrust into the pockets of his suit, tall, slender Brewster Layton squinted against the sunlight.

Graham told police the accident was his fault. "That's what happens when you get into a tough lawsuit. I was thinking about a deposition, decided to take a walk in White Deer Park. An early walk helps me figure things out. At the stop sign, I swear I looked but I didn't see Brewster's car. I hit the gas pedal and wham! I told Brewster, I'll take care of the repairs. I'm glad he wasn't hurt and I'm glad he's an old friend." Graham's big laugh boomed. "I always told Brewster I'd be there when he needed me, but I had no idea how true that would be."

Layton was leaving the Adelaide Golf and Country Club after an early breakfast. "I saw the car, never realized it was Doug's. The sun was in my eyes, but I had reached the stop sign first so I started up. I tried to brake when the car came toward me but I wasn't able to stop in time."

The impact broke the right front axle of the Layton car. Graham waited until a wrecker arrived to remove Layton's vehicle, then he drove Layton to their downtown offices in Graham's car—one old friend giving another a lift.

I tapped the printout. "They had a car wreck."

"If you believe in that kind of coincidence, you're nuts."

"Adelaide's a small town." I was impatient. Maybe Jimmy had lost his nose for news. "What are the odds if you have a car wreck you might know the other driver? Or know someone who knows him or her? Or went to school with the driver's sister? Or—"

"Or maybe you set the crash up in advance. Look where the accident happened. Neither had any usual reason to be on those particular streets at that particular time. What makes the time special? Country Club Drive curls around through some woods and intersects Reverie Lane. Who's out there at seven in the morning? Maybe some walkers or runners but they're probably in the park. Maybe somebody going to or coming from the country club. I understand the club has a breakfast buffet to die for but I was never well enough connected to be invited. But there's no hustle and bustle on that road. Very easy to wait until there are no cars and no runners in view. Let's look at downtown at seven a.m. Even ass-busting lawyers don't get to their offices any earlier than seven. If they tried to stage this downtown, there would have been people all over the place. So they cooked up Master Thinker communing at White Deer and Layton having breakfast at the club. That means they could meet up in a secluded area and stage a wreck."

"If the crash broke the axle of Layton's car, it had to be a pretty hard impact."

"Probably a jolt for both of them. But I'll believe in dancing unicorns wearing tutus before I'll think this was an accident. So, why the charade? Why was it important for Layton's car to get smashed and smashed real good?"

I drank several gulps of Dr Pepper. "I'm sure you have an answer."

"That's when it gets interesting. At first I thought this was just odd. Then I remembered something else—Megan talking about how Layton and Graham avoided each other."

I was suddenly attentive. Megan had spoken of the apparent dislike between the two partners.

"According to the *Gazette* story, they were partners and great chums. We know they aren't. I kept thinking about the wreck and why would it happen. I went downstairs and went through back issues of the *Gazette* for the week before the wreck. Check out this story."

BICYCLIST DEAD AFTER HIT-AND-RUN

Joan Crandall

Goddard senior Alison Terry, 21, was declared dead on arrival at Adelaide General Hospital shortly after 7 p.m. Friday night. According to police, Terry was apparently the victim of a hit-and-run accident on Country Club Drive.

Terry was found by a passing motorist who called 911. The motorist tried unsuccessfully to resuscitate her.

The motorist, Jason Field, told officers he saw a smashed bicycle near the side of Country Club Drive. He stopped to investigate and found the college senior unresponsive a few feet from the bicycle.

Police today said Terry died of a broken neck. Investigators believe Terry's bicycle was struck from behind by a car traveling east on Country Club Drive. Police believe the right side of the car would have suffered damage from the impact. Police are alerting local body shops to report any car brought in with damage if the driver cannot submit a copy of an accident report.

According to police, the bicycle had a red warning reflector on the rear fender. Terry was wearing a white T-shirt and should have been visible to a motorist. Moreover, the bicycle was equipped with a small battery-powered light on the front fender.

Investigating officer T. B. Drake said the driver may have come around a curve and not seen the bicyclist. However, Officer Drake emphasized the driver could not have been unaware of the impact.

Police Chief Sam Cobb said leaving the scene of an accident that results in a death is a felony and the office of the district attorney will be prepared to file charges if the driver is apprehended.

Terry was an education major from Sallisaw. Jan Bliss, the chair of the education department, said she has spoken with Terry's parents, Mr. and Mrs. Gordon Terry. Professor Bliss remembers Terry as an outstanding student, eager to begin her career as a teacher. A memorial service will be scheduled at the Goddard Student Union next week.

Classmates plan a candle vigil at 7 o'clock tonight in the gardens at Rose Bower, the extensive estate which adjoins the campus and is the site of many college functions.

Terry's roommate, Cordell senior Pamela Parrish, said tearfully, "No one was kinder than Alison. She loved kids, loved teaching. How could someone hurt her and leave her there to die?"

Police are asking anyone with information about the car or driver to contact them. The police declined to say if they have any leads to the driver's identity.

I felt a wash of sadness. A life ended much too soon. When bad things happen to good people, those who grieve mournfully wonder why. Even as a Heavenly resident, I have no answer. I know only that all who die, whether just beginning, in their prime, or withered by age, are surrounded by glory and there is fullness and completion of all their possibilities. Heaven—but I must hew to Precept Seven: "Information about Heaven is not yours to impart. Simply smile and say, 'Time will tell.'" I asked, though I rather thought I knew the answer, "Was the driver found?"

"No. Here's the kicker. I did a word search on Layton. The *Gazette* runs all the obituaries on the same page. That page also has a column on one side: 'In Memoriam.' On the date of the hit-and-run, October 17, 2014, here's one of the memorial tributes." A paper rose in the air. He read aloud:

"'In Memory of Marie Denise Layton. January 3, 1955, to October 17, 2013. Your smile lighted my life. The touch of your hand brought comfort. The sound of your voice sings in my heart. The days are gray without you. I love you—'"

Jimmy's voice slowed.

"'—forever. Brewster.'"

Forever dropped like an autumn leaf. Jimmy understood a man who loved and still loved. "People—even good people—make mistakes. But"—Jimmy was stern—"he shouldn't have run away from the accident. I think he probably stopped and got out and the girl was dead. You don't linger with a broken neck. Even so, he would have stayed but I'll bet he was drunk as a skunk. The anniversary of his wife's death."

Jimmy slapped the sheet on the table and now he talked fast. "Anyway, the cops should find out where he was tonight."

⌇

Early morning sunlight slanted into Sam Cobb's office through the wide windows that overlooked Main Street. My night at Rose Bower had been quite comfortable, and breakfast at Lulu's, as always, delicious. I expected Sam to arrive any minute. I was sure he was already well aware of last night's homicide and familiar with the circumstances.

I stood in front of his old-fashioned blackboard that required chalk. No whiteboards for Sam despite pressure from the mayor. Sam had gruffly told her he used chalk when he taught high school algebra and he would use chalk until they pried a stub out of his cold, dead fingers. The Honorable Neva Lumpkin wanted to jettison Sam right along with the blackboard. Lurking in the background, eager to be chief, was her favorite detective, Howie Harris.

I wrote swiftly:

October 17, 2014—Anniversary of the death of Marie Layton

October 17, 2014—Hit-and-run accident with fatality

October 20, 2014—Car accident at Country Club Drive and Rev—

"You're back." A click as the door closed.

I turned, chalk still in one hand.

"Funny thing." His tone was conversational. "Hanging chalk makes me feel like a kid and it's midnight and my folks are out and the cellar stairs creaked."

As I would point out to Wiggins, it was he who set forth the Precepts, and Precept Six was clear: "Make every effort not to alarm earthly creatures."

I immediately swirled present. I was feeling festive and chose an embroidered blue tunic, an elegant flower pattern with matching designs on the lower sleeves, white slacks, and blue strapless heels. Very high. I settled on a straight chair in front of Sam's desk, crossed one leg over the other, beamed at him.

Sam is a sturdy bear of a man, big head with grizzled black hair, large strong face with bold features, burly shoulders. He wouldn't know fashion if he met it on a runway, but I saw a flicker of admiration in his brown eyes as he settled in his large desk chair. "Bailey Ruth." He gave me a welcoming nod, but I saw concern in his dark eyes. "Everything gets—" He paused.

I assumed he was recasting his sentence. Had he started to say, *Everything gets screwed up . . .* or *Everything gets a little strange . . .* or *Everything gets turned upside down . . .*

Sam cleared his throat, started over. "I thought we had a simple case. Boss threatens to fire young lawyer. Young lawyer shoots him."

I started to speak, but he held up a large hand. "The evidence is compelling. Text on Doug Graham's phone orders Megan Wynn to show up or he will pursue termination. If there's a handy explanation, she couldn't seem to find it. She declined to explain. Plus, a neighbor across the street puttered out onto his porch a little before nine. He was sitting in the dark on a screened-in porch, sipping a rum and Coke, enjoying the cicadas—"

I remembered wondrous moonlit nights, swinging slowly in a big hammock with Bobby Mac, listening to cicadas sing the song of summer, smelling the scent of fresh-mown grass, Adelaide at its happiest.

"—with a clear view of the Graham house. A car stopped at the front curb, an old yellow Thunderbird. A tall, lanky guy walked up to the front porch, jabbed the bell, waited, rang again, waited, rang, finally gave up. As that car pulled away, another car arrived, turned into the driveway, parked behind Graham's Porsche."

"The murderer came from the golf course."

Sam's gaze was hopeful. "Who was it?"

I waved a hand in airy dismissal of any suggestion I'd been on the scene. "I didn't *see* the murderer. I know this is what happened because Megan Wynn found Doug Graham dead."

"Were you there when she found him?"

I regretted that I'd been restless and left Megan's apartment, seeking Jimmy. "I can't vouch for the actual moment."

"Spell it out."

He listened, gave me a probing look. "You landed at the Graham house while she was scrubbing blood from her hands. And you think she's innocent?"

"There was no weapon in the room."

Sam shrugged. "She'd already run outside and hidden it."

I couldn't prove she hadn't, though Megan was much too fastidious to ignore blood on her hands. "Why did she have blood on her hands?"

"You tell me."

"She was trying to see if he was alive and her touch caused his body to fall sideways and when she tried to prevent that fall, blood got on her hands and blouse. If she shot him, why would she want to see if she could help him?"

Sam wasn't impressed. "Maybe she wanted to make sure he was dead."

"The timing isn't right. Do you think she shot him, ran outside and hid the gun, came back and approached the body? Why come back?"

Sam's voice was cool. "Maybe she wanted to get at his cell phone and that's how she got in a mess with the body."

It was quite likely Jimmy accompanied Megan to the house. But if Sam was uneasy with floating chalk, I didn't think introducing a dead reporter as a witness would be pleasing to him. Or convincing. Especially if he learned Jimmy adored Megan.

I tried another tack. "Someone crept into the den and blew off the back of Doug's head. You will agree that makes the murder premeditated. Would a smart person drive up to his house in a distinctive old Dodge and park it like a tour bus in the driveway?"

His thick black brows beetled.

I took this as a sign he was open to persuasion. "It's obvious from the facts that the murderer used a stealthy approach, which wouldn't include parking on the driveway to slip into the den where a man was sitting in a leather chair watching a ball game. I'm positive Graham never heard anyone approach, had no idea he was in danger, knew nothing until a bullet slammed into his skull. Further, the text to Megan and the nine-one-one call were designed to have her in the house when the police arrived."

Sam's stare was intent. "You think he was already dead when the text was sent to Wynn from his cell?"

I was patient. "Obviously."

His eyes narrowed. "If that's right, he was dead a few minutes before nine, then the killer used his cell to text Megan Wynn and the house line to dial nine-one-one, report a murder."

I gave him an approving smile. "Exactly. The murderer then exited through the back, crossed the terrace to the golf course, and followed a cart path to a street where a car was parked."

Sam looked dour. "Glad you know what happened. Where's the proof?"

"Megan is innocent."

"You say."

"I do." I was firm. "You need to look elsewhere." I was pleased to know I was making his path forward much clearer.

I would like to say Sam was energized by my pronouncement. Instead, he shook his head, muttered to himself. I might have caught the word *screwy* and heard a weary *looked so simple.*

"Okay." Deep breath. "You claim—"

"I don't claim." I was sweetly reasonable. "I'm certain."

"You may be certain, but I can't ignore a black-and-white case. And the mayor's already after Wynn."

"The mayor?"

"You got it. She called me this morning. *Sam, I'll hold a news conference—*"

His imitation of Neva Lumpkin's supercilious tone was perfection.

"*—and announce that the city of Adelaide once again exhibits its excellence in protecting its citizens with the prompt arrest of a murderess—*"

The door squeaked open.

Sam stopped in midsentence.

As I disappeared, the mayor burst inside. She hurtled toward Sam's desk, much too excited to notice dissipating colors.

Sam heaved himself to his feet, his face smooth and unreadable.

Neva Lumpkin was a sturdy (to be kind) middle-aged woman with too much blonde hair, vivid makeup, and an imposing bust unfortunately emphasized by a tight-fitting orange jersey blouse. This morning she exuded good humor, not an attitude I associated with her.

"Sam"—a sudden transformation of her plastic politician face into momentary respect for the dead—"a dreadful blow to our community. Doug Graham was a fine man, always committed to civic duty. But"—her expression was sunny again—"once again Adelaide swiftly deals with adversity, our finest"—a nod at Sam to make clear the accolade to the police department—"capturing the dastardly assassin within moments. Of course, I want you to be present at the press—"

"Uh, Neva. Please sit down." He gestured at the chair where I sat.

I quickly moved but not quite fast enough to avoid contact with her equally imposing girdled rear.

She remained midway down to the chair, an impressive feat given her heft. She swept a hand behind her.

I quivered.

Neva jerked upright, whirled, stared at the empty chair. "I felt something . . . odd."

Sam was courteous. "The air comes out of that register kind of funny." He gestured vaguely toward the ceiling.

"Oh. Well, talk to maintenance about it." She plumped into the chair. "I've called all the stations. Looks like we'll have the city channels here, too. The coverage should be great. I'll run home and change. I think my blue polka dot silk dress and navy pumps. Dignity, you know." She squinted at Sam. "Your suit's—"

"Wrinkled. Claire's out of town. About that press conference, Neva, here's our situation. We have some unexpected leads, so it would be premature to say the lawyer's a person of interest."

I would have hugged Sam for giving my claim merit, but didn't want to startle him.

Neva's lower lip protruded in obvious petulance. "That's not what Howie Harris told me."

Sam's face remained bland, but I saw the slight tightening of his jaw. Detective Howie Harris was Neva's pick to be police chief, if and when she got rid of Sam. Moreover, Howie was her mole into department doings, which had to gall Sam.

He didn't rise to the bait. Instead, he nodded sagely. "Howie will be brought up to date this morning. Everything has changed since last night."

She looked like a dirigible with a leak, heavy shoulders slumping. "What am I going to do about the press conference?"

"Neva, this is a great opportunity for you. I'll supply you with a layout of the crime scene. Reporters love that kind of inside information. Detective Sergeant Price will be in your office twenty minutes before the press conference. He'll brief you from top to bott—" He paused, rephrased. "Detective Sergeant Price will provide details, and here's the best part. You can say you are on top of the action and you expect a breakthrough in the case over the weekend. That way you'll be on the news tonight and Monday night both."

Neva's pale blue eyes gleamed with the happy light of a shark scenting blood, TV twice on good ratings nights. But she was wary. "Reporters won't come more than twice. I'll tell them today the police have questions for many close to Doug Graham, including Megan Wynn, an associate at the dead man's law firm who was found at the scene of the crime, and that the murder suspect will be named at eleven o'clock Monday morning." She rose. "Since word has already been leaked to the press"—she had the grace to look uncomfortable—"about Ms. Wynn, this keeps her onstage but widens the field."

She was at the door. She looked back. "Eleven o'clock Monday, Sam."

The door shut behind her.

I thankfully returned to the chair. I swirled present, took an instant to admire the intricate embroidery on the sleeves of my tunic.

Sam glowered. "If somebody finds Howie Harris strangled with his bow tie one of these days, I better have an alibi. He not only whispered in Neva's ear, he's already sicced the press on Wynn. When they get the details—lawyer shot, associate found at scene, the text—they'll write stories where any kindergartner could figure she's suspect-in-chief." He tugged on his shirt collar as if it were too tight. "I'm at the poker table without even a pair in my hand and I'm supposed to present a perp on a platter Monday morning. Moreover, if you weren't scre—messing things up, I could charge the obvious suspect."

I was gentle. "You don't want to arrest the wrong person. Megan Wynn isn't the only person with a motive. Yesterday——"

Sam took notes as I described Megan's chance at a new job. "But Doug Graham knew a softy when he saw one. He threatened to fire Anita Davis, a secretary, if Megan left. Anita needs the firm health insurance because her daughter is very ill. A different insurer might not include their doctor or hospital."

I didn't tell Sam that Anita overheard the threat, knew her job was in peril. After all, Megan had immediately reassured Anita that she was remaining at the firm and Anita's job was secure. Moreover, Megan declined to explain to the police the text that brought her to Doug's house to find him dead. Megan hadn't told Blaine the background, either, and I doubted she intended to do so.

If I informed Sam and he confronted Anita, as he certainly would, Anita would think Megan had revealed everything. I couldn't break Megan's promise. Besides, it was apparent that Megan didn't connect Anita to Doug's murder.

I pushed away the thought that Anita wouldn't be afraid of losing her insurance if Doug Graham died.

A rumble as the chief cleared his throat. "Cat got your tongue?" He was eyeing me closely. "Are you seeing how the evidence stacks up against Megan Wynn?"

I realized my silence was unfortunate. It gave Sam plenty of time to envision how angry and disappointed Megan must have been. I tried for a diversion. "I wonder if a clever cat snaked out a paw and snagged a beef tongue from a banquet table?"

Sam's voice was dry. "That's as good an answer as any. Keeps it simple. I like simple. Employee wants to quit. Boss issues threat. Boss shot that night. Like one plus one equals two. Bad boss snuffed. Secretary's job is safe. Lawyer can quit."

He was being stubborn. "Don't close your mind yet." I described young and very angry Keith Porter and his parting words, which amounted to a threat, a loudmouthed oilman and a fabulously expensive diamond ring, Graham's impending engagement to a wealthy widow, the ex-wife who got the short end of the stick in a settlement, Graham writing and crumpling message after message to someone obviously angry or unhappy with him, the hit-and-run death of a bicyclist and a curiously timed car crash—

Sam stopped me there. "What's Layton's motive?"

"Maybe Graham was threatening to expose him as the driver who killed the student."

Sam raised a dark brow. "If Graham kept quiet since 2014, why would he open up now? Besides, Graham would be a coconspirator in covering up a crime, which could get him disbarred."

I hated to see Jimmy's theory ignored. "Graham's death means no one can ever prove anything about that accident."

"Still, why last night? What's different about last night and any other night since the hit-and-run?"

"Possibly nothing. But there was something wrong between Graham and Layton. I don't know if it had to do with the hit-and-run. Layton should have been grateful to Graham. Instead, Layton disliked Graham. Layton avoided him. They ignored each other when they passed in the hall. Maybe Graham was threatening Layton in some fashion."

Sam shrugged "That's pretty vague. I talked to Brewster this morning."

I looked at Sam in surprise.

His face was unreadable. "Brewster called me at home. I've known him a long time. Rotary. He said a friend heard about the murder on the morning news, informed him. Brewster asked what happened. I told him the investigation was in the early stages, that Megan Wynn claimed to have found the body. I asked him if he thought Wynn and Graham were having an affair. He was pretty sharp with me, said, *Absolutely not.* I asked him if they planned to fire her. He said, *Absolutely not.* Of course, now I know what termination Graham meant. But Wynn had to be furious that she was being blackmailed into staying at the firm, so the fact that she wasn't losing a job doesn't matter."

I jousted right back. "A well-balanced young woman doesn't shoot a man because she is forced to stay in a job. She might despise him. She wouldn't shoot him."

"The DA could argue she had to turn down the chance of a lifetime, partnership in a new young firm."

We looked at each other. Stalemate. Sam wasn't about to dismiss Megan from a list of suspects.

"But you are a fair man. You'll look at every possibility."

His smile was slow in coming, but it came. "Yeah. I'll find out everything I can about Graham and the people around him."

I felt a huge relief. Sam was a man of his word. "You'll want to talk to his secretary, Sharon King. She looks smart, as a legal secretary would. Plus, nobody knows a man like his secretary. If Graham was crossways with anyone, she'll know. Then there's Nancy Murray, the paralegal. I don't think she misses much. Louise Raymond, the receptionist, likely has a good sense of everyone in the office. And you'll enjoy getting Geraldine Jackson's take on him. She's another secretary, and the kind of woman every man notices. You can't spend five minutes around her without imagining her at the bar with a beer, shouting a rowdy song. You'll enjoy the time whether you learn anything or not."

"Now that I'm a married man"—his tone was amused—"I make it a point not to enjoy other women. I'll talk to all of them."

I didn't include Anita Davis. Surely a young mother wouldn't commit murder. But mothers will do what they have to do to protect their children.

"Sounds like an interesting office. But"—his smile fled—"the facts look lousy for Megan Wynn. He was dead, she was there. She had a double-barreled motive."

I was emphatic. "He was dead when she got there. She didn't call nine-one-one. So somebody else knew he was dead. What about that nine-one-one call?"

Sam grunted and leaned forward toward his monitor, clicked several times. "Night dispatcher took the call at 9:04 p.m. The caller whispered." His eyes narrowed. "That's fishy. People who call nine-one-one can be hysterical, struggling for breath, shouting, crying. They don't whisper unless an intruder's in the next room. But we have to remember, we're dealing with a lawyer. She might be rigging the whole thing."

My mouth opened.

"I know." Sam was impatient. "You think she's an innocent

bystander, but I'm telling you how the same facts can be read by somebody like Neva. Or me." His tone was grouchy. "The caller could have whispered just to make us crazy when we are trying to figure it out. Anyway, a whisper disguises sex, so the caller could have been a man or woman." He stared at the screen. "Here's what the caller whispered: *Doug Graham house. Ninety-three Tudor Lane. Dead man. Shot.*"

I raised an eyebrow. "That's it?"

"That's it."

I was thoughtful. "I think the murderer texted Megan on Graham's cell, called nine-one-one, and left by the back door, knowing Megan would arrive and likely be in the house when the police got there. Or if Megan found him and left, her car might be seen—as it was—and she would be in big trouble. Plus, there was the text message on Graham's cell to point a finger at her. But"—I was emphatic—"no gun."

Sam's eyes glinted. "You seem to know everything. Where is the gun?"

"I'm not a psychic. The murderer may have hidden the gun in the woods or perhaps the murderer took the gun."

"Thank you." He was sarcastic.

"Always glad to help." I sent him a cheery smile.

He remained somber. "Your ideas are interesting. But you can see that Megan Wynn's obviously suspect number one. Unfortunately, you can never appear"—slight emphasis—"as a witness, so to anyone not privy to your input—"

Obviously he referred to the mayor.

"—Wynn is *the* person of interest."

"On a positive note, please don't waste time suspecting her." I was still worrying about the gun. I felt certain the murder was pre-meditated, so the murderer surely wore gloves to avoid gun smoke residue. Unless the gun could be traced to the killer, it would have been smart to half hide the gun in the woods along with contaminated gloves. Traces of DNA could have been avoided by wearing a double layer of vinyl gloves and leaving with only the inner pair. The intent to embroil Megan was clear from the text on Graham's phone and the 911 call. Megan would immediately have been suspected if the gun were found hidden in a shallow hole in the woods. So far, a search hadn't uncovered it, and I was sure the police had used metal detectors and turned up every rusted can in a half-mile radius. It appeared instead that the murderer took the gun. Why?

Sam massaged one cheek. "The investigating officer thinks Wynn was muddying the water when she claimed she didn't call nine-one-one. Wynn could have taken the gun and buried it in the woods, then made the call. We'll keep looking out there. She had to do something to explain away the text message. Anyway, that's all in the officer's report. You can bet the mayor's already read it. Unless I find somebody else, Neva will insist I arrest Wynn. I'll question Wynn this morning and—"

The phone on his desk shrilled.

Sam leaned over and punched speakerphone. "Cobb here."

"Break-in reported at law offices of Layton, Graham, Morse and Morse. Two cars en route—"

Sam interrupted. "On my way."

I disappeared.

Chapter 8

Brewster Layton's ascetic face was somber. The older man's shoulders slumped in a habitual stoop. His posture suggested a man burdened by years of care, a man who had lost vigor and hope. He cupped one hand to his goatee, likely a familiar gesture when concentrating.

Johnny Cain, trim and handsome in the Adelaide police uniform, light blue shirt and French blue trousers with a black stripe, gazed at Brewster respectfully but intently. "... find evidence of unauthorized entry?"

A rotund middle-aged blonde, Officer A. Benson, stood at Johnny's shoulder, gaze darting, attentive, wary.

Brewster gestured toward the open door at the end of the hall. "Someone broke a window in Doug's office, came in that way. I'll show you." He turned to lead the way.

In two quick strides, Johnny moved ahead of him. "Let me take a look, sir. If you'll wait in the doorway." He was polite but definite. "We want to avoid contaminating any evidence."

Johnny stopped just inside the door to survey the office. In the wall to the left of Graham's desk, there was a single window. The lower portion was raised. A pane was missing. Pieces of glass sprinkled the floor beneath the window. The window looked out to the alley. Two windows in the wall behind Graham's desk were closed and appeared undamaged.

I reached the alley window before Johnny came around the end of the desk. The other officer waited near the door, checking the surroundings. As directed, Brewster Layton watched from the hall.

Johnny stopped a few feet away from the window, careful not to walk into pieces of glass lying on the floor.

I hovered next to the open window. On closer inspection, I saw a portion of metal screen hanging loose. The screen was ajar. I pictured the alleyway late at night, a dark figure standing, waiting, listening. When sure no one was near, one gloved hand likely focused the beam of a flashlight on the window and the other raised a knife to rend the screen. One sharp rip and the screen lapped down. The knife would be put away, the latch on the sill twisted so the screen could be lifted. Now a gloved hand, holding a stone or brick, knocked out the glass pane, including any shards on the perimeter of the wood. It was easy then to reach through, twist the window lock, push up the window, climb inside.

I surveyed Graham's office.

Nothing appeared disturbed.

Johnny's gaze focused on glass particles that appeared ground into the carpet. "It looks like someone broke the window, entered this way." He turned to Brewster. "Do you know if anything is missing?"

Brewster's thin shoulders lifted and fell in a shrug. "I have no idea. This was my partner's office. Doug Graham. You know—"

"Yes, sir." Johnny's expression remained unchanged, respectful, and his tone was courteous. "Is this your usual time to arrive at work?"

Brewster hesitated an instant too long. "I'm earlier than usual."

Johnny waited, his expression expectant.

The two men stared at each other, Johnny clearly making the point that it would be interesting from a police point of view if Layton's schedule had changed on this particular morning, Layton understanding that Officer Cain was imaginative and intelligent and not to be underestimated.

Brewster said, I thought rather carefully, "I'd received word about Doug and I felt I should be here when the staff arrived. Some of them should be coming in soon."

Johnny asked pleasantly, "How did you happen to find the break-in?"

Brewster Layton was too experienced an attorney to betray surprise or concern. Perhaps, in his lawyerly way, he had foreseen the question. *Why did you go into Doug Graham's office?* It did not automatically follow that Brewster's first act the morning after his partner was murdered would be to arrive early and go directly to Doug Graham's office. "I thought I would check Doug's appointments for today and arrange for our receptionist to call and inform the clients of Doug's death."

Johnny Cain persisted, his voice still pleasant, but with bulldog tenacity, "Did Mr. Graham use an appointment ledger?"

Hanging between the policeman and the lawyer was the reality of today's world, the electronic world, schedules kept on phones, tablets, iPads, possibly in a computer, rarely on paper.

I knew someday Johnny Cain would be Detective Johnny Cain. He had realized at once that Brewster's early arrival and immediate entrance to Graham's office deserved scrutiny.

Brewster's gaze was chilly, but he managed a slight smile. "I suppose I wasn't thinking clearly. Shock, you know. I still keep an appointment pad on my desk. I looked in the center drawer of Doug's desk. I didn't find an appointment book. But it doesn't matter. The receptionist will be here soon and she can attend to the matter. In any event, I'm glad I discovered the break-in."

Johnny's gaze swept around the apparently untouched office. "Do you have any idea what someone might have been looking for?"

I wondered what Brewster Layton had been seeking in his early visit and whether he found it. I rather doubted he had summoned the police the instant he discovered the break-in. If he hoped to find something in particular, a file, a paper, surely he'd taken time to make his search before he called. He had been quick to say he'd opened the drawer of Doug's desk, and that would explain the presence of his fingerprints there.

I decided he was clever and quick.

I studied the right pocket of his suit jacket. There might be something in that pocket, something slim, the size of a passport. Or a small envelope containing several sheets of paper.

Brewster stood with his hands loose at his sides. Consciously relaxed? Perhaps. He spoke slowly. "Nothing appears disturbed. Doug had one or two things of considerable value." He nodded toward the desk. "That's an original Tiffany lamp and the ivory Buddha is quite valuable." He frowned. He was silent for a moment, then said slowly, reluctantly, "I don't know if there is a connection, but yesterday a client of Doug's made quite a production of displaying a ring Doug intended to give to Lisbeth Carew. I need to contact Lisbeth. She's in Europe, due home next week."

Johnny was alert. Lisbeth Carew was a name to reckon with in Adelaide. "She's in Europe now?"

Brewster nodded. "In Lucerne. That's where her daughter lives. I'll call her." He glanced at his watch, figuring the time there to be late afternoon. "From what the client said, I believe Doug kept the ring in his desk drawer." He frowned. "I don't believe I recall seeing the ring case when I opened the drawer. If you'd like, I can check." He stepped into the office.

Johnny held up a warning hand. "I'll look." He took three quick steps, tugging a pair of vinyl gloves from a back pocket. He pulled the gloves on, said briskly, "With your permission, I'll open the drawer."

Brewster slowly nodded.

Johnny picked up a pen from the desktop, slipped the ballpoint behind the pull, eased the drawer out as far as it would go.

Brewster watched him closely. "The ring is in a red velvet case."

Johnny crouched, peered into the drawer. "There's no ring case. Was the ring valuable?"

Brewster's tone was dry. "So I understand. A diamond ring. Apparently it cost a hundred thousand dollars."

Johnny had the look of a poker player who'd just drawn an ace to complete a royal flush.

Brewster cautioned him. "Doug may have taken the ring with him when he left the office yesterday. Perhaps his secretary can help when she—"

"Hello." An uncertain voice was raised in the hallway. "Is anyone—"

Brewster called out. "We're in here, Lou." He turned to Johnny. "Perhaps we might step out into the hall."

Johnny followed Brewster into the hall with Officer Benson close behind. Johnny closed the door, the crime scene off-limits until the techs arrived to fingerprint and search.

Louise Raymond, her round face shocked, was just inside the back entrance. "Oh my goodness. There's a police car in the parking lot. And police here." Lou was an appealing figure with her white hair and kind round face. "What's happened?"

The back door opened again. Anita Davis, chestnut curls windstirred, stopped beside Lou. "There's a police car in the—" She broke off, staring at the uniformed officers. Close behind her was Nancy Murray, the paralegal, her eyes huge and staring. She edged even with Anita. "Is something wrong?" Her voice was high. Nancy's outfit likely was new, a pale yellow linen blouse and cream linen slacks. Butterfly bow heels added a saucy flair.

Geraldine Jackson peered around the group. "What's up?" Her tone was raucous. "Looks like we're being raided. What're they looking for? Slots? Porn? A weed stash from the Rockies?"

Megan Wynn edged past the cluster of secretaries. Her heart-shaped face was composed, but dark patches beneath her eyes suggested a sleepless night.

"Excuse me. Coming through." Sam Cobb's deep voice was a clarion. The women moved aside as the chief strode into the hallway, Detective Sergeant Hal Price at his shoulder.

I saw two other familiar faces, Detective Don Smith, tall, dark, and handsome, and Detective Judy Weitz, sturdy and impassive with bright alert eyes.

Sam stopped in front of Brewster Layton. "Morning, Brewster. You've had a break-in?"

"Break-in?" Nancy took a step back. Lou Raymond clutched Anita's arm. "Oh my goodness." Geraldine's heavily mascaraed eyes widened. Megan looked startled, then thoughtful.

Johnny Cain stepped forward. "Sir, Mr. Layton found a broken window in the office occupied by Doug Graham. Mr. Layton called nine-one-one. The screen on the window to the alley was slashed and is hanging loose. A pane of glass has been removed, apparently broken out, from the lower half of the window. That made it possible to unlock the window. The lower half of the window is up. It appears someone entered the office from the alley. The intruder stepped on broken glass in the process. Mr. Layton said the office looked as it had the last time he saw it with no obvious disarray. However, Mr. Layton reports that Mr. Graham had a ring case in his desk drawer yesterday. There is no ring case in the drawer now."

Lou Raymond placed fingertips against her lips. "How dreadful." Anita Davis looked shocked. "Oh, it cost so much money." Nancy Murray shook her head. "I thought he was going to take the ring to the bank." Geraldine Jackson slapped her hands on her hips and her caftan top swirled. "That's a hell of a thing."

I thought Nancy remembered Jack Sherman warning Doug to put the ring in the bank and made the leap in her own mind that Graham intended to place the ring in a safety deposit box.

"The ring's gone?" Some of the tension eased out of Megan's face. Clearly Megan hoped the murder and the disappearance of the ring were linked.

"If the ring was left in the desk overnight, apparently it was stolen. However, that hasn't been confirmed." Johnny continued in an uninflected tone, "Mr. Layton said he went into Doug Graham's office this morning to see if Graham had appointments scheduled for the day. He looked in the desk for an appointment book, but did not find one. At that time, he didn't notice whether the ring case was in the drawer. Mr. Layton arrived this morning earlier than usual." No emphasis, no expression, information shared.

Chief Cobb gave Johnny an approving glance and turned to Brewster. "What time—"

Before Sam could finish, Sharon King hurried through the back entrance. She saw the police. Her slender face held shock and disbelief. One hand touched her throat. She moved slowly up the hallway, stopped before Brewster Layton. "I just heard on the radio that Mr. Graham is dead. Is it true? Is that why the police are here? Is Mr. Graham dead?" Her voice was shaky.

Brewster was somber. He slowly nodded. "Someone shot Doug last night. We're all shocked."

I had a good view of all the women.

Sharon King's dark eyes held horror and disbelief. Lou Raymond's mouth rounded in a breathless *O.* Geraldine Jackson's where's-the-bubbly? facade crumpled and her plump face sagged. Nancy Murray pressed a hand against her lips. Anita folded her arms across her front. "How awful."

Only Megan appeared unsurprised, her young face carefully expressionless, her lips in a tight line, her thin shoulders rigid. Her eyes held the memory of a slumped body. Suddenly she tensed, jerked her arm, then froze motionless.

I didn't need neon to announce Jimmy's arrival. He was there, tugging on Megan's arm, and she, sensibly, resisted.

As Anita continued to murmur, I reached Megan, swept my hand, clutched at a muscular invisible arm. I stood on tiptoe, whispered as lightly as possible, "Megan's office. We'll be there in a minute."

He wriggled with impatience.

"Don't talk. Go. Now."

For an instant there was the feel of resistant muscle beneath my fingers, then nothing.

No one had noticed or heard, my whisper lost in the sound of the shocked women and their stricken sentences. "Was it a burglar?" "Who did it?" "When was he killed?"

Sharon blinked her large brown eyes. "He was so happy yesterday." Her voice trembled. "Later that afternoon he showed me the ring again, asked if I thought Mrs. Carew would like it. He—" She broke off, a quick drawn breath. "Has anyone called Rhoda?"

Sam Cobb stepped toward her. "Rhoda?"

"His former wife." Sharon half turned, stared at Lou. "Perhaps you should go and be with her."

There was an odd flicker in Lou's eyes.

Why had Sharon immediately turned to Lou? Why not Brewster Layton? I looked at Lou more closely. The sudden smoothing of her face told me she knew something which involved Doug Graham's former wife.

Sam Cobb said firmly, "Detective Smith will speak with the former Mrs. Graham." Sam gave Don Smith a glance that told him: *Find her, talk to her, find out where she was last night.* Don nodded and moved quickly toward the door.

Sam kept his deep voice calm, reassuring. "For the moment, we will appreciate everyone who works here remaining present.

Detective Smith will be thoughtful when he speaks with Mrs. Graham." Sam cleared his throat. "For those of you who are not aware of the circumstances, Doug Graham was killed by a gunshot last night at his home. Megan Wynn was at the Graham home when police arrived—"

Megan's heart-shaped face was utterly still, but her body tensed.

Brewster Layton gave Megan an affirmative nod. Lou's eyebrows rose in surprise. Anita appeared shocked. Nancy shook her head back and forth as if bewildered. Geraldine's gaze was speculative. Sharon half turned to stare at Megan, her eyes wide.

Megan elevated her chin.

"—in response to a nine-one-one call reporting a man shot. Ms. Wynn told police she was summoned to the house by a text message from Mr. Graham. She drove to his house, parked in the driveway, followed the instructions in the text to enter the house from the terrace. She reported finding Mr. Graham dead in a leather chair facing a television screen. The television was turned on. She denies calling nine-one-one, told investigating officers she saw no one at the house. We are here to interview everyone who was in contact with Mr. Graham yesterday. In addition, we will investigate the apparent break-in discovered this morning. Who can tell me more about the ring that may be missing?"

No one spoke.

Geraldine raised an eyebrow. "Might as well lay it out on the table. Hell of it is, we all thought we were having fun." She described the previous morning, the bigger-than-life oilman hoisting the ring case, lid raised, for everyone to see. "He said Mr. Graham paid a hundred thousand dollars for the ring."

Brewster swung toward Sharon King. "Was the ring in Doug's desk last night?"

"It was there in midafternoon. I don't know about last night."

"What time did Mr. Graham leave the office?"

She glanced about, but no one else appeared eager to speak. "About ten to five, I believe."

"Was he carrying the ring with him?"

She gave a slight shrug. "I have no idea. I suppose it could have been in his pocket." But her answer was almost mechanical. She was clearly struggling with shock. But so were they all.

Yesterday in this hallway Jack Sherman hoisted a ruby red ring case in one big hand amid gasps of eager interest. Today the ring seemed unimportant, faraway, a footnote.

Brewster Layton's eyes were sunk in a thin face, his lips in a tight, hard line. Sharon King's long slender fingers clenched and unclenched. Lou Raymond's sweet mouth trembled. Anita Davis kept shaking her head, as if this moment were a bad dream that would soon end. Anita wasn't disheveled today. She'd obviously taken some pains with her appearance, chestnut curls tidily brushed, makeup neatly applied. Her white peasant blouse was crisp, her skirt wrinkle free, but she looked tense and worried. Geraldine Jackson was like a flag at half-mast, her unaccustomed gravity making her look older. Nancy Murray's eyes darted up and down the hallway. Was she remembering yesterday morning? Megan's expression was thoughtful. Was she thinking about the ring and what its disappearance might mean?

More sounds at the back door. Two crime techs entered, each carrying a small black case. One was a wiry man likely no taller than five feet five with a mop of fire red hair. His companion could have been a lineman on any coach's team, well over six feet, pushing three hundred pounds, bald-headed with small blue eyes. The two men walked up to the chief. I wondered how many big guy–little guy jokes they'd heard. On closer inspection, the little man looked tough as a boot and only a fool would tangle with the big man.

Sam was brisk. "Fingerprints. Photographs. Check the contents of the center desk drawer. Save and catalog everything in it."

I was pleased Sam hadn't forgotten the crumpled notes Doug Graham had written yesterday morning and I'd retrieved from the wastebasket and placed in the drawer, which reminded me that the ring case had definitely been there late last night.

Sam jerked a thumb. Johnny Cain nodded and led the techs to Doug Graham's office, held the door for them. They stepped inside. The door closed firmly.

"Lou, check Doug's appointments." Brewster Layton sounded weary. "Call and cancel. In fact, I think it would be good if all appointments were canceled today. As soon as each person has spoken to the police, you are free to leave. The office is closed for the day."

Brewster Layton frowned, eyes narrowed, then said quietly, "We are all struggling with the shock of Doug's death. If anyone has information that will help in the investigation, please speak to the police. Moreover, I'll ask everyone to respond to any requests the police make." He touched his goatee. "Does anyone have any objection to a police search for the ring case?" He looked from face to face.

Sharon was clearly disinterested. "They can look in my desk. I don't care."

Anita nodded in agreement. Nancy spoke quickly, "Sure." Geraldine turned thumbs-up. "Feel free. I haven't had any secrets since my second divorce." It was a pale imitation of her usual boisterous attitude. But Lou Raymond's face turned a bright pink and she burst out, "The thief broke into Mr. Graham's office. Why look for the ring in the rest of the offices?"

Anita made a sympathetic coo. "They're just being thorough, Lou. Don't you ever watch detective shows on TV? They have to think ahead, and someday somebody might want to know why they didn't look for the ring. Just in case."

Lou's voice wobbled. "Just in case one of us took it?"

Brewster was soothing. "No one is suggesting anyone here is involved in the theft. As Anita says, the police are just being thorough." He looked at Sam. "That's the situation, isn't it?"

Sam's expression was genial. "We always try to be thorough."

Megan's clear voice was crisp. "A good idea."

"And, of course, my office as well." Brewster's tone was wry. "No need for a warrant. Have your people look where they wish. Although I doubt a thief broke in and left without the ring." He looked at Sam. "Use our conference room for your interviews." He gestured toward a closed oak door midway up the hall.

Sam nodded his thanks. "Officer Cain will check all offices for signs of entry and then make a careful search for the ring case. I'll interview each person separately in the conference room. At that time, I would appreciate permission from each person to take your fingerprints." His expression was bland. "We know members of the firm and staff often have occasion in be in various offices. The fingerprints will help us determine if there are any unidentified fingerprints in Mr. Graham's office. I trust no one has any objection?"

Brewster was quick to approve. "We will assist you in any way we can."

Sam nodded his thanks. "Before we begin the interviews, I invite anyone to step forward if they believe they have pertinent information."

No one moved.

Sam's genial expression didn't change. "For convenience, I will see each person in—"

The back door swung in. Blaine Smith, with a patch of sunburn on each cheek, stepped inside. He saw Megan and started up the hall, relief evident in his bony face.

Johnny Cain took a step toward him. "Sir, we are investigating a crime and the premises are currently closed."

Blaine was pleasant, but had a look of bulldog determination, head jutting forward. "Sorry, Officer. I need to speak with Ms. Wynn." He took three long strides, was at her side. "I just heard on the radio. They said you arrived a few minutes after nine last night." He turned, nodded at Chief Cobb. "Hello, Sam. I went by Doug's house last night. The house was lighted. I saw his car in the drive. It was the only car in the drive." He stopped for emphasis, held Sam's gaze. "It was a couple of minutes before nine. I rang and knocked. There was no answer."

Megan's face brightened. "I saw the taillights of a car driving away as I arrived. Now I know why they looked familiar."

Sam looked from one to the other, wary, possibly skeptical. "You mentioned taillights. Now you think it might have been Mr. Smith's car?" On easier days, he might have spoken of the young lawyer as Blaine. Not today. Not here.

Megan's nod was decisive. "Yes."

Sam turned back to Blaine. "Good of you to come forward.

Please step into the conference room." He glanced at Detective Weitz, who immediately moved toward Blaine.

The tall, gangly lawyer gripped Megan's arm. "Hell of a thing to happen. Hard for you. I'll talk to you in a little while."

"Thank you, Blaine." Her face and posture were suddenly stronger.

I understood. His arrival here meant she didn't have to be afraid, very afraid, that his departure from Graham's house last night implicated him. She, of course, believed what Blaine said. Would Sam Cobb? Or would Sam suspect Blaine equally with Megan?

Blaine followed Detective Weitz to the oak door.

Inside the conference room was a long golden oak table with chairs at the head and foot, four on either side. A pad of paper and pen sat in front of each place. Quickly I grabbed a pad, wrote: *The ring case was in Graham's desk last night at shortly before midnight.* I ripped off the sheet as the door opened. I heard Sam's carrying voice. "After I speak with Mr. Smith, I'll see each of you in alphabetical order. Please do not make or receive any telephone calls or texts until the interviews are done."

I felt a deeper quiver of worry. The alphabetical listing might seem simply an easy matter of order. I doubted that was Sam's reasoning. Megan Wynn would be the last person to be interviewed. Before then, Sam intended to dig for any and every scrap of information that could be negative for Megan.

I stood next to the head of the table, holding my sheet below the table surface out of sight.

Detective Weitz held the door for Blaine Smith. "Please take a seat on one side."

Blaine walked to the near side, settled in a chair. He looked determined and combative.

Detective Weitz went around the table. She was carrying a dark briefcase. She pulled out a tape recorder, placed the black plastic machine on the table, lifted out an electronic fingerprinting machine that scanned fingerprints digitally, and positioned it to one side. She slid into a chair as Sam and Hal entered. Hal closed the door to the hall. He strolled around the table and sat next to Weitz.

Sam pulled out the end chair, lowered his bulky frame into the high-backed chair.

As soon as Sam was seated and had one hand below the surface of the table, I slipped the note into his hand. I admired Sam's presence of mind. He never changed expression, instead took a quick glance down, gave an infinitesimal nod.

I returned to the hallway. Anita, Nancy, and Lou huddled close together near the back entrance.

Brewster Layton walked up the hallway, placed a gentle hand on Sharon King's shoulder. "I'll ask Chief Cobb if he could see you first. I know how many years you've worked for Doug."

Sharon King managed a tremulous smile. "That's all right, Mr. Layton. I want to stay and try to help. I'll see about his work, send it to you or Megan."

"Thank you, Sharon." He lifted his voice. "Everyone might as well go to their desk until the police are ready for you. I'll be in my office." He turned and walked, shoulders slumping, toward his door.

Megan looked at Sharon with sympathy. "We'll all do whatever we can, Sharon. I'll be in my office." Her face still somber and drawn, she walked briskly to her office. She paused with her hand on the knob.

I knew she was girding for an encounter with Jimmy. I was interested to know what brought him here, other than Megan and murder, of course. But first I wanted to see if I could discover the reason for the slight bulge in Brewster Layton's jacket. When I reached his office, he was turning away from a far corner of the room. He looked like a man relieved of a burden. There was an element of satisfaction in his long face. He walked to his desk and sank into his chair.

I was pleased to see he was in his shirtsleeves. I spotted his jacket on a coat tree near the door. I watched him carefully as I eased my hand down the lapel to the pocket. The left pocket had bulged.

No bulge.

I slipped my hand into the pocket.

Empty. Nothing there.

Could I have been mistaken? Was it the right pocket?

Nothing.

I was too late. The moment I'd taken to alert Sam about the ring had been enough. Brewster Layton entered his office, closed the door, immediately removed something—a packet, a letter—from his pocket. He'd come early to the office, knowing his partner was dead. He'd had a ready explanation for fingerprints on the center drawer to Doug's desk. I was convinced Brewster arrived early intent upon removing something from Graham's desk. The material could be hidden anywhere in this room, possibly secreted deep within a file. As I struggled with disappointment, I scanned the room. My gaze stopped at the corner where he'd stood when I'd entered. A small machine sat there.

In an instant, I was at the corner, studying the lid. There were two slots, one larger than the other. I glanced over my shoulder.

Brewster cupped his goatee, his expression intense. He looked like a man with a problem, working out how to respond. Was he struggling with a legal challenge or did he have murder on his mind?

I ran my fingers across the top of the small machine. Why had he come directly to this corner when he entered his office? His pocket was now empty. Something about this machine . . . I looked at a button marked Power. I pushed with my index finger. A loud whirr shocked me. I yanked my hand back. The whirr ceased.

Brewster's chair whacked back against the wall. He was on his feet and striding across the room.

I quickly moved out of the way, bent forward to watch.

He stared at the now-silent machine, his face furrowed with concern. He reached down, grabbed a handle, lifted. He tilted the gray metal base, looked inside.

I looked, too, and saw shredded shiny strips in a mound at the bottom of the plastic container. Other strips hung from the bottom of the lower portion of the lid.

Still frowning, he eased the obviously heavy lid with its under-carriage back into place. He turned away, paused, looked back, shrugged.

It is always helpful to know that ordinary people, when con-fronted with the inexplicable, work their way to an answer. A short circuit. Something wrong with the machine. He gave a decisive nod. He hurried to his desk, pulled free a couple of sheets of lined yellow paper from a legal pad, returned to the corner, folded the sheets, punched Power, fed the sheets into the machine.

How clever. The machine reduced pages into thin narrow long strips. I had seen enough of the previously shredded material to have a very good idea what Brewster Layton had hurried to destroy. Sam would be interested.

Out in the hallway, I hesitated. I wanted to find out why Jimmy had tugged at Megan in the hallway, but I decided first to see how the crime techs were doing in Doug Graham's office. I hovered just inside the doorway to Graham's office, now the scene of painstaking forensic investigation. The short red-haired tech was checking the grayish residue of fingerprint powder on the surfaces of the broken window. "Bunch of smudges mostly. I'll see what I can pick up."

The big guy grunted. "Maybe there will be some microscopic glass particles in the perp's shoes. If he wore sneakers."

The redhead was wry. "Got to find the perp first. Can't check all the sneakers in Adelaide."

I scarcely heard. Next the techs would check the desk drawer. I suspected last night's silent intruder had been careful, very careful, the drawer pulled out by a gloved hand, the ring case scooped up, a quick turn, a cautious check of the alleyway, then out into the night, running lightly, the ring case securely in a pocket, or possibly a cautious exit from Doug's office to the hallway and out the back door to melt into the shadows.

I looked at the gleaming surface of the desk and a silver-framed photograph of a quite beautiful older woman, elegant, patrician. I felt sure it was a portrait of Lisbeth Carew. Doug Graham had planned to give her a magnificent ring. What was her feeling for him? He was handsome and could be charming. Perhaps he was entertaining and interesting, a good companion. If he had lived and they had married, she might never have known that he was a man who had little compunction for others if they failed to please him. I imagine he would have continued to be charming to Lisbeth Carew.

I realized with dismay that I'd not until this moment paused to think about those who might grieve for Doug Graham. His ex-wife had once loved him. His children knew him as their father. I took a moment to wish his soul well. *Requiescat in pace.*

For now, my focus was on the living. I wondered about Rhoda Graham. The expression on Lou Raymond's face told me Lou knew something she did not want to divulge about the ex-wife. Detective Don Smith was likely at Rhoda Graham's house or office at this moment, telling her of her ex-husband's death. I would give him time to finish his visit and then I intended to see what I could find out.

Out in the hallway again, I hesitated. I could not be everywhere at once. Not even a ghost can manage that feat. I would check with Sam later to see if he discovered anything new from the interviews. And Jimmy might know something helpful.

In Megan's office, she stood with her back to the door, glaring toward the window. ". . . out of your mind?"

Jimmy's young voice was offended. "You should start paying attention to what I say. I told you not to go to Graham's house last night."

The fight drained out of Megan. She walked tiredly across the room, dropped her cotton shoulder bag onto the desktop, slipped into her chair. "I thought I had to go. For Anita." She lifted her chin. "How was I supposed to know somebody was going to kill him?"

"Okay, okay." Jimmy was exasperated. "I get it. But one of these days you have to stop riding to the rescue of widows and orphans. But hey"—now his voice was soft—"I guess that's why I love you. But you should do what I say now. Hold a press conference. You need to get your side of the story out. The mayor dumped on you big-time at the news conference this morning. Right now reporters are sending in their leads, like: *Megan Wynn, associate at the law firm of Layton, Graham, Morse and Morse, claims senior partner Doug Graham was dead when she arrived after dark at his house in response to a text ordering her to come.* New paragraph. *The text sent on Graham's cell phone to Ms. Wynn's cell phone threatened to proceed with the termination Graham and Wynn discussed that morning. Wynn refused to explain the text and denied she faced dismissal from the firm.* This will convince readers your arrest is pending."

Her voice was stiff. "I hope to practice law for about fifty more years, and notoriety doesn't become lawyers. Besides"—now her tone was practical—"what am I going to say to reporters? I got a text. Yes, that's what the text said. No, it wasn't my termination. So they ask whose termination, and there's where I say I have no further comment. I'd be better off to ignore all of it."

Jimmy knew newspapers. He knew once tarred it's hard to rehabilitate an image. I chimed in. "Jimmy's right. You should put out a statement to the press."

Her head jerked. "You're here, too? Two voices offering tidbits of wisdom, not just one. Some people have an imaginary friend. Me, I have two. Am I ever special." Her voice was strained.

I kept my voice quiet, pleasant. "If you had a client unjustly suspected of murder and clearly identified by authorities as a person of interest, what would you advise?"

Megan's expression altered. She was interested, intrigued. "I would tell my client to provide the press with the following statement: I am assisting the police—"

I settled in the chair in front of her desk, picked up a pad and pen, began to write.

Her voice faltered for an instant as the legal pad rose and apparently settled on an unseen lap, then she gave a brief nod and continued.

I wrote fast, caught up.

"—in their investigation of the murder of Doug Graham. I discovered Mr. Graham's body Thursday evening when responding to a text about a business matter he and I had discussed at the office Thursday morning. I am not at liberty to divulge the contents of that talk. I can, however, provide details of my actions last night. I was at home reading when I received Mr. Graham's text. I drove to his home, arriving at shortly after nine p.m. I observed a car pulling away from the front of his house. I pulled into the driveway, parked behind Mr. Graham's car. Following the directions in the text, I went through a gate, crossed a terrace, and came to the back door. When I stepped inside, I saw Mr. Graham slumped to one side in a chair. He had suffered some kind of head wound. I hurried across the room, tried to find a pulse. There was no pulse. When I dropped his hand, his body toppled over. I was unable to prevent him from falling to the floor. In the process, my blouse and hands were stained with his blood. I used newspaper sheets to try and clean my hands so that I could get my cell phone out of my purse and call nine-one-one. I had just picked up my cell phone when I heard sirens and realized police were coming to the house. I have no idea who called nine-one-one. I didn't hear a shot when I arrived. I neither saw nor heard anyone as I approached the house or when I was in the terrace room. When I heard the sirens, I hurried out to the driveway and met the police as they arrived. I have no idea who shot Mr. Graham. I do not own a gun or pistol and have never owned a gun or pistol or had one in my possession. I have never held a gun or shot a gun of any kind. I hope the police succeed in discovering the identity of the person who killed Mr. Graham."

"That's a girl." Jimmy was pleased. "Now, get on your computer and zap that to Joan Crandall at the *Gazette*: jcrandall@thegazette.com. Ditto to the newsroom at the *Oklahoman* and to AP. Print out a copy for that big hulk of a police chief."

I didn't like Jimmy's disrespectful description, but he likely sensed that Sam was after Megan, and he knew the mayor wanted a quick arrest.

I ripped off the sheet from the legal pad, slid it across the desktop.

Megan looked cheered. Battling back often has that effect. She started to take the sheet and her hand brushed her purse. She looked at it in mild surprise, grabbed the strap, and pulled open the lower right-hand drawer. She swung the purse down, stopped. The purse hung there, midway to the drawer, immobile.

Chapter 9

I reached Megan's side, stared down, too.

Jimmy crowded next to me. "Oh hell."

I realized I was clutching my invisible throat.

I'd thought the situation could not get worse for Megan.

I was wrong.

A gun rested neatly on the bottom of the drawer. I stared at the shiny stainless steel barrel and ridged black grip.

"Top of the line." Jimmy sounded choked. "A Ruger Mark III target pistol. Twenty-two caliber."

"Did you do target shooting?" In a moment of shock perhaps a foolish question could be forgiven.

"Yeah, yeah, yeah."

Megan stood rigid, purse hanging above the drawer. Sudden fear marked her heart-shaped face.

Jimmy exploded, half-mad, half-scared. "That's all the cops need. The gun might as well have a tag on it: *Murder weapon used in Graham homicide.* We have to get rid of it." Jimmy's elbow jabbed my hip. He pushed me out of the way, and I grabbed at the desk to keep from falling.

The gun rose in the air, the barrel gleaming bright silver in the light from the overhead fluorescents.

"Jimmy, stop." Megan knocked over her chair as she raced around the desk, hands outstretched.

The gun rose to the ceiling, far out of reach.

I went up after the gun and Jimmy. I gripped his arm. "Don't be a fool. She has to tell the police."

Jimmy yanked away from me. As we struggled and the gun dipped toward the floor, I clung to his muscular forearm. The gun went off, the sound of the shot loud as thunder in the small office. The bullet gouged a streak across the wooden floor, ricocheted to the window, shattering the glass.

The gun clattered to the floor.

Through the office door there were sudden shouts, the pound of running feet.

Megan darted to the gun, snatched it up. Her hand shook as she aimed the barrel at the floor. Her face was taut with stress. The gun looked huge in her small hand.

The door burst open, slammed against the wall. "Hands up. Police." In a half crouch, Johnny Cain moved fast at an oblique angle, gun drawn, leveled at Megan. "Drop that gun." Officer Anderson, also crouching, gun drawn, moved to his left, covering him, gun trained immediately on Megan. Her face was empty of expression, her eyes alert.

Megan looked at the gun in her right hand. Her words were jerky, fast, breathless. "I found it. It went off. An accident. I'll put it down." She bent forward and cautiously placed the gun on the floor, slowly straightened, backed away, hands partially raised.

The doorway seemed full of people, Sam and Hal Price and behind them the office staff and Brewster Layton.

Megan, her face stricken, stared at the service revolver aimed at her. She knew her position was untenable, unexplainable.

Burly Sam, white-blond Hal, and frowsy-haired Weitz bunched just inside the doorway, alert, wary, poised to draw weapons.

"Hey, what the hell." All elbows and knees, moving like a half-back looking for an open field, Blaine Smith wriggled past them despite Sam's stern order to get back.

Blaine reached Megan. "What happened?"

Johnny moved fast, never taking his eyes off Megan. He stood over the gun. "Step away. That's right. Stop there." He pointed with his free hand at a space three feet from the gun.

Blaine moved with her, gripped one elbow. He was struggling with uneven breathing. "That shot . . . what happened?"

"I found that gun." She scarcely managed a whisper.

Sam's heavy face was rock hard. "Stay exactly where you are, Ms. Wynn. You, too, Smith." He studied them for a moment, Megan wide-eyed and shaking, Blaine bewildered but glaring at Johnny and his service revolver. "There's no need for a gun. Put that away before somebody gets hurt."

Sam slowly nodded, glanced at Johnny. "At ease, Officer." He and Hal Price and Judy Weitz moved forward, making the office seem small and crowded.

Johnny sheathed his gun, but remained standing over the .22 lying on the floor.

Brewster Layton spoke from the doorway. "Is everyone all right?"

Sam continued to stare at Megan, but his booming voice could clearly be heard by those crowded behind Brewster. "A gun went off accidentally. There is no danger."

Sam gestured at Weitz. "Get the techs." He walked across the room, studied the gouge on the hardwood floor, looked up at the shattered window. "Ms. Wynn——"

Blaine had his arm around her shoulders. "Wait a minute. Can't you see she's upset?"

Megan spoke quickly, her voice firm. "It's all right, Blaine." She looked up, knowing he was there, knowing he was her champion, knowing she needed a champion. She gazed directly at Sam. "I found the gun." Her voice was stronger, clearer. Her stare was level, unflinching. "I pulled out my lower right-hand desk drawer to put my purse in. I saw that gun. I did not put the gun there. I know nothing about that gun. That is not my gun. I have never seen the gun before and——"

Sam held up a hand. "We will speak to you in the conference room. Come this way."

Layton and the staff, Anita Davis, Geraldine Jackson, Sharon King, Nancy Murray, Lou Raymond, heard every word.

Megan stood straight and as tall as her five feet one inch permitted. "I have a right to tell you what happened."

Weitz pulled a pad and pen from her pocket, began to write.

Megan's words came in short bursts. "I was startled. Without thinking I picked up the gun. I don't know much about guns. I was going to bring it to you and it went off. I have never seen that gun before. It was not in my desk last night. I did not put the gun in my desk."

I would like to think she was persuasive, but I knew Sam didn't believe a word. That was devastating because every word was true except for the disposition of the gun after she opened the drawer.

Sam folded his arms. "You knew that no weapon was found at the Graham house."

"Yes." She spoke evenly, but she looked small, vulnerable, beleaguered.

"You knew Officer Cain was going to search all of the offices." She took a quick breath. "Yes."

It hung unspoken between them, the fact that a search was coming. If she knew about the gun in her desk drawer, she had to do something about it. If she was indeed surprised when she opened the drawer, why had she picked up the weapon?

Sam was brusque. "We'll take your statement now in the conference room."

Blaine stepped forward. "Ms. Wynn is my client. I will be conferring with her. We will be at the police station at one o'clock."

There was a taut silence while Blaine and Sam looked at each other. Finally, his face grim, Sam nodded. "One o'clock."

Blaine nodded at Megan. She picked up her purse and they walked together into the hall as the watching staff moved back. No one spoke.

⟢

The door to the hall closed. Megan's office was empty now.

"I screwed up." Jimmy's lugubrious voice came from the corner of Megan's desk near the window.

I moved near, reached out, patted his shoulder. "These things happen."

"If you hadn't grabbed my arm——"

"I know." I was well aware I bore some responsibility. "But what is, is. Blaine will protect her."

A heavy sigh. "I guess he's not such a dweeb."

I could hear a dream dying.

Another heavy sigh. "Megan probably never wants to hear from me again."

"She knows you mean well."

"Yeah." The reply was bleak.

Maybe I'm a sucker for love. Okay. I admit it. I am a sucker for love, especially a love that endured past living.

The shining steps in the corner of the room became brighter, the golden glow deeper.

"I guess I'll—"

I reached out, gripped a muscular forearm. "Not yet, Jimmy. Megan needs you." When he climbed the stairs to Heaven, I wanted him to know he'd made a difference for Megan, and she would always remember him with a smile. I hunched my shoulders, expecting at any instant to hear the thrum of wheels on rails, the whoo of the Rescue Express. I talked fast, justifying myself to Wiggins, appealing to Jimmy. "The gun in her office puts her at risk of arrest." Sam Cobb had been suspicious before. The discovery of the gun in Megan's office might be the critical fact he needed. At the very least, she would have vaulted to suspect number one even if she'd immediately rushed out and alerted the police to the gun. Likely, the gun had been polished shiny clean without any identifying or identifiable prints. Now, of course, the grip was liberally plastered with Megan's prints. Sam could also reasonably infer she had been afraid there might be some scrap of a print still on the gun and decided to handle the gun to excuse those prints.

If Megan was to be saved, I had to work fast. "You know how to dig out information on people."

"Yeah." He was still bleak.

I thought out loud. "Was Graham killed because somebody wanted to steal the ring or—"

"Somebody did steal the ring." He used a comforting tone appropriate for a doddering elderly relative.

"I know that. Why shoot him?"

"The thief figured Graham would know who took the ring."

I wasn't convinced. "That's a stretch. Graham was killed around nine o'clock. I know the ring case was in his desk drawer around midnight. If the murderer is the thief, he or she waited a couple of hours or more before coming here, breaking in, and taking the ring."

Jimmy was patronizing. "If you were going to steal something from an office, wouldn't you wait until midnight or later to sneak into an alley and break a window? The later at night, the less likely anyone would be around to notice anything."

Jimmy had a point. I still didn't see why theft required murder. "Why kill him?"

"Like I said, maybe Graham would have had a pretty good idea who took the ring. Maybe the thief was betting on murder making a missing ring look unimportant. Maybe he was killed for another reason and the ring stolen to make it look like theft was the motive. Maybe the ring made somebody mad."

I instantly wondered about Graham's ex-wife. How would she feel about a hundred-thousand-dollar ring for a wealthy woman? If she had no feelings left for him, did she resent his affluence, begrudge his spending that kind of money?

A thought wriggled in my mind, sinuous as a water moccasin in a dark pond. I didn't know the disposition of his estate, but very likely his children inherited everything. Jimmy was blunt. "Coincidence sucks."

His pronouncement was short on charm, but unerring in judgment.

He continued forcefully, "Graham's oil buddy flashes that rock around the office and that night Graham's shot. Why else would he be shot? That ring caused the whole thing."

Cause and effect: The ring unveiled to watching eyes. A shot in the back of the head. Whether the ring set off the events that followed, it was certain that Graham's murderer broke into the office and put the murder weapon in Megan's desk. Did the murderer then take the ring, and was the ring the reason for murder? Or did the murderer take the ring to obscure the real motive for Graham's death?

Perhaps the reason the ring was taken didn't matter. But the theft was a huge pointer to the killer's identity. The ring case and its contents had been prominently displayed yesterday morning to an avid audience. I remembered the crowded hallway, Brewster Layton and his client Winifred Kellogg, angry young Keith Porter, Megan and the staff, stressed-out Anita Davis, roguish Geraldine Jackson, surprised Sharon King, fascinated Nancy Murray, dazzled Lou Raymond.

If the ring set off the events that followed, the list of those aware of the ring's location was short. But there were other possibilities. Doug Graham wrote several messages, obviously intended for someone angry with him. He apparently had a whirlwind romance with Lisbeth Carew, but he didn't seem the kind of man to be celibate, and I wondered if he'd found a lover after his divorce.

I would ask, but the people I intended to see were tense and

anxious. I needed to find someone who knew Graham well, someone who had nothing to fear by speaking openly with an investigator. It was like pieces of a puzzle slotting together. "Carl and
Ginny Morse!"

"I don't think you've heard a word I said." Jimmy was aggrieved.
"I asked you why can't you do some kind of stuff—like the way
you go places and hear things—and find that damn ring?"

"I'm not a ring dowser."

"A what?"

I didn't have time to explain the old-fashioned concept of people
gifted with an ability to divine water or oil or gold or whatever
they sought by fashioning a V-shaped rod from hazelwood or willow, holding the ends, and traversing the search area until the rod
dipped to indicate the location of the sought-after object. "We don't
need the ring. We need information."

Carl and Ginny Morse were relaxing in Italy, far distant from
the tension and fear that burdened those now speaking one by one
with the police. Did they know anything that mattered? Perhaps
not. But they were partners in the firm and knew everyone involved.
They might be able to help.

I had a moment of self-doubt. Was I seeking a reason to expand
my activities to Italy? I remembered a trip there with Bobby Mac
and, of course, each of us tossing a coin into Trevi Fountain.

I always wanted to be an emissary in a romantic locale. Not that
Adelaide isn't romantic, but you know what I mean. Adelaide is
home. Had I considered Carl and Ginny simply because they were
far away in *bella* Italia?

Bella Italia. I remembered Jimmy's idyllic spring in Tuscany
with Megan. I had plenty to do in Adelaide. And Wiggins, if he

ever had an inkling that I'd been tempted, oh so tempted, to enjoy a summer evening in Florence, would be pleased I remained on duty in Adelaide. Besides, there was no telling how Jimmy might react or what he might do if he felt Megan was being unfairly treated by the police. It would be better to direct his energies.

However, there was a small problem.

If I went to Florence, I could appear. Not that Wiggins was ever pleased at that choice, but I had the option. Even Wiggins would admit Carl and Ginny Morse would not react well to a disembodied voice.

I had to make up my mind. Fast.

Sam and Hal were in the conference room, seeing each person in the office in alphabetical order with Detective Weitz recording the questions and answers. Likely it was Weitz who would take each person's fingerprints. As soon as each session ended, that person would be free to leave. Sam and Hal would be efficient, knowing that Blaine and Megan were coming to the police station at one. Moreover, though they would always pursue every possibility, right now Megan was their prime suspect. I wouldn't go so far as to think the inquiries would be pro forma. In fact, the questions might even focus on Megan's relationship with Doug Graham, with emphasis on the question of "termination."

The witnesses would enter one by one. I saw them in my mind: Anita Davis, who had dressed so carefully for today; Geraldine Jackson, sensual, ready to play, now pondering mortality; Sharon King, who'd been shocked to learn of murder on her car radio; Brewster Layton, who came to the office earlier than usual; Nancy Murray, shaken by her close proximity to sudden death; matronly Louise Raymond, whose gaze suddenly shifted when she was linked to Rhoda Graham.

I bid farewell to an image of a golden evening in Florence. "Jimmy, you know some Italian."

"I know the Italian that counts." His tone was light.

"I mean, you're comfortable in Italy. I want you to go to Florence. Carl and Ginny Morse have rented a villa. Go to the *Gazette*, find a phone in an out-of-the-way place, call Lou Raymond, and ask for the address of the villa where the Morses are staying. There's no reason why she wouldn't give you the information. Then—"

"Like, think Italy and there I am?" He was seriously amused. "Sure. Maybe I could swing by Mount Everest on the way."

I was diverted. "Do you mountain climb, too?"

"That was on my bucket list, but I ran out of time." He was wistful. "I did some rock climbing in the Dolomites. Went up the north face of Cima Grande."

I didn't know Cima Grande from a grand cinema, but the casual tone of his voice told me he'd managed an admirable feat.

"Obviously, no challenge is too great for you." I was sincere. "That's why you can handle Italy and the Morses. As soon as you get the address, go there—"

"Like I get the address, think the address, and I'm at a villa in Florence? Like I thought about Graham's pool and there I was?" He was skeptical, but there was a considering tone in his voice. That maneuver worked with the pool. . . .

"Precisely."

"What do I do then? I can see it now. I knock on the door and somebody opens it and nobody's there and the door slams shut."

I envisioned a huge red *X* scratched across my file at the Department of Good Intentions. No more telegrams. No more adventures. If only Wiggins were truly perplexed in Tumbulgum and perhaps remained unaware. However, Wiggins had an uncanny ability to arrive when I transgressed. But an emissary must do what an emissary must do.

"Jimmy, cross your heart, will you follow my directions?"

"Like, take a hike to the stairs?" He sounded morose.

"Not yet. I want you to appear—"

"Appear?" A bitter laugh. "Oh sure. Anything you—"

"Concentrate. Think: *Here.*"

"Think *here?*"

"Yes. I will think *here* also." Colors swirled as I appeared. "I'm choosing my costume. I'll be talking to several people as a police detective." I chose an amethyst blue silk top with silver checks, a white summer blazer, and a navy skirt. Low heels, of course. Serviceable. But flattering to a redhead.

"You're *here.*" His voice was young and stunned.

"Think *here,*" I ordered. "Appear in something a young member of the staff at the U.S. Consulate might wear."

"*Here.*" His tone was tentative.

His form took shape, dark hair, a sensitive, intelligent, appealing face. He wore a blue blazer, white shirt, blue knit tie, gray slacks, navy loafers with tassels. He looked down at his hands, flexed them. "Here!"

"Very good." It was my turn to be impressed. "You *are* handsome." I'm not au courant with Hollywood stars. I remember Gregory Peck and James Stewart and Van Johnson. Now I knew Ansel Elgort must indeed be extraordinarily handsome.

Jimmy smoothed the jacket of a blue blazer. He was definitely presentable. I thought he was most likely irresistible to most women.

He gave me a dazzling smile. "I wish I'd known I could do this. I wonder what Megan—"

I hurried to rein him in. I hoped. "You are appearing solely to help clear Megan. You will have a specific task. In Florence, not Adelaide. Imagine how unnerving it would be if someone who knew you saw you walking down a street in Adelaide."

He had a wicked gleam in his eyes. "That might be fun."

"Jimmy." I suppose my voice reflected a shade of panic.

"Just saying." His tone was airy. "Okay. I go to Florence and look up the Morses."

I smiled in relief. "Use your charm"—I looked at him critically; charm he had in abundance—"to find out why Brewster Layton and Doug Graham didn't like each other and when that dislike became obvious. Get a time frame if possible. Also, maybe you should try to talk to Ginny Morse without her husband." I never doubted Jimmy could attract any woman from seven to seventy. "Women pick up on things. See if she knows if Graham was involved with anyone when he was married to Rhoda. Or after his divorce. Also"—I looked at him and had no doubt in my mind that he would succeed—"see if you can persuade Ginny to tell you how the money's divvied up in the firm. That may be a challenge."

"Got it. I'll check it all out."

"And Jimmy"—I looked at him steadily—"I want your promise that when I say, *Jimmy, go,* you will disappear on the instant."

"Disappear. Like, in *disappear*?" Colors whirled and there was only space where he had stood. "I can come back." His voice was triumphant. *"Here."* And there he was.

His triple crown grin touched my heart.

"Your promise?" I sniffed, expecting coal smoke.

Slowly his face reformed. The smile was gone. He looked at me with serious brown eyes, brown eyes that held a memory of the girl he loved. "I promise."

I reached out. We solemnly shook hands. His hand was warm and firm and young.

He looked at me expectantly. "I'm ready."

I showed him my small black leather folder that identified me as Detective M. Loy. A very flattering resemblance. In an instant, he held a leather folder with a diplomatic ID for James Taylor. "Remember to be cautious that no one is nearby when appearing or disappearing. Let's meet this afternoon at the cemetery, say around four o'clock. Good luck, Jimmy."

"*Arrivederci. Sto andando.*" His voice was young, eager, fading.

I felt noble, withstanding the lure of bella It—

Coal smoke swirled around me. The thunder of wheels on rails.

I quickly disappeared.

Wiggins was gruff. "Bailey Ruth, climb aboard." No ifs, ands, or buts.

As Mama always told me, "When a man comes home grumpy, make him comfortable, a smile, a steak, an easy chair." "Wiggins, I know you are pleased Jimmy will be in a place where he is totally unknown and can cause no harm. It is your thoughtful approach to problems that inspired me! Where, I wondered, could I send Jimmy to seek information? It was as if I heard mandolins. And I knew what to do." No need to tell Wiggins mandolins came to mind because Jimmy learned phrases of love in his pursuit of Megan. I feared Wiggins might consider my thought processes frivolous. "Jimmy was an investigative reporter. He is charming. No one is better suited to discover if Carl and Ginny Morse possess information that will help find Graham's murderer. I do not feel that I"—great emphasis on the pronoun—"can take credit." Or, if we were going to get serious, blame. "You inspired me, your leadership a beacon, when I made the very difficult decision to instruct Jimmy in how to appear. Definitely, you were first and foremost in my thoughts." I'd envisioned Wiggins's censure from the get-go. "You are always my inspiration." My tone was reverential.

"Oh well, thank you, Bailey Ruth." Still a bit gruff, but much softer.

I think he was touched. As I've often said, Wiggins is a dear man. I hurried on while I had the advantage. "The only drawback," I said, speaking in a tsk-tsk tone, "was the utter necessity"—great emphasis—"of Jimmy appearing. But he will be appearing far, far away. We must hope he succeeds in his quest, because Megan is in danger of imminent arrest. I have very little time to solve both Graham's murder and the theft of the diamond ring from his office, and I need all the help I can get. I know you understand I am pressed on all fronts." If my voice quivered a bit, reflecting intense stress, let that conclusion be in the ear of the listener. "I have made difficult decisions based on necessity." If I sounded a bit stuffy, so be it. I know language that appeals to Wiggins. I don't feel the change in syntax is duplicitous. I would never wish to be accused of manipulating as fine a man as Wiggins. But as Mama often said, "Men admire the soldier who storms the rampart."

I tried to judge his silence. On a positive note, the scent of coal smoke was dissipating and I no longer heard the urgent thrum of wheels on rails. On a less positive note, Wiggins was likely out of patience with my evasions of his dictums.

"Bailey Ruth," he spoke with an edge of despair, "you are as squirmy as an eel in putting a good face on your transgressions of the Precepts."

"God loves eels, too." My voice was small.

A rumble of deep-throated laughter. "Yes, He does."

The clack of wheels on rails faded. I no longer smelled coal smoke. I was alone. Wiggins hadn't offered me carte blanche, but I was still here. I didn't need for Wiggins to give me marching orders. I well knew that he expected me to keep an eye on Jimmy and save Megan.

Chapter 10

It seemed ages ago at the *Gazette* when I dispatched Jimmy to find addresses. True to my reassurance to him, I remembered them without aid of notes. I went first to a small brick house on Elm. Several cars filled the old-fashioned single drive, a Chevy, two Toyotas, and a Ford. As I arrived, a Mazda pulled up at the curb. The driver's door slammed and a tall, thin woman wearing an ivory blouse and tan slacks and carrying a casserole dish moved purposefully toward the porch.

In a hallway, I glanced at an array of framed photographs hanging on the wall, photographs sketching a history of a family, a young, proud Doug with one large hand guiding his bride's as they cut the wedding cake, babies, toddlers, skinny little kids, attractive teenagers. Mom and Dad rolling out bicycles one Christmas. Dad carving a turkey. Rhoda as a bride was tall and willowy with sleek dark hair, a rather long face. In the later photographs, her eyes had lost the glow of happiness. The dark hair was touched by a streak of white. Lines of laughter and likely sorrow flared from her eyes and mouth.

I looked in a living room crowded with women, soft voices rising and falling. The room had no touches of the elegance in her late husband's office. The furniture looked comfortable, worn, two sofas, several easy chairs, a coffee table. I wondered if the office had been redone after their divorce. One wall of bookcases was full to overflowing. Books were stacked next to a couple of the chairs. Another bookcase held more framed photos and art pieces likely created by the children, a lopsided vase, a tooled leather box, a pottery horse that lacked one leg. There was a stain near the bottom of one drape. A venetian blind in one window was slightly bent. Everywhere there was evidence of much use and little money for upkeep.

A large Persian cat rubbed against my invisible leg. I reached down, stroked silky fur, was rewarded with a throaty purr.

Rhoda Graham sat stiffly in a straight-back chair near a small desk. She had obviously dressed for a day at work, a simple cream blouse, a tan belted skirt, brown heels. One hand clung to a long necklace of metal medallions studded with turquoise. The emptiness of her face indicated shock, a struggle for understanding. She spoke haltingly to a plump redhead, who held a pad and pen. "Doug's brother is coming. He will arrange for the funeral. I'm so thankful. That way the—" Three women occupied a nearby sofa, their heads close together as they talked.

I moved outside the house and stepped into the shadow of a cedar. There was no one near, and a tall wooden fence behind me. I appeared and walked briskly to the walk and onto the porch. I knocked three times.

A tiny woman with terrier hair and sharp brown eyes opened the door, saw a stranger. "We've had—"

"Detective M. Loy." I held up the small leather case. "We have just a few more questions for Mrs. Graham. She said she would like to help in the investigation."

"Oh. Well, just a moment." She started to close the door.

I had the screen open, moved forward. "Just a clarification. Perhaps there's a room where we can speak privately for a moment?"

The woman dithered uncertainly, taking a half step one way, then back. "Oh well, there's no one in the sewing room. I'll show you."

She led the way down the hall, opened the door to a small room, stepped aside for me to enter. A sewing machine sat on its stand in one corner. A partially finished lacy eyelet afghan lay on a small love seat. I loved the soft raspberry color of the yarn

I stepped inside. "Thank you. I'll wait."

She scurried away.

In a moment, steps sounded. Rhoda Graham paused on the threshold, took a breath, looked at me uncertainly.

I introduced myself. "Detective Smith sent me. We hope to clarify some information just received."

She walked in, closed the door behind her, remained standing. "What is it? I have so much to do. The children are flying home. I have to drive up to the city and pick them up." She glanced at her watch. "I need to leave in a few minutes."

"Certainly, Mrs. Graham. I'm sorry to take up your time."

She brushed a hand against one cheek. "Of course I want to help." Her tone was wooden. "I still can't believe Doug's . . . gone."

"You know Mrs. Louise Raymond."

Her face was suddenly still. "Yes."

I continued without inflection, but my eyes held her gaze. "Mrs. Raymond was present yesterday morning when an unexpected incident occurred at the law office."

I saw knowledge in her eyes, knowledge and a quick scrambling to decide what to say.

"Please describe your conversation with Mrs. Raymond. We want to make sure our facts are accurate."

She tried to be brisk. "Lou is an old friend. I know she meant well when she called me, but I wasn't interested in hearing about Doug's—"

"Please tell me what she said and your responses."

She brushed back a loop of dark hair with its silvery edge. "I don't know that I can remember word for word. I put it all out of my mind. I was very busy yesterday."

"As nearly as you can remember."

She pressed her lips together for an instant, then spoke in a rapid, clipped voice. "I can't be sure this is exactly right. Lou told me that Jack Sherman, he's an old client of Doug's, had caused quite a scene. Lou said that Jack demanded to see a ring that Doug bought for Lisbeth Carew."

"Did she say how much the ring cost?"

Rhoda Graham's gaze slid away. She looked down at the floor. She obviously saw trouble ahead if she admitted knowing yesterday morning that her former husband had spent a huge sum for a ring. But she had to assume I was there because Lou Raymond had revealed the contents of the phone conversation between Rhoda and Lou. Realizing she'd been silent too long, she looked at me, spoke hurriedly, "Jack claimed Maisie told him the ring cost a hundred thousand dollars." Rhoda tried to keep her voice level, but there was an edge. Anger? Resentment? Jealousy?

"What then?"

"Jack went into Doug's office and came out with the ring and held it up for everyone to see. Apparently he made it quite a show. Then he tossed the ring case back to Doug and left." Full stop.

"What did you say about the ring?"

"I don't remember." Her voice was stiff. "I suppose I said something."

She remembered, but she hoped Lou Raymond hadn't reported their conversation verbatim.

"How much support did your children receive from their father?" This would be a matter of public record in the divorce decree.

"They are both over eighteen."

"Did he pay for their college expenses?"

"No."

"Did he refuse to help them?"

"Yes."

"Why?"

Her face tightened. "He had a new life. He didn't include them."

"Did they want to be included?"

"I can't speak for them."

"Can't? Or won't?"

She made no answer, but her stare was hot with anger, anger with me, anger at the father who'd sloughed off his children. I well knew that even grown children are often bitter over divorce and sometimes blame one parent, cleave to the other.

"Did you resent his refusal to help them?"

"He knew how I felt about that."

"What was the reason for your divorce?"

"What usually causes divorce? People decide to go their separate ways. At this point, it doesn't matter, and I have no intention of discussing the circumstances."

"Was he involved with another woman?"

She shook her head, her lips pressed tightly together. She had every right at this point to decline to talk about Doug Graham. Unless and until there was evidence linking her to his murder, she was justified in her reticence.

I was brisk. "To return to today, you told Lou Raymond you were furious"—this was a guess on my part—"that he spent a hundred thousand dollars on a ring but provided no support to his children."

"I suppose that's how she took my comment."

She was trying to gloss over what she'd said to Lou.

"Obviously"—she chose her words carefully—"I felt Doug was unreasonable to act as he had."

So my guess was correct. When Lou Raymond called with news of the extravagant ring, Rhoda Graham was angry. "Do your children have student loans?"

"What does that have to do with Doug's murder?"

"Do you know the terms of his will?"

Her face smoothed out, was expressionless. Then she laughed, a ragged bitter laugh with a touch of triumph. "Doug never made a will. His father made a will and a week later he died. Doug thought making a will was bad luck. What kind of lawyer is that?"

I didn't know what kind of lawyer that made Doug Graham, but I knew one fact, his children would not have to go into debt now to go to college. I saw that knowledge in her eyes and saw fear as well. With her husband dead and his estate divided by heirs, his children wouldn't have to worry about money.

"What did your husband say when you spoke to him?"

"My former husband." The words again were clipped.

"What did your former husband say when you spoke to him?"

A pulse flickered in her slender throat, but now her response was rapid, definite. "I had no occasion to speak to him." Her gaze was direct, open.

"Were you at home last night at nine o'clock?"

There was a slight hesitation, then she said quickly, "I was home all evening."

I rather thought not. She'd insisted she'd not spoken to him. Her statement suggested there would be no calls to trace to her cell phone or landline. If she had spoken to him—or attempted to speak to him—she must have gone to see him. She claimed she never left the house. She must have felt confident there was no one to contradict her. No one alive.

⁓

The blazing summer sun was not quite midway in the sky. From a celestial perspective it is interesting that earth's inhabitants think of the sun rising and setting, yet the sun is immovable, the earth instead orbiting and rotating. But I was here and thinking in a human way. Perhaps only twenty minutes had passed since I left the law firm, though it seemed longer. Assuming the police interviews averaged fifteen or twenty minutes in length, I should be able to be present when each person arrived home.

I told Jimmy I wasn't a dowser when he suggested I use ethereal magic to find the missing ring, but I intended to make a circuit to observe Anita Davis, Geraldine Jackson, Sharon King, Brewster Layton, Nancy Murray, and Lou Raymond after they were interviewed. I didn't hope to divine a murderer, but whatever the tenor of the interviews, if one of them was the killer, surely maintaining an innocent facade exacted a toll.

I was pleased when I arrived at Anita Davis's small frame house to find the only occupants were Bridget, lying small and thin on a sofa in the living room holding a book in her lap, and in the kitchen a matronly woman humming "The Little Brown Church in the Vale" as she whipped egg whites on a long blue willow pattern platter. I knew at once she was making an angel food cake, an intense labor of love attempted only by very good cooks. I felt at home. I had a sudden picture of Mama, though her hair was red and usually in braids, not a graying straggly bun.

I returned to the living room, noted approvingly that it was immaculate, freshly starched white curtains at the windows, the oval braided rug worn but vacuumed. A small table next to the sofa held several books and a small vase with freshly cut roses. Bridget was propped against cushions. Her face was thin and pale, a fine bone structure, high forehead, slender nose, softly rounded chin. Pale brown hair was pulled back in a ponytail. She wore thick-lens glasses but the frames were a cheerful daffodil yellow. Now the book lay open in her lap and her face held a too-adult look of pain. She gazed unseeingly across the room.

On the porch, I hesitated. But I couldn't shirk this moment. I'd not told Sam that Anita was aware of Doug's threat to fire her. I had to find out whether Anita should be included in the list of suspects. After a quick look about to be sure I was unobserved, I appeared. I knocked gently.

In a moment, the woman, wiping her hands on a capacious apron, opened the door.

"Hello, ma'am." I opened the leather folder. "Detective M. Loy. I understand Mrs. Davis is on her way home." At her look of alarm, I said quickly, "The law office is closed today. Mrs. Davis and others at the office are assisting police in an investigation and, if you don't mind, I'll come in and wait for her."

The woman looked troubled. "You say she's coming home?"

I gave her a reassuring smile. "The office has been closed for the day. Officers are interviewing staff about a crime that occurred last night. Someone broke into the office and committed a theft. The interviews at the office were necessarily short, so I'm here to ask a few more questions. May I come inside and wait for her?"

She reached out, took the leather folder, studied it. "Well, I suppose that's all right. But we have a sick child and she's in the front room."

"I'd love to visit with her until her mother gets home. I like children. I have two."

That seemed to reassure her. She held the door and I stepped into the living room.

She nodded toward a plaid easy chair. "You can sit there if you like. I'll bring you some iced tea while you wait. Sweet or unsweet?"

"Sweet, please." I never knew anyone drank tea cold turkey, so to speak, until I was a grown woman.

Bridget put down her book, looked up with a shy smile. "Are you a friend of Mama's?"

I settled in the chair, smiled in return. "I'm looking forward to meeting your mother."

"What do you do?" She was guileless. She wanted to know. She asked.

"I ask people questions."

"What kind of questions?"

I wished I were far away, preferably aboard the *Serendipity*, not trifling with people's lives. This little girl needed her mother. But my questions would do no harm if Anita was innocent of murder. I felt further comforted because Megan continued to protect Anita. Megan was not a fool. She was well aware Anita had a staggeringly strong motive and yet she kept silent both about Doug Graham's threat and, even more damaging to Anita, the fact that Anita over-heard the exchange between Doug and Megan.

"Sometimes I ask people what they do in the evening. What did you do last night?"

Bridget tipped her head, considering the question. "I played checkers with Mom."

"Was that fun?"

"Kind of. Mom wasn't paying much attention. Mom works for some lawyers. Sometimes she has hard days. I think yesterday was one of those hard days. So I told her she needed to rest up a little. She likes to run errands. There's a nice man who works at Walmart in the evenings and Mom talks to him. His name's Brian. I asked Mom to go get me some Reese's Peanut Butter Cups at Walmart."

"Did she go?"

Bridget beamed and nodded.

"I suppose the nice lady who answered the door was here with you while your mom was gone."

"Mrs. Ellis goes home at five every day."

"You were by yourself?" I suppose surprise showed in my voice.

Bridget was scornful. "I'm not a little kid. If I needed anything, I could call Mom. I have my cell phone." She spoke with pride.

"I suppose she went and came right back."

"I guess." Suddenly she was tired. She sighed and sank back on the pillow. "I don't know when she came back. I fell asleep and I woke up this morning in my bed. Mom carried me there."

The front door opened. Anita stepped inside, looked at me in alarm.

I stood, made sure my voice was relaxed, nonthreatening. "Hello, Mrs. Davis. I'm Detective M. Loy." I had the leather folder out. "I've been having a nice visit with your daughter. I explained to your daughter that I'm a lady who asks questions and you are being very helpful about the break-in at the office last night." My eyes told Anita that there had been no mention of murder, that there would be no mention of murder. I didn't know how someone from Sam's department would have handled this moment, but I had no intention of frightening a child.

Steps sounded from the kitchen. The gray-haired woman stood with a tray. "I fixed tea and a limeade for Bridget." Her gaze at Anita was uncertain.

Anita spoke carefully. "That's very kind, Lela." She crossed the living room, bent down to gently kiss her daughter's cheek. "You okay, honey?"

Bridget's smile was bright. She sat up straighter. It was as if her mother's touch infused her with strength.

Lela placed a glass on a small table next to me, carried the other glasses to the coffee table in front of the sofa. Bridget smiled at

Mrs. Ellis. "Thank you." She picked up the glass, drank. Anita settled next to Bridget. She ignored the tea, stared at me. "I just spoke with the police."

"I know, but their time was limited. I'm simply here to get a little more background about the office. How long have you worked there?"

"Sixteen years." She was wary, worried.

"Do you remember the occasion when Mr. Layton and Mr. Graham were involved in a car accident?" I drank the tea, perfect with a little wisp of mint.

She looked bewildered. Whatever she'd expected, perhaps feared, this question came as a total surprise. The tenseness eased from her shoulders. "Yes."

"After the accident, did there appear to be a change in the relationship between Mr. Graham and Mr. Layton?" I lifted the glass again. The sweet tea was refreshing.

Anita's eyes widened. She squinted in thought. "I never thought about it before. Things did change about that time. But Mr. Layton's had so much happen to him. His wife died the year before that and—" She broke off.

"Julie died in April." Bridget's young voice was thin, but steady. "She stopped coming to school about the same time I did."

Anita turned, took her daughter's hand, held it tight. "She wasn't like you." Her voice was fierce. "There wasn't any medicine that could help Julie. She needed a new heart and there wasn't one. You have a great heart. The doctor said so. You're very strong. The doctor says the new medicine will make everything all right. You are going to get well."

I wished I could wrap my arms about them both, the little girl who knew she was very sick and her mother who willed her to live. I did the next best thing. "That's right. All it takes to get well is the right medicine." And faith. And luck.

None of us knows the number of our days. I always held to the belief that each life is lived until that particular life is complete, whether measured in months or decades. In Heaven each person realizes every gift, every grace, every happiness, and they are the creatures they were destined to be, now perfected, beautiful in God's image. *And God shall wipe away all tears from their eyes, and there shall be no more death, neither sorrow nor crying, neither shall there be any more pain: for the former things have passed away.* And if you thought you knew happiness on earth, well, just wait— But I must remember Precept Seven: "Information about Heaven is not yours to impart. Simply smile and say, 'Time will tell.'"

Anita shot me a look of gratitude. "Exactly. The right medicine."

Bridget looked at me, too.

I nodded vigorously. "You're obviously a very good patient. You'll be amazed how things will change with the new medicine." I hoped the sudden light in her eyes was renewed hope.

I looked at Anita. "After the accident occurred, Graham and Layton began to avoid each other."

Anita slowly nodded.

"And recently?"

Her expression was troubled. "I like Mr. Layton. He's always been wonderful to me."

I waited.

She shook her head. "I haven't paid much attention lately."

She had said all she was going to say.

℘

I like the way the British call a mobile home a caravan. The noun has such a jaunty tone. The drawback to mobile homes in Oklahoma is their tragic vulnerability when tornadoes strike, usually in late spring, sometimes in summer, always a possibility. Tornadoes usually hop and skip, though sometimes massive wall clouds destroy everything in a several-mile swath. Those without shelters and those in mobile homes look at a purple sky, hope for good luck.

But trailer parks thrive. Some dare fate because of necessity. Some shrug away spring storms because they've always lived in a trailer and never been hit. Some see the trade-off between safety and the lure of hitching up and moving on.

This trailer park was cheerful, with a small central playground and lots of shade trees. I passed over several sycamores. A red Camaro was tucked into the parking slot next to Geraldine Jackson's silver trailer. To one side, a bright red awning offered shade for two wicker chairs and a small plastic outdoor table.

Geraldine looked comfortable in a loose blue cotton top, white cropped slacks, and ruffled flip-flops. She was absorbed in hand stitching. I looked over her shoulder, admired the half-finished tree of life in delicate shades of pale green, soft ivory, sunrise rose. The embroidery was elegant and lovely.

I moved to the far side of a weeping willow, checked to make sure no one was near, and appeared. I came around the tree and followed a neat graveled path to her trailer.

She looked up at the sound of my footsteps. Her plump face held no concern, only polite inquiry.

I pulled out my leather folder. "Detective M. Loy. Chief Cobb has a few more questions about Mr. Graham that he didn't have time to cover this morning."

Geraldine placed her wood hoop on the plastic tabletop, gestured toward the wicker chair opposite her. "Sure. Glad to help. It's a real shocker. Then to have that ring disappear!"

I had my notebook on my lap and was writing as she spoke.

Her gaze was shrewd. "Lou's on her high horse. *How dare you search my desk.* But it looks like a pretty short list of people who knew where that ring was. We all heard Jack Sherman stomp into Doug's office and open the desk drawer. I don't suppose"—she squinted at me—"you people found the ring at Doug's house? Maybe it's like one of those boxes in boxes in boxes. Somebody shot him and got the ring out of his pocket and then broke into the office to make it look like one of us had to be a thief."

"We're considering every possibility. The ring may or may not have been the cause of his murder, and the shooting and theft may or may not be related."

She looked a little confused and I didn't blame her. I was far from certain about cause and effect, though I agreed that the likelihood of anyone hearing gossip and breaking in and going directly to Doug Graham's desk and finding the ring was unlikely in the extreme. Geraldine was right. Knowledge mattered, and the location of the ring was known to Jack Sherman, Brewster Layton, Winifred Kellogg, Anita Davis, Geraldine Jackson, Sharon King, Nancy Murray, Lou Raymond, and, through Lou, Rhoda Graham. Jack Sherman was occupied last night with a rig fire. It bordered on the absurd to envision Winifred Kellogg skulking down an alley with her walker, breaking a window, and swinging her walker and herself into Doug's office.

"We are pursuing several leads. Now we need to flesh out our picture of Doug Graham."

She gave a gurgle of laughter. "Flesh out. The sins of the flesh." She saw my surprise. "I may not look like it, honey, but I grew up in an old-fashioned church and we heard all about the sins of the flesh. It was supposed to scare us into chastity belts. Didn't work for some of us." Another hoot of laughter. "Anyway, Doug acted like he was the good husband but he was happy handed when Mr. Layton wasn't looking. Doug had the hot look, you know what I mean? I learned how to handle that kind of guff by the time I was thirteen."

"You said Doug Graham was careful to make sure Mr. Layton wasn't looking?"

"You better believe it. Turns out there was a lawyer at the firm, this was before my time, who had it going hot and heavy with a secretary. Mr. Layton busted him out of the firm and fired the secretary. Mr. Layton"—now her voice was softer—"is a good, good man. He's had a sad life. No"—now her tone was serious—"everything was on the up-and-up in the office. Doug might have gotten a little too close when we stood at the copier, but he knew where his bread was buttered."

"We'd heard Graham was having an affair."

She shrugged. "Usually it's another woman when there's a divorce." Now her green eyes were thoughtful. "But about that time was when Mr. Carew was real sick and Doug was doing a lot of work for them. I'd see Mrs. Carew come to the office, and you would have thought Doug was running for class president and she had all the votes. Man, was he nice." Her voice reflected disdain.

"Did he display a suggestive attitude with all the women in the office?"

"Depended. When Brewster wasn't looking, he was a little flirty with Nancy. He always treated Sharon like she was a spinster teacher. Guess that makes sense. She's the kind of woman who always has her legs crossed. No wonder she never got married. But she took care of her old mother, who died last year. He used to play up to Anita, but after her little girl got sick, he stopped hanging around her desk. Kind of hard to be a sexy dude when a woman's been crying. Of course, Ginny Morse is in the clear because she's in Italy. She's a looker. Not that I ever saw him play up to her. Carl's a pompous ass, but he's pretty possessive and right there on the scene. As for Lou, Doug treated her with kid gloves. Lou and his ex-wife are good friends. Doug knew better than to act like an ass with Megan Wynn." She hitched forward in her chair. "I don't know what's going on, but Megan never shot him. If she said she went to his house because of a text about work, that's why she went. She's not a liar. As for that gun in her desk drawer"—Geraldine's green eyes narrowed, one red-tipped finger tapped on the tabletop—"how about somebody shot him, broke in the office, and put the gun in Megan's desk?" Now she drummed her fingertips on the tabletop, continued almost as if talking to herself. "That would have to be someone familiar with the office, knowing Megan's desk. But her name's on the door." Abruptly she shivered. "Kind of scary. I guess whoever put the gun in that drawer killed Doug."

"Do you know of any reason anyone in the office might have shot him?"

"Not a one." Her answer was a little too quick and a little too smooth.

"Where were you last night at nine o'clock?"

"Right here. I'm working on an embroidery for my granddaughter. She's four. Lives in Amarillo with my daughter and her husband."

I glanced down at my notepad. "I think that covers everything. Oh"—I was casual—"I need a brief personal bio, your background, marriages, divorces."

She arched a dramatically dark brow. "If you want the long version, I'll go in and get a résumé for you. The short? Born in Lawton. Dad in the Army. Grew up, went to school at OSU. Married three times. One daughter. Been in Adelaide eight years. My third husband's hometown. He wanted to move back to the old home place but his idea of comfy was rocking on the front porch and drinking beer while I worked. I liked the job, decided to hang around without him. I moved out here. The living is cheap." She pointed at the sky. "The stars at night knock your socks off. For fun, I run out to the casino and bet a little, have a few drinks at the bar, talk it up with some cowboys."

"Any romantic interests?"

"I'm always ready for a good time. Right now I'm on the lookout."

∽

The trailer park was on a rural road, not far from Sharon King's home. Sharon's modest A-frame cottage was tucked at the end of a straggly gravel road. The structure wasn't visible from the blacktop. The cottage was surrounded by trees, the woods crowded close to a picket fence. Rosebushes bordered the house. The small front yard was enclosed by a picket fence heavy with blooming wisteria. A rocker on the porch afforded a view of the thick woods. The cabin was secluded in its enclosure. Tall evergreens screened a parking area. In the backyard, a stately sycamore shaded a small pond and several Adirondack chairs. An outdoor gas grill stood at one end of the pond. The only sound was the cackle of crows, the chitter of squirrels, the rustle of breeze-stirred leaves. It was a lovely retreat.

The interior of the cottage surprised me. In the living room, the Scandinavian-style furniture was austere. There were no trinkets. One bookcase held mostly histories, classical Rome, medieval England, colonial America, and a few novels, *Green Mansions*, *To the Lighthouse*, *The Great Gatsby*, and *The African Queen*. A framed Still print, irregular swaths in varying shades of sepia and one splotch of ice blue, was the only decoration. The print hung above a spare sofa with thin beige cushions.

The repressed motif was the same in the single bedroom and a second room used as a study. In the bedroom, the walls were the pale blue of a robin's egg. A delicate white frieze emphasized the coolness of the blue. A silk cover on the bed was a matching blue. The vanity held only a silver comb and brush, a porcelain tray with a single perfume atomizer. The closets were neat, blouses, skirts, slacks on one side, dresses on the other. Shoes lined on shelves at the back of the closet.

A car door slammed.

I was in the front yard as Sharon King came around the evergreens. She moved slowly, as if each step required special effort. I looked at her closely. I'd not studied her carefully at the office. There she was a secretary. Here she was a woman who lived alone in meticulous, orderly surroundings.

She reached the gate, one hand on the latch. She gazed about, her dark eyes flicking from the woods to the ground to the small front porch. The gate opened, closed.

I rather thought she had looked for any sign of intrusion, anything out of the ordinary since her departure that morning. She lived in isolated surroundings. She took no chances. Satisfied, she walked slowly toward the steps, her pale face grim and preoccupied. She used the key, opened the door, closed it behind her.

This morning she'd reflected the shock of a woman who'd learned from bright impersonal chatter on a radio newscast of the violent death of someone she knew well. Obviously, she'd been fond of Doug Graham. Her response suggested she'd been employed there for a number of years. Secretaries know a great deal about anyone for whom they work, whether a person is honest, fair, reasonable, thoughtful. Or not. Marital tensions likely were communicated either by occasional comment or overheard phone conversations. I thought Sharon might be just the person to help me discover more about Doug Graham's private life. Was he involved with another woman when his marriage faltered? What kind of communications did he have with his children? Was she aware of any quarrel that would explain the notes he'd begun, crumpled, and discarded? Graham had clearly wanted to appease someone, set some matter straight, resolve a disagreement. Had he said anything to her indicating if he'd contacted the intended recipient of the notes?

I was on the porch, ready to appear, when the silence wrapped itself around me, the midday quiet in the woods emphasized by the high, sweet chatter of birds, the rasp of cicadas. If I appeared, knocked on the door, she would likely answer, though there was no guarantee. There was a peephole in the door. She was a careful woman. She would look. I would present my credentials.

But there was the silence of the country. No sound of a car arriving, the wheels crunching on gravel. No sounds of a car door shutting. No sound of footsteps climbing to the porch. No police cruiser in the drive.

Much as I wanted to talk to Sharon King, I would have to figure out another way.

⁓

Brewster Layton's two-story Georgian brick home was on one of Adelaide's older residential streets. Elms and maples shaded stately structures built in the 1920s, some with screened-in porches that afforded respite from sweltering heat in an era before air-conditioning.

There was no car in the drive. I checked inside the garage. It, too, was empty. Tools hung from pegs on a cork wall in the neat space. There were no oil stains on the concrete floor.

Inside the house in the central hallway, I admired an ormolu-framed mirror above an early American maple side table. There were two lace doilies on the table, one bronze bowl. Several envelopes rested in the bowl. I picked up mail, realized none had been opened. An electric bill, a cable bill, a reminder postcard from a chiropractor, a square white envelope in richly textured paper, likely a wedding invitation. I liked to think perhaps sometimes there was personal mail to carry to a comfortable chair, enjoy. But no one had mentioned family other than his late wife and daughter.

I looked into the shadowy unlit living room. I walked a few steps. The formal living room reflected interest in antiques, a Sheraton secretary, Chinese plates on the fireplace's marble mantel, a collection of China thimbles on a small marble-topped table. Rose damask hangings framed the windows.

Brewster lived in the midst of beauty, but the house felt lonely and quiet. One chair, larger with sturdy arms, was placed in a direct line with the fireplace. I sat down and looked up at a woman's portrait above the mantel. Was this where Brewster spent his evenings, perhaps holding a drink, looking up at a well-loved face, looking at intelligent gray eyes and softly waved brown hair and a gentle smile?

On the table to one side of the chair sat a studio portrait of a girl, perhaps ten or eleven. The girl—Julie—looked lively and eager, healthy, short blonde ringlets, bright blue eyes, a dazzling smile. Her dress was lovely, turquoise blue tulle with cap sleeves and a sequined top. A hair ribbon featured a matching blue bow.

How many evenings did Brewster spend alone with only memories?

I had a sudden picture of a man on the anniversary of his wife's death, drinking alone at a bar, leaving after dark, coming around a curve, not seeing a bicycle in time despite its taillight reflector. The terrible impact. Stopping. Struggling out of the car, hurrying to find a young woman with a broken neck, past help, past caring. A man who knew he'd had too much to drink. A man with a motherless daughter at home. Was Julie already ill at that point? Did he know that her heart could not last, would not last?

I understood why he drove away. Had he called Doug Graham for help? Or had Graham possibly been at the club that night as well. Perhaps he'd driven around the curve, seen Brewster's car in the headlights, stopped. Brewster, unsteady, shaken, perhaps begged Graham to drive on, drive away.

Had Graham agreed? Or perhaps even then Graham hatched a plan. Hide the car in your garage. Don't take it out. Monday morning leave the house early. We'll meet out here. A crash. Both cars heavily damaged. Nothing to show a body shop that there had been previous damage to one car. Both cars hauled in to be repaired. No questions would arise because the accident accounted for a crushed fender, broken grille.

The living room was cool in every respect, from the chill of air-conditioning to the subdued grays and pale blues of the furniture and drapes to a crystal vase on a glass-topped coffee table. The vase held two white roses. I stood and walked near the coffee table, bent forward, was rewarded with a delicate scent. I never doubted Brewster every week chose two white roses from his garden and put them by his side, roses for remembrance.

I heard the front door open, close, slow, heavy steps. Brewster Layton stood in the oval archway to the living room, turned on the lights. The crystal chandelier that hung from the ceiling was not only elegant, its luminous light was pitiless. His sensitive face was drawn, his dark eyes bleak. He walked to the chair, obviously his chair, sank down. He looked up at the portrait. "You always admired me for telling the truth." He lifted a hand to rub against the front of his goatee. "I never wanted to disappoint you."

He was talking to his dead wife. Was that his solace now? To come home from the office, settle into his chair, and tell her what he had done that day? That's what spouses do. Good days or bad, especially bad, there is a willing heart to listen, to encourage, some-times to absolve.

Now Brewster Layton was alone, except for two white roses. But the yearning to share remained.

He continued to gaze at the unseeing lovely face. "There are lies of omission and commission. Do you suppose hellfire singes as hard for sins of omission? I did what I thought I had to do. Some-how I hated him even more after Julie died." He pushed up from the chair, walked across the room to a bottle of Dewar's sitting on a table. He half filled a glass, added no soda, carried the glass back to his chair. He sat, lifted the glass, drank several swallows. The whisky seemed to go down easily, a man who was accustomed to drinking straight Scotch. Again he spoke aloud. "I hope he burns in hell." His face crumpled. "I'm sorry, Marie. I'm not the man you always admired. God forgive me."

I returned to the porch, hesitated. Detective M. Loy could gain entry. But to what avail? Brewster Layton was a lawyer. More than that, he was a man with secrets held hard and fast. I'd come away with nothing. But there was one thing I could do and should do while the police were still occupied at the law firm.

Chapter 11

Sam's office was empty, as I expected. I glanced at the wall clock. A quarter to twelve. Likely Sam and Hal were nearing the end of the interviews at the law firm. I was afraid Sam's focus was on Megan's interrogation at one o'clock. I hoped she sensed that I was doing my best to find out facts leading away from her. I found a current Adelaide phone directory in the center drawer of Sam's desk, flipped to the *L*'s, dialed, knew caller ID would read: *Adelaide Police Department*.

"Layton, Graham, Morse and Morse." Lou Raymond's voice was a little higher than normal.

I was pleasant but firm. "Please inform Chief Cobb that Detective Loy wishes to speak to him. Ask him to call"—I glanced at the number on Sam's phone—"333-3333." Nice alliteration. I wondered if Sam liked threes, as in *third time's the charm, three to make ready, three Musketeers, three's a crowd*. "Thank you." I hung up.

Lou might, if it were an ordinary day, be surprised a detective didn't call the chief directly, but this was no ordinary day there. She would take the message to Sam.

I settled comfortably in Sam's chair, opened the lower left-hand drawer, found his M&M'S sack, filched a handful. The phone rang. I finished a munch and answered cheerfully, "Hi, Sam. I hope the interviews are going well." It is always well to encourage people in their endeavors.

"Making yourself at home?" The query was sardonic.

"It is the responsibility of all good citizens to assist the authorities. Please instruct the crime techs to go to Brewster Layton's office and take into evidence the scraps from his little machine that chews up paper. Label the evidence bag with the date and a notation the material was taken from whatever kind of machine—"

"Paper shredder."

"—paper shredder in the office of Brewster Layton. It may turn out to be important evidence."

"Evidence of what?"

"That's to be determined. And—"

"Are you trying to distract me?"

"I am aiding the investigation. The material is relevant to the case in the event Brewster Layton is the murderer."

An irritated breath. "I'm in a hurry to get to my"—emphasis on the pronoun—"office and interrogate the primary suspect. At this point, there are no other suspects. Let me remind you that Megan Wynn responded to a text. You think Graham didn't send the text. I think he did. There are no prints but his on the cell phone—"

"The murderer wore gloves." My tone suggested this was Perp Behavior 101. "Were Graham's prints smudged on the cell?"

"He kept the cell in his back pocket."

"Smudged?"

"Of course."

"Rest my case."

"A diversion."

Some comments do not deserve a reply. "Speaking of pockets, was there a note in his handwriting, the one about *Let's talk again, we can work this out*, found either in the pocket of the suit he wore that day or in his clothing when he was killed?"

"We checked his suit and a white shirt tossed in a hamper. No note. Clothes worn at time of death: billfold with the usual contents including one hundred and forty-eight dollars, eighty-two cents in change, car keys, cell, two peppermints wrapped in cellophane. No note."

I was excited. "He gave the note to someone. Maybe set up a meeting at his house."

"He was shot in the back of the head. Never knew what hit him."

"He was grim about that note. He worked and worked on it, tried a lot of versions. The note has to mean something."

"Maybe. Or maybe he talked to someone on the phone, smoothed out whatever it was. Or maybe he changed his mind, tossed the note in the trash. Some other trash," he added hastily. "What matters in this case is the text sent from Graham's cell to Wynn's cell. Wynn responded to the text, hotfooted it right out to his house. She was there and he was shot. Sure, the termination wasn't her own, but she was the one who had to kiss off a job she wanted. I got the whole picture when the Legal Knight came jousting to protect his Lady. There's more than work in the air here. So Wynn gets this text. She's already mad. She goes out there, shoots him—"

"Where was the gun when the police arrived?"

His reply was prompt. "Hidden in the woods."

"The gun was found in her desk."

"Yeah. She hid it in the woods, got nervous, decided to retrieve it."

"Then proceeded to her office to put the gun in a drawer in her desk? Do you think she's an idiot as well as a murderer? Why not go toss it out in the lake?"

"I think she's out of balance, hardly knows what she's doing, probably thought there would be no reason for anyone to search the law office. Maybe she thought she might need it again."

"How about the ring?"

"Somebody stole the ring." His tone indicated theft was a side issue. "Probably not her. It only takes one motive for murder. We may never find out who broke in and took the ring. You can bet Jack Sherman's performance was the talk of Adelaide by midafternoon. Somebody heard about the ring—Jack shouting about the ring being in Graham's desk—anyway somebody decided to steal the ring."

"The law offices must have been pretty busy last night. The ring taken. The gun placed in Megan's desk." Not to mention the fanged rat encountered by the cleaning crew.

"The night's long."

I tucked that thought away for future consideration. "I think someone heard about the ring—a hundred-thousand-dollar ring— and decided to steal it."

Sam wasn't impressed. "The hundred thousand sounds like a ticket to easy street but a thief couldn't hope to get that amount for stolen property."

"Maybe this was a thief with a brain. Steal the ring. Lay low with it. In a few months, take it to a jeweler in another city, say the design has never been quite right and how about putting in a few small emeralds and changing the band in some way. After the work is done, ask for an appraisal, use the appraisal to sell the ring to a store in another city, clear at least eighty K."

"Why kill Graham?" He slapped out the words like tossing an ace over a king. "There was no need. Sure, he might have been suspicious of people who saw the ring that morning, but he would never be able to prove anything. And"—his tone was grudging—"maybe the thief does have a brain. I like that plan, get the ring redesigned, sell it after a while." A pause. "Right now you're an irritant, like a horsefly at a picnic, but I'm glad you haven't taken to crime."

I took his comment as a compliment. "Not yet." It wouldn't do for him to be complacent. "Will you see to the material in Layton's shredder?"

"Sure. But you're whistling for a dog that isn't there. We're almost done here. I've asked all of them about Megan Wynn's demeanor yesterday. Since you have your chips on her, you'll be pleased to know they all like her. Nobody wants to say anything negative, but I kept after them. It's clear Wynn went into Graham's office cheerful, came out looking grim. I covered my a— I hit all the bases, asked if anybody else seemed upset yesterday. Again, there's a consensus. Everybody was fine except for Anita Davis, and the fact that she was upset wasn't unusual because she has a really sick kid."

"Are you asking about Doug Graham's enemies and whether he was having an affair when his wife divorced him?"

"Be my guest. It will keep you busy. And maybe out of my office. Meanwhile, I'm—"

I would have to tell Sam on some other occasion that heavy irony obscures rational thought.

"—building a case. The facts are what they are. You backed the wrong horse in this race. You'd think with your connections you'd have a heads-up. Sorry."

The connection ended.

Always before, I'd worked in concert with Sam. Now I was on my own. He'd made up his mind. It was only a matter of time before Megan was arrested, charged, jailed. Blaine Smith would fight hard to keep her free, but by Monday at the latest—the press conference was set for eleven a.m.—Sam would make his move.

Unless I came up with the murderer first.

But now I knew what to ask about. Apparently there had been no questions in the sessions this morning about Doug's romantic interests or any recent quarrels. I didn't fault Sam. There was plenty of evidence against Megan. There was motive. Moreover, he knew that murder usually results from an immediate trigger.

I agreed, but he and I saw different triggers. Yesterday morning the diamond intended for Lisbeth Carew glittered in the harsh light from the overhead fluorescent bars. I remembered the intensity of that moment. Sam was focused on Megan's anger with Doug Graham. He believed murder resulted because Megan saw her future blocked. I believed the ring gleaming in the hallway somehow, someway triggered the deadly night.

I picked up the phone book, found Sharon King's number, dialed.

"Hello." Her voice was wary.

Once again caller ID was my entrée. No one even peripherally involved in a murder investigation will ignore a call from the police.

"Sharon King?" My voice was pleasant.

"This is she." Her low voice was precise, cool.

"Ms. King, this is Detective M. Loy. We are expanding our inquiries into Mr. Graham's personal life—"

"I was his secretary." The interruption was sharp. "If you want information about his personal life, I suggest you contact his former wife or talk to Mr. Layton."

I wished I were there in her immaculate, well-ordered house. I wished I could see the play of emotion—if there was emotion—on her fine-boned, intelligent face. Voices can be revealing, but expressions much more so. "How many years did you work for him?"

"Nine."

"You were his secretary when he and Rhoda Graham separated and later divorced?"

"Yes." She sounded faintly surprised. "Why?"

"It's important to find out as much about his private life as possible. Were you aware that he was having marital difficulties?"

"There was a period"—she appeared to be picking her words carefully—"when he wasn't as cheerful as usual."

"Did you overhear any angry exchanges between Graham and his wife?"

"Not really. And that was a long time ago."

"When was he divorced?"

Certainly his secretary would be aware of that kind of life event. "About a year and a half ago."

"Not so long ago."

She didn't respond.

"We heard there's a possibility he was involved in an affair. Do you have any idea of the identity of his lover?"

"Look, I work there. People's private lives are their private lives." She was clearly resistant. "I've always made it a point not to get involved in personal issues."

"If you worked for him for nine years, you must be aware that he was the kind of man who was very interested in women. In fact, we understand he was a little too familiar at times with women in the office."

"Some men are always a little too familiar with women."

"Did he ever stand too close to you?"

"Of course not." The retort was sharp, immediate. Quickly, she added, "He knew how Mr. Layton felt about office behavior."

"You're single." My tone was mollifying. "I supposed he might be more"—I paused—"attentive to single women."

"He always treated me with respect." Her voice was stiff and cold. "I am an excellent secretary."

I felt stymied. "So in the last few years, you have no idea whether he was having an affair?"

She was crisp. "I was his secretary, not his friend. I didn't snoop in Doug Graham's private papers or eavesdrop on personal conversations. If he was having an affair, I know nothing about it."

"You seemed upset this morning when you learned of his death."

"Of course I was upset. He was my boss. He treated me well. I'm driving to work and it's an ordinary day and I'm thinking about the manicure I'll get after work and I hear on the radio that somebody's shot him! It's unthinkable, unimaginable. Mr. Graham, of all people."

"Why 'of all people'?"

"He was so alive." There was a tremor in her voice.

She remembered a man moving, living, breathing, and now his body lay on a slab in a mortuary.

"This is a small town. Did you ever hear gossip linking him to someone?"

"We didn't run in the same circles. I wouldn't be likely to hear gossip about him. Besides, people might not say anything because they knew I worked for him. I have no reason to think he was having an affair. When he was out of town, I called his cell if anything arose that needed his attention. I never had any trouble getting in touch with him."

"If he was having an affair, why do you suppose he was so careful to keep the fact hidden?"

"Maybe he wasn't." She was matter-of-fact. "Maybe the gossip is wrong. Why don't you ask his ex-wife?"

"We will. What do you think about Rhoda?"

"Think about her?"

"The kind of person."

"I don't really know her. I had the impression from him that she was kind of fussy and earnest, awfully serious, one of those helicopter mothers. He got awfully impatient because she'd call about the silliest things, what a teacher said or a scraped knee. Sometimes," she added hastily, "he'd blow off steam about that."

Was she explaining how she knew this personal information,

yet was unaware of angry exchanges with a spouse or involvement in an affair?

"But"—and now she was once again cool, collected—"I suggest you ask people who knew him socially about another woman."

"Were you aware he was romantically involved with Lisbeth Carew?"

"That was a surprise. But obviously I didn't know much about his personal life. If that's all you—"

I interrupted. "There's another area where we need help. Why was Keith Porter angry with Graham?"

"Money." She answered without hesitation. "Keith wanted money, big money. Mr. Graham told him no. Mr. Graham was the guardian of a trust set up by Keith's parents, Betty and Mark Porter. They died in a plane crash a couple of years ago, and Mr. Graham administered the estate. It's in trust until Keith turns thirty. He's twenty-five. The terms of the trust are generous, ten thousand dollars a month. Keith spends every penny. This time he's got an idea for some kind of app. He wants a couple hundred thousand to set up a company, thinks he'll end up big rich. Mr. Graham turned him down."

"What happens now?"

"It may be"—again that considering tone—"that Keith's luck has turned. Judge Mosley has an Apple Watch. He loves electronic gadgets. He may appoint a new trustee who will think Keith's idea is terrific."

Was it a matter of luck? Was Keith Porter so angry at Doug's refusal to advance the money Keith wanted that he slipped across a golf course with a gun and murdered the man he saw as a roadblock? How could Keith know about Megan's confrontation with Doug? If

Keith contacted Doug later in the day, again pled for money, had Doug laughed and described Megan's intent to quit and his threat to fire Anita as proof that no one defied him without paying a price?

Clearly, Doug Graham told his killer about the confrontation with Megan, making the spurious text possible. Likely, the murderer considered the text exceedingly clever. Not only did the text bring Megan to the house, the contents put her in a very difficult position. Had Doug shared the facts of his threat to Megan out of malicious pride at his bullying success? Or had he intended to warn someone not to push him, *Here's what happens if you do?*

Someone was angry enough with Doug Graham to kill him. I knew Keith Porter was angry. Later that morning, Doug struggled to compose a note. He wanted to smooth things over with someone. Had the note reached the intended person? I didn't think the note on legal paper was intended for Keith. Graham had no intention of seeking reconciliation with him. Reconciliation . . . "Ms. King, yesterday Graham threw away several drafts of a personal message. Those drafts were found in his wastebasket. He wrote: *I never promised anything. If you make claims, I'll deny everything. Let me explain. Scandal won't help anybo*— We have reason to believe he gave a note to someone with this message: *Let's talk again. We can work this out.* He'd tucked that final bland version in his shirt pocket. That note hadn't been found by the police."

"I don't know anything about that."

"You have no idea who might be angry with him?"

"Do you mean yesterday or generally?"

"Old quarrels don't usually result in violence. I want to know about current disagreements."

"Other than Keith Porter, I'm not aware of any quarrels."

"Do you know if he spoke to his ex-wife yesterday?"

"No."

"How do you think she'd feel about the hundred-thousand-dollar ring?"

"I suggest you ask her."

"Was Anita Davis in trouble for slipping out of the office at times to go home and see about her daughter?"

Her response was sharp. "I don't know what anyone's said but Anita does her work."

"Graham was unhappy with her."

"Anita would never hurt anyone."

"What do you think about the gun in Megan Wynn's desk?"

"I can't imagine." The words came slowly. "Megan is a very nice girl. I don't believe for a minute she had anything to do with the murder."

"She was at the house."

"She must have had a good reason." Now her voice wasn't quite so certain.

I thanked her, urged her to contact police immediately if she thought of anything useful. I took one more scoop of M&M'S, relished the bursts of sweetness, reviewed the conversation. Sharon King was a very careful woman. She saw, heard, and spoke no evil. Could a boss carry on a clandestine affair without a secretary having any inkling?

Perhaps. Or perhaps in fact there was no affair. If Graham carried on an affair, he managed to do so without knowledge of it becoming public. Geraldine dismissed the possibility of involvement with anyone in the office because Brewster Layton frowned on liaisons at work. It might be that Graham had no intention of a long-term commitment and was careful to give a lover no legal basis to claim, especially after he became single, that there was a common-law marriage. That suggested he was always focused on himself, looked long term. One of the note drafts read: *I never promised anything. If you make claims, I'll deny everything.* Of course those words applied equally well to a wager, a promise, an agreement.

Chapter 12

Adelaide's prosperity, due in part to the successes of the Chickasaw Nation, has resulted in the construction of several new and fancy apartment complexes. Glenwood Apartments was a two-story stacked stone structure with several fountains and a statue of a bronze deer. Deck chairs surrounded a sparkling pool in the interior grounds.

Unit 22 was on the ground floor in the north wing. I concentrated on geography and placed the apartment complex on one side of White Deer Park. Perhaps that accounted for the deer statue. At the back of the parking lot, a neatly graveled path into the woods would lead to the park. I imagined proximity to White Deer Park was a selling point. Residents could easily walk to the park and enjoy the public tennis courts as well as the lake.

I walked briskly through the parking lot. I didn't have to worry about the lack of a police car, because the entrances to the apartments

were in the interior. Three wings were built around a central courtyard and pool.

The fragrance of wisteria mingled with a strong smell of chlo-
rine as I passed the pool. I watched the numbers, veered to my
right. My footsteps clicked on the cement walk. I stopped at number 22, knocked. There was no answer. I waited a moment, knocked
again, spoke firmly. "Police."

The door eased open. Nancy Murray was summer bright in a
vivid pink blouse, set off by a magenta and pink scarf knotted at
the throat, a white pleated skirt, and adorable flower slides in a
matching pink. But her face was starkly white, her dark eyes wary.
She said nothing, stared at me.

I flipped open the leather shield. "Detective M. Loy. Some further questions for you." I stepped forward as if there was no uncertainty about my admittance.

Nancy backed away. She watched me approach as if I were a
cobra gliding, head erect, hood flared, tongue flickering.

The living room was airy and spacious. There were only a few
pieces of furniture but those were quite nice, a sofa with fine linen,
a restored early American rocking chair, a simple Danish easy
chair. The Persian rug was vivid in blues and golds and only a close
inspection would reveal some threadbare spots. Either the rug was
a family heirloom or a trophy from an estate sale.

Again, I felt my perceptions shift just as they had with Sharon
King when I saw her as an individual in her own world, not as a
secretary in an office. Now I saw more than Nancy Murray, paralegal. I saw the taste and thought she'd put into her surroundings,
and I saw a stiffly uneasy woman. Was she afraid of the police?

I gestured toward the sofa. "If we might sit down?"

"I told the police everything I know." Clearly she did not want to talk to me.

"We are expanding our investigation. The interview this morning established what occurred yesterday at the office. Now we need more personal information." I walked to the sofa, sat.

Nancy moved slowly to the easy chair, perched on the edge, all the while her gaze locked on me.

Uneasiness was not an unusual response to a police inquiry. But possibly there was something more here. When she entered the office this morning, she'd been shocked to find the police, but it was the fact of Doug Graham's murder that seemed to terrorize her. I was almost sure her fear stemmed from the actual fact of homicide, not from the investigation. Of course, murder is terrifying.

I returned her stare. "Who do you think killed him?"

The stark question hung between us.

"I can't imagine anyone doing a thing like that." Her voice shook. "It's terrible. To come to work and find out someone shot him." Her face held a look of incredulity. "I keep thinking it's a bad dream and I'll wake up. I've never been around anything like this." She took a shaking breath. "I never read about bad things. Never. I don't watch the news, people blowing people up, so many terrible things. I can't stand movies where people get hurt. Mr. Graham shot." She wrapped her arms across her front as if trying to ward off evil.

My expression softened. She was very young. Mid-twenties. I spoke gently. "Murder is awful. Someone is alive. A moment later life ends. That's why we are trying to find the person who shot Mr. Graham."

She pressed her lips together as if trying not to cry, then spoke raggedly. "I don't mean not to be helpful." Her voice was wobbly. "But I can't get over how awful it is."

"We've been told that Mr. Graham and Mr. Layton didn't like each other."

"Mr. Layton wouldn't shoot anybody." Her reply was hot, her defense definite.

"But there was coolness between them?"

Reluctantly she nodded.

"Did anyone else in the office have any quarrel with Mr. Graham?"

There was a flicker in her eyes, but her head shake was immediate. "Oh no."

"Anita Davis?"

Again her reply was firm. "Anita is an excellent secretary." But she obviously knew Anita had been reprimanded for leaving the office on personal matters.

"We've heard Mr. Graham may have been having an affair before his divorce."

She almost managed a weak smile. "You'll have to ask people who knew him. I just worked there. I don't know anything about his personal life."

There didn't seem to be much more ground to cover, but I persisted. "Do you know anyone who had quarreled with him?"

She looked uncertain. "I don't know if you'd call it a quarrel. He was the trustee for an estate and the heir, Keith Porter, was upset." She wasn't sympathetic. "Keith's a mess."

"Do you know him?"

"I was in high school with him. He always acted like he was

special. He's really rich. But Mr. Graham wouldn't let him have the money he wanted." There was a touch of malice in her tone.

"Where were you last night?"

"When Mr. Graham was killed?" Again she looked upset. "I was here."

"Alone?"

She nodded. "Right here." Her voice was louder.

I rose. "If you remember anything, think of anything that could help in the investigation, please contact us immediately." I gave her Sam's number.

I stepped out the front door.

As the door closed, I heard the safety latch click into place. Nancy Murray might not have watched the nightly news with its emphasis on murder, robbery, cruelty, and death, but the nightly news had come to her.

⁕

Lou Raymond's house was in a quiet neighborhood near the old high school. The small, mostly brick homes were well maintained, fresh paint on shutters, several with new roofs, likely the result of spring storms, neatly mowed grass, plenty of petunias, zinnias, black-eyed Susans, peonies, and daylilies, old trees, elms, oaks, sycamores, and magnolias.

A brown Ford sedan was in the drive. Since Lou had been the last person scheduled to be interviewed at the law firm, finding her at home meant Megan Wynn was now answering question after question at the police station. I paused in the deep shade of a huge magnolia and appeared.

I was careful to avoid a miniature toy car on the second step and skirted a mound of alphabet blocks on the porch. I rang the bell, admired a Whitmani fern in a huge pot next to the door, noted two stained Popsicle sticks resting on a frond.

The door opened. Lou Raymond's white hair was pulled back under a red kerchief. She wore a flour sack apron decorated with a plump gray tabby perched on a yellow stool, lower legs crossed, strumming a guitar. A verse extolling delight in bites of mice floated above the cat's head. There was a smudge of flour on one cheek.

"Yes?" She was polite, but clearly impatient to return to her kitchen.

"Mrs. Raymond," I said, holding up my leather folder, "Detective M. Loy. May I speak to you for a few minutes?"

She looked flustered. "I'm right in the middle of making a pie."

I gave her my most charming smile. "I just have a few questions. Can we visit while you are cooking?"

"Oh, if that's all right." She opened the screen, glanced at the fern. "Oh, that Jason." She stepped onto the porch, picked up the Popsicle sticks, held the screen for me. "My grandson. I pick him up—"

I followed her down a sparkling hallway to a wide kitchen with white tile counters, white refrigerator and gas stove, white cabinets with chrome handles, a white kitchen table. Daisy-patterned chintz curtains were fresh and crisp above the kitchen sink window. A blue wooden high chair sat at one end of the table. There was a scent of melted butter, freshly cut apples, and nutmeg.

"—after day care every evening. My daughter works 'til nine. Oh, watch out for his gears."

I stepped over a haphazard mix of yellow, red, and green plastic rings, cranks, and pillars.

She reached a pulled-out pastry board. A rolling pin rested by a mound of pie dough. She began to work the dough, looked over her shoulder. "I suppose it's about Doug Graham."

I moved until I was in her vision. "Yes. I've spoken with Mrs. Graham."

Lou stopped rolling, stared at me.

"You called and told her about the diamond ring for Lisbeth Carew." My tone was matter-of-fact.

There was a flash of relief in her blue eyes. The police knew what she'd done. She was free to admit the call. "I thought she ought to know." Her tone was a little defensive.

"Of course. That's understandable since you and she are old friends. I suppose it's been a struggle for her financially since the divorce."

She thought about the question, said cautiously, "Women always have a hard time after a divorce. But"—resentment was evident—"it doesn't seem right that Doug started making a lot more money right after the divorce. He built that fancy house. Just for him!"

"He didn't help his children with college."

"He knew how they felt about him. They sided with their mom. As they should have." She was emphatic.

"There seems to be some question whether he actually was involved in an affair when he was married."

Her cheeks flushed. "Rhoda told me she found a note once in the pocket of his jacket. It was, well, she said she couldn't believe what she was reading, describing . . . well, she didn't finish. She asked him. And"—now her outrage flamed—"he twisted her arm and took the note and threw it in the fire."

"If he had an affair"—there was doubt in my voice—"he apparently was extremely careful never to be seen in public with anyone. Why take those kinds of precautions?"

The pink faded in Lou's face. "It would be just like him. He always had to run everything. He was probably involved with someone who wasn't his social equal and he wanted the people at the country club to think he was cool. Or maybe he was just being careful and didn't want to get hooked. Whoever she was, I think she was either too nuts about him to care or maybe she had some reason to sneak around. Or maybe he always had his eye on the big picture."

"Big picture?"

"Lisbeth Carew. He'd done legal work for the Carews for years. She's only been a widow for a year. Maybe he had an idea he could charm her. It wouldn't look good if he had a messy divorce and there was stuff in the paper about an extramarital affair. I don't know Lisbeth Carew but she's big at church and her husband was very devoted to her. Never any hint of scandal."

"Very interesting. I certainly appreciate—" I paused as if struck by a late thought. "Oh, one more point. Can you please repeat what you said to Mrs. Graham in your phone call and her replies? Just for the record."

She carefully smoothed out a thin strip of dough, didn't look at me. "I don't know that I recall exactly. Let's see, I told her how everyone gathered in the hallway and Jack Sherman made such a spectacle of himself. I think the whole episode made Doug mad. I guess he didn't want word to get out about the ring. A hundred thousand dollars." She spoke with disgust. "Jack kept on and on and got the ring and everybody saw it. Anyway, I told Rhoda because I thought she'd want to know and not have someone tell her in public, though people like Rhoda and maybe no one would have."

"What did she say?"

Lou stared down at the pie dough, spoke very carefully. "She was upset. For the kids. A hundred thousand could make such a huge difference for them. They're both piling up student debt. It isn't that she cared anymore what Doug did or about Lisbeth Carew. That was all over for her with Doug."

She was burying me in words but not directly quoting Rhoda.

"What were her exact words?"

Lou made a fluttery gesture with one hand. "Oh, I don't know. That she couldn't believe he'd spend money like that, but why should she be surprised since he built that house."

"Did you leave the house last night?"

She eased a sheet of crust in the pie plate. "I took Jason home, then I came home."

"What time was that?"

"A little before nine."

"How long did you stay at Rhoda's?"

She caught her breath, turned to stare. "How did you know?"

"Neighbors keep an eye out for each other." She was being careful with her words and so was I. It was certainly not dishonest to make a general observation. "I suppose you were disappointed she wasn't home?"

"I just went by on the chance she'd be there." Lou made her voice careless, as if it didn't matter that Rhoda was unaccounted for during the period when someone shot her ex-husband and forever changed the financial prospects for her children. "I'll take the pie over in a little while and have a chance to visit with her before I pick up Jason." I made my good-byes and didn't ask if she intended to relate our conversation to Rhoda. If she did, Rhoda might be very worried, and that might all be to the good.

⌒

The next home was quite different from the others I'd visited. The circa-1980s creamy stucco mansion stood on the crest of a hill. A wing extended on either side of the central block, embracing a terrace with a spectacular view of the lush valley that fell away below. A rectangular pool looked inviting, the water a sparkling blue. The house was three stories with a shining expanse of windows. Everything about the house and grounds was quite perfect from the immaculate front lawn to the curving drive paved with yellow bricks to imported Italian cypresses that bordered each side of the terrace.

When I'd learned that Keith Porter enjoyed an income of ten thousand dollars a month from the trust, I'd been puzzled that he'd pressed for a substantial advance for his entrepreneurial ambitions. No longer. Maintaining this home would require substantial monthly expenditures. There was no assurance a new trustee would make a different decision, but there was the possibility. If Keith Porter committed murder, it would likely have been prompted equally by thinking a different trustee might advance the money and fury at being thwarted in getting what he wanted.

The lower floor was very quiet. Water splashed softly in a small pool in the huge entryway. A potted palm sat to one side. The golden marble floor featured an intricate design of palms on the borders. I went through richly furnished spacious rooms, found no one. I reached a stainless steel kitchen with all the warmth of an operating room. In a small adjacent office, a housekeeper sat at a desk making out a list. She was fiftyish and plump with a pleasant round face.

I looked over her shoulder at the list. The sight of homely items, ketchup, bread-and-butter pickles, mixed nuts, flour, offered the only evidence that real people inhabited the huge formal house.

A buzz.

She looked at an intercom. A light flashed red above silver letters: *POOL*. She pushed a button. "Yes, Master Keith?" Her voice was rather high and sweet and her tone very kind. I felt sure she'd worked here for many years, known Keith Porter since he was a small boy, was fond of him.

"Mag, I won't be in for dinner. Think I'll run up to the city, eat at Mantel's."

Her face crinkled. "I hope you stay over. I worry about you driving on the dark roads after you get off the interstate. There might be a deer crossing the highway."

"And what you're really saying is you know I'll have a few drinks so please don't drive." There was no irritation in his voice, instead good humor. "Oh, all right. I'll stay at that new boutique hotel. I've heard it's cool. Why not?" He clicked off.

She bent back to her list, smiling, content.

I found Keith sprawled comfortably on a cushioned hammock shaded by an elm tree. His South Sea Island swim trunks were dry. He rested with one knee raised, a pad propped on the bent knee, a felt pen in his right hand. He was actually quite nice-looking, dark brown hair, thickly lashed brown eyes, a narrow, sensitive face. He wrote rapidly, paused, wrote again, nodded approval.

Before I could read his notes, he flipped a page, scrawled: *Check out business plan with Dave.* He underlined the sentence three times. He rolled to one side, dropped the pad on a glass-topped table. He levered up on an elbow, picked up a Bud Light, drank.

At the far side of the Italian cypresses, out of his view, I appeared. I walked past the end of the row of trees to the flagstone terrace.

He heard my steps, looked across the pool in surprise.

I moved fast, pulling out my leather ID folder. "Glad to catch you, Mr. Porter. I'm Detective M. Loy." I came around the end of the pool.

He was standing by the hammock, looking puzzled. He looked very young, an unlined face, a slender build. "A detective?"

I stood a few feet from him, smelled a mixture of suntan lotion and beer. "We need an accounting of your movements last night."

"Me?" He sounded truly astonished.

I wondered if he was as guileless as he appeared. "Describe your actions from a quarter to nine last night until"—I made a guess, the cleaning people departed the law office around midnight, the theft and planting of the murder weapon likely occurred around one or two in the morning—"three a.m."

He folded slender arms. "I don't get this. Why are you asking me where I was last night?"

I gave him a stolid stare. "Doug Graham was shot last night at approximately nine p.m."

His eyes widened. He lifted a thin hand to rub the knuckles against his chin. "You got to be kidding." His voice almost cracked.

"You quarreled with Mr. Graham yesterday morning. You threatened him before you left the law office."

"Hey"—the words tumbled out—"sure he was a louse and he

was screwing everything up for me, but it's crazy to say I would shoot him. Or anybody."

"What telephone calls have you made this morning?"

"I called some people on business."

I pulled out a notepad and pen. "Names. Numbers."

"What I did this morning isn't any of your business."

"The calls were about business, right?"

"So what?"

"You want to start a new company. You need money. Graham wouldn't let you have the money. Now he's dead. He can't stand in your way. You called some investors to start putting together a deal."

He watched me as if I were a magician pulling out snakes instead of rabbits.

"How did you know he was dead?"

He massaged one cheek. "I saw the news on TV this morning."

"Does your housekeeper live in?"

"Yeah," he answered cautiously.

"Her name?"

"Margaret Baker."

"Where were you last night?"

"I was"—he paused and perhaps realized the housekeeper would be asked to confirm his presence in the house if he claimed he had been home—"hanging out some places."

I waited.

"Drove around. It was a nice night. I had the top down. I wasn't paying attention to the time. I dropped in at the Red Rooster, had a couple of beers. I probably got home about ten."

"Did you leave the house again last night or early this morning?"

This answer came more quickly, confidently. "I watched a movie, ate a sandwich. I didn't go anywhere."

⟡

Sam's office was empty. I went directly down the hall past the central area with desks and monitors, several of them occupied though it was late afternoon. I didn't see any familiar faces. The doors in the hallway were closed. I checked out two interrogation rooms, tan walls, a single table with several chairs on one side. Two straight wooden chairs on the other. A gooseneck lamp stood next to the table. The beam could be directed at the wooden chairs.

I'd once observed an interrogation, brusque questions, one after another, the same thing asked different ways, always seeking a stumble, a contradiction, a revelation. Both interrogation rooms were empty.

I wasn't yet relieved. I moved to the cell block behind a steel door. Three cells. All were empty.

I pumped my fist. Megan was still free.

⟡

I landed in Megan's living room. The calico cat lifted her head and stared at me. I heard a murmur of voices from the kitchen. I hurried to the doorway, hugely relieved. However the afternoon had gone, the inquisition at the police station was over, she was home, she was not in a cell.

Megan poured tea into two tall tumblers filled with ice. Blaine sat at the kitchen table, watching her.

There is such a thing as love light. His brown eyes were soft. They said, *You're wonderful. You're the best. You have courage and grace and character and I'll fight for you.*

Megan carried the glasses to the table, sat opposite him. She still wore the navy linen blouse, white skirt, and navy pumps in which she'd started the day. I admired her pearl earrings and short pearl necklace, which nicely accented the white skirt. Very stylish.

Blaine lifted the tumbler. "Good job today, Counselor." His big hand made the glass look small.

For an instant her composure wavered. "I never thought I'd be a suspect in a murder case." Her voice was thin. "Now if I have a client who looks like he—or she—is dripping with guilt, I'll stop and think for a minute about circumstantial evidence. You remember in law school? Of course crimes can be proven with circumstantial evidence. Not to worry. The evidence must be convincing, compelling, irrefutable. Hey, that's swell unless you're the one trying to explain facts that almost everybody—and especially the police—consider utterly damning."

"You did a great job." He reached out, one big hand gripping a small one. "You were absolutely consistent."

"Oh yes." She sighed. "I was consistent. I was telling the truth. It's not hard to be consistent when it's true. That small point appears to have escaped everybody else's notice." She pulled her hand free, lifted the glass, drank and drank. "Anyway, that"—her tone was determinedly cheerful—"is enough about me. We've worried this bone to splinters. There's nothing to say we haven't said. You came galloping to my rescue this morning. You've spent the day fending off the cops." She smiled at him, a gentle, grateful smile. "You're the one who did great, Counselor. I'm not in jail. Now, how many unfinished tasks did you leave on your desk this morning?"

A big hand flapped, dismissing what he'd left behind, but Megan placed her elbows on the tabletop. "You know you're in a big hole.

You will make me feel much better about myself if you charge to your office and catch up on your work."

"I thought we'd——"

"No more. *No más. Sufficiendo.* I don't want to think about last night. I want to do a Double-Crostic and pretend I'm planning a trip to Padre Island or The Galleria in Houston or the Alamo. Somewhere. Anywhere. Far from Adelaide and sudden death." Her voice quivered. "I can't think about it anymore."

His long face squeezed in apology. "You're right. You need a break. I'll get over to the office, take care of some things. I'll bring pizza about seven. You like anchovies, right?" He stood. "Promise me you won't worry. Everything will be all right."

She rose, too, forced a bright smile. "Sure. We'll shake on it." She held out a small hand.

He took her hand in his big hand, then pulled her close. She stood on tiptoe. He bent toward her.

Some moments are not meant for others. As I departed, I heard her murmur, "Oh, Blaine . . ."

Chapter 13

The sun was a hot red ball hanging low in the sky. Jimmy and I had agreed to meet around four. At the cemetery, I took a slight detour to the Prichard mausoleum. I'd dropped in when I first arrived, but I now felt I needed all the luck I could get. Though the air was hot and still in the mausoleum, it was lovely to be out of the direct sunlight. I gave the greyhound two soft strokes, stepped to my right and patted the top of the cat's head. I was definitely grateful, I nodded at the dog and cat, that Megan wasn't in a cell, but from the conversation between Megan and Blaine it was clear the police still thought she was guilty. I'd found out some interesting facts, but nothing to persuade Sam to consider other suspects.

I hoped Jimmy had learned something of value. I moved to his grave site and squinted against the sunlight glittering on his granite stone. "Jimmy?"

No answer.

I sought the shade of the sycamore, leaned against the trunk.

I knew Jimmy wanted to do his best for Megan, but he'd been so eager to return to Italy and was so excited he could appear, I feared he'd be tempted to extend his stay. "Jimmy?"

No answer.

I began to pace, counted to a hundred, was at ninety-three—

"Hey, Bailey Ruth." His call was loud enough to be heard near the grave, too soft to carry far.

I blurted, "Jimmy," in obvious relief.

"Did you think I wasn't coming?"

"Well, Italy—"

"I went to some of our favorite places." His voice held yearning layered with melancholy, the understanding that what had once been could never be again, that caring and regret and passion can't change reality, that the past is forever beyond reach.

"I'm sorry." I was. I understood. The present, however precious, is ephemeral. Take a breath, the moment is gone.

"It took me a while with Ginny Morse. That's why I was late. What's happened? Where's Megan?"

"The police didn't hold her."

I heard a soft whuff of relief. "Where is she?"

"At her apartment."

"I guess The Suit's with her." He sounded midway between forlorn and disdainful.

"Blaine stayed with her all day, first at the law firm, then at the police station."

"I guess he did a pretty good job." Midway between relieved and jealous.

"She isn't in jail."

"I guess she thinks he's pretty swell." Definitely forlorn.

I didn't want to make him unhappier than he was so I didn't say anything.

"Okay." A man accepting an unpalatable truth. "That's good. She needs somebody to help her. If I could be there, I would. But I can't. I'll pin a medal on him if he gets her out of this." An effort at a laugh. "Never thought you'd hear me say that, right? But she's in a hell of a mess. All because she tried to help somebody, do the right thing. She won't explain that to the cops. They see that text on Graham's phone and they think they've got her on a platter. You'd think anybody could look at Megan and know it's nuts to imagine she'd sneak into a house and shoot somebody in the back of the head. Maybe they'll wise up."

I had to be honest. "They aren't looking at anyone else. I don't know why she hasn't been arrested yet."

"Sam Cobb's careful." Jimmy spoke with the authority of a reporter who knew his city officials. "He gathers all the evidence before he huddles with the DA. You can bet he's trying to find out more about Megan. He'll see what he's got Monday, then talk to the DA."

I hoped the facts I'd gathered today would be enough to interest Sam. I quickly sketched my day for Jimmy.

He was silent for a moment, considering what I'd told him. Finally he said, "Kind of feminine intuition on your conclusions. Not that I don't think women have a sort of inner Ouija board—"

I didn't disagree.

"—but I got something Cobb can get his teeth into. I got to the villa in late afternoon and the Morses were there. I introduced myself. They couldn't have been nicer to the young guy from the consulate. I played it great. But Carl Morse is about as big a stuffed shirt as I've ever met. He chooses his words like he's stacking tooth-picks. *Doug was a fine fellow. Never heard anyone say anything bad about Doug.* When I asked what caused the deep freeze between Graham and Layton, he looked shocked. *Why, his partners were gentlemen, never a cross word between them.* I was watching her. She's a babe, a stacked honey blonde. There isn't a man on the planet who wouldn't make a move on her if he had the chance. She looks at her husband and she's got this little smile, like, *Honey, you are so much baloney.* He turned to her every so often to say, *Don't you agree, Ginny?* She'd murmur *Mmmmm.* Here's where I'm a genius. I got finished and she's walking me down the hall and I said *I left my car at the bottom of the hill, do you think you could give me a lift down there?* She did, and she wasn't quite so lovey-dovey about their wonderful partners. I invited her to have a glass of Chianti at this neat trattoria, kind of like the one where Megan and I used to go. I laid it on, how she looked like a woman who picked up on nuances. First I tried to get her to open up about the law firm staff. Did anyone have it in for Graham? How about Anita Davis? Ginny got this bland look, sometimes husbands and wives look like each other and she was pure stuffed shirt . . . *a wonderful staff, everybody on the best of terms, especially some of them . . .* I picked up on that, pressed her but she backed off. I don't know exactly what she meant but she had something in mind. I told her we knew there'd been a change in how Layton and Graham treated each other. That set her off. No more collegiality. She has these deep green eyes. It was like watching a cartoon and the good-looking dame has dollar signs instead of pupils as she adds up what the penniless widow owes her. Scratch all that comity puff from hubby. The bottom line is"—Jimmy's tone was wry—"what it always is, the bottom line. She and Carl are ostensibly 'partners' in the law firm. In reality, they were assured a certain amount of what they billed and collected. If the aggregate firm income was up, they were assured of a bonus in line with their contribution to the firm's net income for a year. Last December they had the annual money confab. Their billings were up by about three hundred thousand over the previous year and the Morses were thinking maybe they'd buy a vacation place at Grand Lake. Instead, Graham got a big boost and they each got an extra ten thou. Layton took the biggest hit, but you'd have thought somebody cut out her heart. She looked at me out of those big green eyes, those dollar signs flashing like a candle on a slot, and said it didn't make sense Layton would channel extra profit to Graham, especially since he didn't like the son of a bitch."

The leaves in the cottonwood rustled, reminding me of the slap of bills on a wooden counter when we cashed out after a nice winning spree at a casino in Vegas. We always bought a hundred dollars' worth of chips and quit when we lost our stake. That time we won. Eighty-six dollars. That was a lot of money in our day. Maybe Ginny Morse could hear the slap of bills and imagine them rising in front of Doug Graham.

"Why didn't she and her husband form their own firm?"

"Third glass of the dark red, she talked about the payments on her BMW and how they were probably making more even when they were getting screwed than if they started over on their own. They'd had a small firm and joined up with Layton and Graham about five years ago."

I honed in on the red meat. "Jimmy, you found out what matters. Layton ponied up big-time the year there was the hit-and-run.

A clever form of blackmail. Layton's an angry man." I thought about the look of despair in his civilized face as he spoke to his dead wife. The hundred-thousand-dollar ring for the rich widow might have been enough to push him to murder. Not to protect himself at this point, but for revenge against a man who took advantage when Layton hid the truth to be able to stay with his daughter. Julie was gone now. Perhaps Brewster Layton no longer cared what happened to him.

But the morning after the murder he came to the office early, destroyed something he'd taken from Graham's office. The substance of the slick strips in the shredder suggested photos to me. It would have been just like Doug Graham to use his cell, take pictures of the crumpled fender on Layton's car, print them out. Those pictures would be quite at variance with the damage recorded by the insurance adjuster after the cars collided that Monday morning.

"Hello." The tone was aggrieved. "Have you left?"

I realized Jimmy had been talking. "Sorry. I was thinking."

"Yeah." His voice rose with hope. "You have a plan?"

I didn't want to admit my thoughts were scattered. I was anxious—very anxious—about Megan's prospects. I'd followed every lead I had. Would anything I'd learned interest Sam Cobb? All I could do was try. But the morale of the troops depends upon the leader. It was no time to display lack of confidence. "I'll make a report to Chief Cobb."

"Does that big ham-faced guy listen to voices out of nowhere?"

"I have a method for communicating with the chief." Words can obfuscate as well as enlighten. "You know how anyone can call up and leave information anonymously?" I wasn't claiming that was my method.

"I did a feature on it. The Tip Line, guaranteed anonymous. The headline read: 'A Tip a Day Keeps the Bad Guys Away.' Yeah, I wrote a good one."

"Exactly."

"So you call the cops. What do I do?"

"You've helped a lot. Why don't you relax for the evening?"

"Relax? I can hear the handcuffs snapping shut. That's what they'll do." His voice was suddenly wobbly. "They'll take these damn big metal handcuffs and clamp her wrists. And I can't do anything about it."

"There's something you can do tonight. If you were sitting on a sofa, maybe eating pizza and drinking a beer, and Megan came in the room behind you, you'd know she was there. You wouldn't have to turn around and look. That's how it is with someone you love. You don't have to see someone to know they're there. Just go. Be there. She won't know why, but she'll feel better."

We only know we've been brushed by an angel's wing when for no apparent reason we feel warmth, reassurance. Jimmy was no angel, but he loved Megan very much.

"I'd give anything—" He broke off.

He wanted to stand at her door, knock, be there in person, reach out, take her hands, hold her small hands warm in his.

"But I can't be where she sees me. I can't do that to her." There was a maturity in his voice that I'd never heard. "She really cared about me, but I'm done. We would have had a good life." He was silent again.

I spoke gently. "She will have a good life with Blaine."

"He's an okay guy. He's doing everything he can to take care of her. And pretty soon—"

I glimpsed the shining curve of golden stairs, brighter than blazing sunlight, and knew Jimmy saw the stairway, too.

"—I'll be on my way. But until then, even if *he's* there, I can be with Megan."

I was alone.

✍

Sam's office was dim. I was careful to close the venetian blinds before I turned on the gooseneck lamp on his desk and twisted the shade to illuminate the blackboard. I picked up a piece of chalk. Should I relate what I'd learned in chronological order or list conclusions in the order of importance? Sam would not be interested in a play-by-play description of Detective Loy's activities. Very well. I wrote in block letters:

Doug Graham was blackmailing—

"Like Yogi Berra said, 'Déjà vu all over again.' I'm pretty sure that's how my day started. Chalk hanging in the air." His deep voice held a mixture of exasperation and fatigue. There was no *Glad you're here, Bailey Ruth.*

I swung around.

He closed the hall door behind him. "Have you been hanging out here all day?" He moved toward the table that sat between his desk and the brown leather sofa. The sofa faced the two windows that overlooked Main Street. His steps were slower than this morning, his suit more wrinkled, his heavy face shadowed by the stubble that requires some men to shave twice daily, especially if planning a night out. He was carrying a sack and a plastic cup. He plopped the sack on the table, pulled out a chair, sank into it with a thud, a big man running out of steam. He flipped the lid off the cup, drank thirstily. "Claire keeps after me to drink more water. Tells me iced tea is dehydrating. Lulu's has the best damn iced tea I've ever tasted, just like my mother used to make."

I knew the kind of tea he remembered, a rich amber chilled by clear ice cubes, brewed from boiling water poured over Lipton tea bags.

He reached for the sack as I pulled out the chair opposite him. His hand stayed midway to the sack. "It's been a long day. Chalk in the air. Chairs pulling out unaided."

A new outfit always gives me a lift. I admired the texture of the Italian silk blouse, the colors quite perfect, varying shades of green from topaz to emerald in indeterminate cloudlike swaths, and wide-legged cream linen trousers, and strap sandals in a matching cream.

He was tired, but not too tired to notice. "Claire has a shirt like that but hers is kind of orangey." He grabbed the sack, frowned. "I can split the cheeseburger with you."

I hastened to reassure him. "Thanks, Sam, but I'm looking forward to stopping at Lulu's in a while."

That cheered him. "So you haven't taken up permanent residence in here." He opened the sack.

"I needed to use the phone."

"Glad we could help." He split the sack, used the paper as a plate. He spilled out french fries, squeezed ketchup from a packet, tore open the little packets of salt and pepper, unwrapped the cheeseburger. He took a big bite, jerked his head toward the blackboard. "I got the point about Layton when you told me about the hit-and-run."

"Now there's proof." I described the change in Graham's income the December after the hit-and-run. "You can confirm this by interviewing Ginny Morse."

Sam took another gulp of tea. "I thought they were in Italy."

"They are. I have sources."

He raised an eyebrow, but he looked in a better humor. His eyes had their familiar sharp glint. He was gaining energy from the food. "I wouldn't bother to listen, but I have to say I was impressed with Wynn. I know she's smart. I've checked her out. Law review. Order of the Coif. Graduated third in her class. They always say women lawyers are smarter than men lawyers because they have to be. But she for sure has no criminal background and she never stumbled. She told the same story at the end of three hours of interrogation as she did at the beginning. It wasn't the old decline-to-answer-on-the-grounds-of-self-incrimination dodge. She answered everything fully, completely, and unhesitatingly. Her responses never changed about the text she received. Yes, she and Doug Graham discussed termination. No, it was not her termination. No, she was not at liberty to say whose termination. I know from you that she was protecting Anita Davis. I'd be inclined to believe her but the facts haven't changed, either. She was there. She had blood on her clothes. The murder weapon was found in her desk drawer. The first two she can explain. The third she can't. And a very scared guy, Sammy Rodriguez, was cutting the hedge at Graham's place Thursday and he heard a woman and a man talking at the pool, plotting his murder. The guy said it was time somebody killed him, and he mentioned Megan."

"People who overhear conversations often misconstrue what they heard. The gardener heard my voice and that of a young friend of mine, and I can assure you we were not plotting murder."

"Too bad I can't take your statement, yours and your friend's. Until then we have Sammy's statement down in black and white, and the mayor intends to trumpet this on Monday. But most of all, Wynn can't wish away that gun in her desk drawer."

"Someone else—"

He jabbed a french fry into a mound of ketchup liberally laced with pepper. "Yeah, yeah, yeah. In popped the jewel thief and just happened to have the murder weapon and decided to leave it in her desk. When you can show me why anybody would kill Graham to steal the ring, I'll pay attention. What else have you got?"

"Rhoda Graham knew about the ring. Lou Raymond told her. Rhoda wasn't at home at the time of the murder. With his death, her kids will inherit and they won't have to worry about college loans."

He gave me a level glance. "Yeah. But now they don't have a dad. A dad's a dad even if they got mad when he divorced their mom."

I knew then that Sam in his careful way was seeking information about everyone who might have been involved. "Anita Davis was on a Reese's Peanut Butter Cup run when Graham was killed."

He spoke over a mouthful of fries. "I can see it now, the DA telling the jury how this heinous criminal shot her boss then stopped at Walmart to buy candy for a kid with cancer. I don't think so."

"Geraldine Jackson said Graham was pretty touchy-feely with the help but never went too far. She said Brewster Layton had strict ideas about behavior at the office."

Sam munched a french fry. "After the hit-and-run, Graham could have felt a little freer. Maybe that's proof he didn't have anything going on with anyone."

I wasn't quite ready to give up on the possibility of a love affair gone wrong. "Or maybe he kept everything quiet because he saw a pot of gold over the horizon."

"Lisbeth Carew? That might make any guy toe the line."

I nodded. "Sharon King claims she has no idea if he was involved in an affair. You'd think his main secretary would know. But she won't say anything bad about anyone. Maybe she knows more than she's telling."

Sam wiped his mouth with a paper napkin. "Afraid nothing rings my bell. The facts haven't changed."

I was up against cold, hard reason and the kind of evidence a DA loved. All I had left were Nancy Murray, a scared rabbit, and Keith Porter, who turned out to be likable. Was that why I believed—

Sam's cell phone rang. He grabbed another napkin to wipe his hand, dug in his pocket, pulled out the cell. He checked caller ID and was abruptly alert, gaze intent, shoulders tight. "Chief Cobb." He listened, swiped Speaker, held the cell between us.

Megan Wynn's husky voice was slightly breathless. ". . . Blaine said I had to call you. But I promised Nancy I wouldn't—"

"Start at the beginning. Who's Nancy?"

A deep breath. "My phone rang a few minutes ago. My home phone. I looked to see who was calling. It was Nancy Murray. The paralegal at the office."

"Were you expecting a call from her?"

"No." She sounded surprised, a little puzzled.

"Does she often call you?"

"No."

"Why did you answer?" It was a brusque demand.

"I don't know. I usually answer the phone when someone I know calls. I thought perhaps she was calling to tell me she didn't believe I had anything to do with— Oh, it doesn't matter what I thought or why I answered. Let me tell you what she said." Megan's voice was thin, strained. "Nancy was whispering. I don't know if she thought someone might hear, but she was whispering and she talked really fast. She said, *Megan, I have to see you. Please come. Don't tell the police. I need help. I'm afraid—* She broke off. It was as if she put her hand over the speaker. The line went dead. I called back. There wasn't any answer. I got dressed and called again and the phone rang and rang until the recorder came on. I ran outside to my car and Blaine came up and wanted to know where I was going and I told him and he said I had to call you. We're in his car and we're almost there."

Sam headed for the door, moving fast for a big man. "I'm coming."

I disappeared.

I stood in Nancy Murray's brilliantly lit living room just inside the open front door. Light spilled out into the night. Nancy would no longer mark day and night. She lay crumpled on one side of the old Persian rug. Blood and tissue matted her left temple. The unmarked portion of her face was slack and white. Her eyes stared into eternity.

I was abruptly angry with myself. I'd taken her fear as a sheltered young woman's recoil from murder. Obviously there was a basis for fear beyond the fact of violence. Why had she been afraid? What did she know about Doug Graham's murder that had placed her in danger, brought death to this tastefully furnished room?

Voices sounded, Sam's deep and brisk. He reached the open doorway, then looked to his left, snapped a sharp command. "Stay right there, you two. Don't move."

I knew the order was directed at Blaine and Megan.

The door had been wide open when I arrived. Obviously Blaine and Megan reached the apartment before the police. Had they found the door ajar? Did Blaine knock? Call out? Had the force of his knock caused the door to slowly swing away and reveal Nancy lying on the floor? She was visible from the doorway. Blaine's first act would have been to call Sam again. He, in turn, would use his radio to call for backup. Sirens squalled.

Sam waited where he was. The ME would be the first to enter, and then the slow, careful forensic investigation would begin.

More sirens. Car doors slammed. Brisk steps. The rumble of voices.

I looked again at the body. From its position, Nancy apparently had been walking toward the door. She had been struck on the left temple, crumpled to the floor. Whoever wielded the weapon must have been slightly to her left and a step behind her. This was in keeping with a hostess moving to open the door to a departing guest. Had she been so eager for her visitor to depart that she'd stared ahead at the door, reached out, ready to turn the knob, pull the door open? If that were so, she would not have been half turned to see the person behind her, would not have been aware if a hand slipped into a purse or pocket, pulled out a weapon, lifted an arm, and swung. Swung hard.

It was a critical determination. If she had been attacked as she walked to the door, that meant she had admitted someone, they had spoken, and now the guest was departing.

When I left her apartment that afternoon, the chain lock snapped into place. That precaution underlined her fear. That was what I carried away from our talk. Nancy Murray was afraid. I held to that thought. What had frightened her?

Cocky steps and the ME, Jacob Brandt, arrived. How can steps be cocky? He was a slender guy with a jaded face, but he carried himself like James Cagney as George M. Cohan. In your face. *Get out of my way. I'm a hell of a guy.* He was scruffy. Slight stubble of beard. Shaggy hair that needed a cut. A hole in the shoulder of his tee, baggy shorts, sandals. He stopped a foot away, studied the body on the floor. He pulled plastic gloves from a pocket, knelt, checked for a pulse. "Dead within the last thirty, forty minutes. Blunt trauma. One good hard whack was all it took. Neurocranium smashed." He rocked back on his heels, jerked a thumb toward the floor, and a dark object.

I moved nearer, recognized a man's sock, thick and solid from toe to heel, the upper portion limp and empty.

"Looks like a dandy little homemade blackjack." He peered down. "Yeah. I see blood and hair. A man's black dress sock, nylon, filled with dirt or sand, tied with a twist. Simple. Untraceable." He pushed up from the floor. "She's all yours. You know the press is going to give you hell? I can see the headline now: 'Killer Terrorizes Adelaide. Is Anyone Safe?' They'll write about the second homicide in as many days, what's happening to our fair city." With that he plunged out into the night, his sandals slapping on the concrete walk.

The forensic investigation began, an officer with a sketch pad, another with a camera. Sam gave low-voiced instructions. Movement at the door and two officers stepped aside for Detective Sergeant Hal Price. Hal had obviously been at home relaxing. He was his always remarkably handsome self in a Hawaiian shirt and khaki pants. Sam gestured for him to come near and spoke for a moment, then the two of them turned to step outside.

The light on the walkway along the first-floor apartments was muted, no blazing glare at night, enough illumination for safety and ease of passage, no more. Lampposts dotted the courtyard but their golden glow emphasized the darkness of the shadows. Two figures stood in a swath of shadow a few feet away from Nancy's open door. Blaine Smith was hard to see in a navy polo, jeans, and dark running shoes. He stood with his head jutting forward, one arm protectively curled around Megan's slight shoulders. She huddled against him, much more visible in a cream T-shirt and white slacks and sandals.

Hal headed on a path to the swimming pool. Sam strode toward Blaine and Megan.

A nearby door opened. "What's going on? I heard sirens." Other doors opened, voices rose. "What's happened?" "Is there a fire?" "Fire! I don't smell smoke." "Is somebody hurt?" "Why all the cops?"

Sam lifted his voice. "There is no emergency. Repeat, there is no emergency. Police have responded to a nine-one-one call that affects apartment 22 only. Residents and visitors are asked to remain in their apartments. We appreciate your cooperation. Apartment 22 is a crime scene. An active investigation is under way. There is no danger to other residents. Anyone with information regarding the occupant of apartment 22 or who saw anyone enter or leave apartment 22 within the past hour is asked to come to the pool area. Detective Sergeant Price will interview residents. Again, we are interested in a description of person or persons seen entering or leaving apartment 22 within the last hour. Thank you."

Sam reached Blaine and Megan. "In twenty minutes, we'll go down to the station. I'll ask you to accompany me, Ms. Wynn. Smith, you can follow in your car. We can do it on that basis or I'll take Ms. Wynn into custody."

"I'm her attorney." Blaine had moved nearer Sam, was a bulwark between Sam and Megan.

"I got that. You can be present when I question her. I will also question you. You can also decide if you want counsel. Lawyer up if you want to."

Megan reached out, touched Blaine's arm. "I'll go with Chief Cobb. I have nothing to hide. I have never been to this apartment complex or to Nancy's apartment until you and I came here together tonight."

The chief's face was in shadow, but I thought I saw a slight nod of admiration.

A sudden light blazed. "Great shot, Chief. You and the Black Widow Lawyer, who shows up at every murder in Adelaide. I'll sell this for a bundle."

Sam's face turned dull red. His big hands clenched. "This is a crime scene, Carson. No press releases—"

I remembered an encounter with Deke Carson during Sam's investigation into the murder of a man whose greed cost him his life. The weedy freelancer was Adelaide's equivalent to celebrity-haunting paparazzi, the bottom-feeders in the news business. Carson sneered. "So last century, Sam the Man. Who needs press releases? I got a scanner. Murder. Glenwood Apartments. Number 22. Occupied by Nancy Murray, paralegal at firm of Layton, Graham, Morse and Morse. Inside skinny says Black Widow Lawyer Megan Wynn was on the scene of the murder of partner Doug Graham. Now she's on the scene"—Carson lifted his Leica, another burst of brightness—"of murder two. Looks like they're dropping like flies at that firm. Black Widows eat flies, don't they?"

Sam took two quick steps, stared down into Deke Carson's weaselly face. "Get behind the police lines or go to jail."

Carson backed away, one arm wrapped around his camera. "Sure, sure, sure. And you have a fun ride to the cop shop with the Black Widow. Hope you make it." With that he turned and loped across the courtyard. The pool was in his way. He started to veer left. Suddenly he took a header. Just as if someone stood in his way and thrust out a leg.

Carson catapulted forward, stumbling, flailing, his momentum carrying him to the edge of the pool and over. He struck the water. The camera was pulled loose from his hands just as he toppled. The camera hovered for an instant before it plummeted straight down and disappeared beneath the surface.

I understood immediately. I was thrilled to see sleaze justly rewarded and even more thrilled to know Jimmy's location. I was there in an instant. I called out, my voice low and urgent. "I need to talk to you."

The hoarse reply was belligerent. "He deserv——"

"Of course he did. Good job. I need your help. The end of the pier at White Deer."

Chapter 14

I perched at the end of the pier. The moon hung high and luminous. Its radiance painted a swath across the lake. A refreshing breeze stirred my hair. Water lapped against the pilings. Frogs croaked in a nearby inlet. Their deep throaty bellows dominated the night, drowning out even the rasping cicadas. As Bobby Mac delighted in explaining, male frogs serenade ladies to get a little action going. Why was I not surprised?

"I got to get down to the station." Jimmy was frantic. "Ham Face is taking her in his car. Like she's some kind of felon."

"It's okay, Jimmy. The photo creep had all his facts wrong, except for one. Megan's a lawyer. She can handle Sam. She'll be fine—"

"Fine?" He was explosive. "What planet do you live on? He's going to third degree her."

"You read too much Mickey Spillane."

"Who's that? Look, Cobb's—"

I refrained from asking what planet he lived on. I knew the answer. Earth, twenty-first century. His cultural icons and mine were decades apart. Life goes on, never the same, but always similar, the age-old quests for happiness and success, whether the seeker wears a doublet, breeches, and high leather boots or a Tommy Bahama breezer shirt, plaid Bermuda shorts, and leather loafers without socks.

"—about to pull into the back of the cop shop. I got to get down there—"

I reached out, gripped his arm. "Steady, Jimmy. I'll find out about Megan's status. ASAP. But I have an idea—"

"I *told* her not to go out."

His frustrated complaint caught my attention. "Were you there when she got the phone call from Nancy?"

"Oh yeah. The evening was great for a little while." His voice softened. "She'd had a bath and she came out of the bathroom and her face was kind of pink and her hair was wrapped in a towel and she had on this cute short terry cloth robe and she was barefoot. If I hadn't cracked up in those rapids, I think she would have married me, and that's how it could have been, me and Megan at home." The cry for what could have been, could never be. "I kept quiet. I didn't bother her or say anything. She didn't know I was there, but that was okay. It was great just to be there with her. Sometimes she'd bend over and give Sweetie a kiss. I don't mind when she kisses Sweetie. Anyway, we were there without *him*. When the phone rang, I thought maybe it was him. But I should have known. He'd call her cell. This was the landline. I went over and looked at caller ID,

Nancy Murray. Megan picked up the phone and she looked surprised, then she frowned. I knew this wasn't good. In fact, I had a feeling it was real bad and was I ever right. Anyway, Megan started to speak, then broke off. She held the phone and stared at it. She'd been cut off. She ended the call, punched to call back. She held on and on, I guess until the recorder picked up, then shook her head and slammed down the phone. She whirled around and ran to her bedroom, dropping the robe. In a minute she'd pulled on some clothes and was stepping into her shoes and brushing her hair at the same time. I asked her what was going on, where did she think she was going? She was shocked to hear my voice. She said Nancy was upset and she had to go see what was wrong. I was chasing after her as she ran down the stairs. I told her not to hurry off like she did when she got the text from Graham's cell. I grabbed her arm when she got to the foyer, told her only dumb broads fell for the same line twice—"

I agreed with Jimmy. The call was a setup, just like the text. The caller may or may not have been Nancy. A whispering voice . . .

"—and she better not hare off to somebody's apartment and maybe it was time to ring up The Suit. I hated to ask her to call him. She said she couldn't bother Blaine anymore, that he'd missed a whole day's work because of her, and he was probably at his office catching up. She said she'd put him to too much trouble already and there was no reason why she couldn't talk to Nancy. By that time we were almost to her car and all of a sudden *he* loomed up in a dark shirt and jeans, kind of melted out of the shadows. He asked where she was going. She told him and he said they'd take his car." Pause. "Cool car. I rode with them and he told her to call Ham Face."

"That's wonderful!" If I'd been visible, I would have done a high kick. Nobody cancans with more verve than I. You should have seen me play Claudine in a summer theater production at White Deer Park. I wondered if the local theater group still thrived. We'd had a great group for a number of years. I began to hum "If You Loved Me Truly."

"Oh yeah, let's high-five. Good move, make sure the cops arrive to find you at the scene of the crime."

"That's the point." I was hugely relieved. "Blaine was at her apartment house. He saw Megan come out. It's clear he was on guard. He can swear her car never left the parking lot."

"What are the odds Ham Face will listen?" Jimmy was hostile.

"He will." Sam would listen. So far everything had looked black against Megan, but now there was a witness to give her an alibi. "Thank God for Blaine. If he watched her car from the time he left her apartment until she came out, she'll be in the clear."

"I get it. They can time when the call came to her apartment. That will prove when she was there, and he can testify when she came outside, and she was with him all the way to Nancy's."

"Right. It doesn't matter whether the call came from Nancy or her killer, the call had to have been made by one or the other, and Megan is alibied before and after the call."

"Maybe the killer wasn't so damn smart." Jimmy was pumped. "But"—there was a thoughtful pause—"Megan would be up a creek if Blaine hadn't hung around. I guess he was letting her rest. Not getting in her face. But he stayed around to make sure nothing happened to her. Now he can swear she couldn't have been at Nancy's. I guess he was going to hang out there all night. I guess"—a longer pause—"he's a pretty good man."

Tonight someone stood in Nancy's apartment, called Megan's number. The reason was obvious. Megan was clearly a suspect in Doug Graham's murder. Put Megan on the scene of Nancy Murray's murder, tie it up with a pretty bow for the police. "The fact that Nancy let the murderer inside her apartment doesn't make sense."

"Somebody knocked on the door. She opened the door."

I was impatient. "When I talked to her, she was frightened. She claimed she was upset because of the fact of murder, knowing someone who'd been killed. Obviously it was more than that. She suspected someone of committing the crime. But how did the murderer know Nancy was suspicious? And if Nancy was so scared, why did she let the murderer in?"

"Maybe she called the killer, said I can talk to the cops unless you slip me a cool ten thou and I'll have amnesia."

"She was too frightened to call the killer." I remembered the pall of fear around her.

Jimmy was exasperated. "She let the killer in her apartment."

If I was right that knowledge of the killer accounted for her fear, how had she known who killed Doug Graham? There had never been any suggestion Nancy Murray had a motive for killing Doug Graham. There was no reason she would be at his house to see someone approach or had been present when the murder occurred. How then did Nancy learn the murderer's identity? And, if Nancy hadn't attempted blackmail, how did the murderer know she posed a threat? If Nancy hadn't contacted the killer, then the killer came to her apartment unannounced.

Why did Nancy open the door?

Did the killer reassure Nancy? Or did the killer threaten Nancy? What could the killer possibly know that made Nancy feel she had no choice but to open the door?

It was like watching slots click click click.

"Oh. Oh!"

"Spit it out." Jimmy must have heard the sudden understanding in my voice.

I reached out, grabbed Jimmy's arm. "Meet me in Megan's office."

~

I turned on the light. Megan's desk was just as she'd left it, a folder open on the desktop, the bottom-right drawer pulled out. There were traces of fingerprint powder on the desk. I didn't doubt there were fingerprints. Megan's fingerprints. The killer most assuredly wore vinyl gloves Thursday night. There would be no telltale fingerprints of the murderer.

"Jimmy, where were you when the door burst open after the gun went off?"

"I was right in front of that cop, ready to kick his gun out of his hand."

"You were facing the door?"

"Yeah."

"Sam and Hal and Weitz were right behind Johnny. Then came Layton and the staff. Everybody was there, watching. You heard Megan tell Sam that she'd found the gun in her desk?"

"Yeah. She had to cover for me shooting the gun off, and her explanation fell flat."

"That's the critical moment."

"The gun going off?"

"Megan saying she found the gun in her desk drawer. Were you looking toward the door?"

"I was right beside Megan. She was looking at the door, talking to Cobb. I saw Cobb. I saw all of them. It was like I was a 60x zoom Nikon. I got it in a freeze-frame. Some things you never forget. I was the butt who got smart with the gun and set the posse after Megan. The whole sorry thing runs over and over in my mind. The guy cop's blue eyes looked like ice. The woman cop had her arm out and the muscle in her forearm bunched like a fist. Ham Face already had stubble on his chin. Reminded me of hunting with my uncle, a big man, too. When Unc lined up Bambi in his sights, he had the same tough got-you-now look like Ham Face. The Blond God cop had his hand an inch from his gun. Brewster Layton stared at the gun on the floor like it was a snake and might come after him. Anita Davis's mouth kept opening and closing, and she was making little oh-oh-oh noises. Geraldine Jackson stood on her toes for a better view. Sharon King looked into the room, then she glanced away. Lou Raymond clapped her hand over her mouth. Nancy Murray—"

He broke off. "Oh wow."

He and I held the same memory.

Jimmy talked fast. "Nancy was at the door. She was holding on to the jamb. She wasn't looking at Megan or the gun. She was look-ing at someone near her. That person looked toward her. They stared at each other for an instant, then Nancy jerked her gaze away. It must have been obvious in Nancy's face. *I saw you put the gun in Megan's office.* But how did Nancy know the moment the gun was found?"

It was as neat as $x + y$. "What happened Thursday night?"

Jimmy was impatient. "That's when the killer put the gun in Megan's office."

"What else happened that night?"

His retort was quick. "The ring was stolen. But"—he worked it out in his mind—"the killer didn't care about the ring. The killer wanted to see Megan arrested. So the killer didn't take the ring. Someone else took the ring. Oh sure. It was Nancy. She stole the ring. She broke through the window. She wanted the theft to look like an outside job. She came down the alley and broke the window and climbed in. She got the ring. And then when she was getting ready to leave, maybe she decided to take the easy way out, use the back door, and she started to open Doug's office door and somebody else was there, somebody who had a key, somebody who came in and walked to Megan's office and went in and then came out. Nancy was probably scared to death she was going to be caught. She stood there and watched someone she knew leave by the back door. Friday, when the gun was found, she knew who put it there." Jimmy heaved a huge sigh of relief. "You can tell Ham Face, and everything will be all right."

It wasn't going to be that easy. "I'll point Sam in the right direction. He has to find proof. I won't tell him who Nancy saw."

"Why not?" He was irritated. "Why toss out bread crumbs for him to follow? Why not tell him what we saw? I swear dames have to make everything complicated. Tell the man."

"Let me see," I said in a musing tone, "I can say, 'Sam, you know

I was watching when Megan explained how she found the murder weapon in her desk drawer. Everyone in the office heard what she said. By the way, there was another ghost present who can confirm what I saw. He and I both observed Nancy Murray and her killer looking at each other. Straightforward as can be."

The desk chair tilted back. "You mean Ham Face likes facts. Okay. Do what you have to do. Get busy with your bread crumbs."

Now I was crisp. "I'll talk to Sam. I need for you to go to the *Gazette*, check out some dates."

He listened as I explained. "Easy."

"We'll meet at seven in the morning." I wanted to start Saturday in the best possible fashion. "When you were here—"

"Like *here?*" Colors swirled. Jimmy, in a blue polo and madras shorts, lounged in Megan's chair, one leg draped over an arm.

I was struck again with the extraordinary sensitivity of his face beneath a mop of brown hair, a smooth high forehead, deep-set brown eyes, straight nose, a tiny mole just below and to the right of his lips, rounded chin. His expression reflected delight. He was *here.*

"Where did you eat breakfast?"

He raised those brown brows. "A new game? What's your favorite ball club? Do you drink Bud Light or Coors? Have you ever picked up a tarantula? Rangers. Bud Light. Hell, no. Breakfast? Usually a granola bar and coffee at my desk. Starbucks Red Eye. Sometimes I'd meet Megan at Panera. Anything else on your mind?"

"So no one would be likely to recognize you at Lulu's?"

"Geezer City, lady."

"See you there."

The interrogation rooms were dark and empty. I found Megan and Blaine in Sam's office. I was a little surprised Detective Weitz wasn't there. Sam was settled in his swivel chair.

Megan and Blaine sat in the straight chairs facing the desk. Megan's gaze was steady, her expression serious but unintimidated. Blaine kept a protective hand on the back of her chair.

Sam was in his shirtsleeves, his rumpled brown suit jacket hanging from the coat tree by the door. The stubble on his jaws was darker, but his dark eyes were alert and intent. I noted a recorder on Sam's desk, saw the lighted panel. Sam was speaking. "I'll have the statements you make transcribed."

I was surprised at the geniality of his tone.

"I know it's late but I'd like to hear what happened one more time."

There had been a change between his hard-faced appraisal of Megan and Blaine at Nancy's apartment to this almost informal—except for the whirring recorder—conference in his office. Was this a variation on the good cop, bad cop routine?

Whatever. I needed to get Sam's attention before the police left Nancy Murray's apartment. The blackboard was behind Megan and Blaine but the chalk might make a scratchy sound. I scanned Sam's desktop, saw a legal pad and pen, but a pen moving independently would scarcely escape their notice.

I dropped to the floor, tugged on Sam's trouser cuff.

He never took his gaze away from Megan and Blaine, simply wriggled his foot.

Blaine leaned forward, big hands splayed on his knees. His long bony face was confident, his deep voice emphatic. "We finished our pizza about seven. Megan was exhausted. I told her to relax, said good night. When I got down to my car, I was thinking about Thursday night. Somebody went to a lot of trouble to get her out to Graham's house. Somebody planted the gun in her desk drawer. Somebody wants her to go to jail. I don't know what—"

This time I tapped on Sam's knee.

His gaze fell. One big hand reached out, gripped my wrist. He gave my arm a little shake. I took it to mean, *Wait a minute, let me finish here.*

"—I expected, but I decided not to take any chances. I wasn't going anywhere. If anybody came, I'd see them. I parked where I could see her car. I could see her windows on the second floor. I even had a good view of the back of the apartment house. The front and back are well lit. Some people went out the front, a couple came in the front, nobody went out the back. It was about nine thirty when Megan came bursting out of the front door. I got to her car when she was opening the door. I can tell you her car never left the lot between the time I came about seven and the time she came downstairs. She told me about the call. I said I'd take her to see Nancy but she had to call you, anything else was nuts. I drove and she called you. We got to Nancy's. I knocked—"

Their arrival had unfolded as I imagined.

"—on the door. No answer, but the door swung in. We saw her. I called you. That's all we know."

Sam's big face was thoughtful. "You are prepared to swear to these facts in a courtroom." It was a statement, not a question.

"I am."

Sam heaved himself to his feet. "You're free to go."

For an instant, two faces stared at him. Blaine's sandy brows lifted in surprise, then his bony face held triumph. Megan's tense posture eased. *She was the little girl at the vet and the doctor is saying her cat will live.*

They rose, Blaine's hand firm on Megan's elbow. Blaine's voice was a little uneven. "You won't regret tonight."

Sam was matter-of-fact. "Just doing my job."

By the time the hall door closed, I was visible on the sofa in a cheerful cotton top, a bamboo print with graceful pale blue blossoms and matching pale blue cropped trousers. I admired my light beige sandals with faux sapphire trim. "I'm over here."

The bottom drawer in his desk squeaked. He plucked out the bag of M&M'S, crossed to the sofa.

I held out my hand. As Mama always said, "When a man offers his favorite food accept with an appreciative smile."

Sam settled heavily at one end of the sofa, poured a mound in a big palm. "You can say *I told you so.* Megan Wynn's in the clear." He didn't sound happy.

"What happened on the ride to the station?"

He munched, spoke a little unclearly. "Nothing she said changed anything. It was what I expected. What I didn't know until I talked to both of them was that Blaine was watching her apartment and her car. That puts her in the clear, because she answered a call from the Murray apartment. Doesn't matter who made the call. What matters is the time. She answered and a couple of minutes later she flies out of her apartment house. Blaine stops her at her car. The Murray woman is dead when they find her about eight minutes later. Wynn's out of it." Crunch. Crunch. "I was a scout-master for a long time. Blaine was in my troop. Eagle Scout. If he says he was there, he was there."

There are advantages to living in a small town. People know each other.

A weary sigh. "Glad for him. He's head over heels. But now I have to start over. The facts had seemed pretty clear." He rubbed his knuckles on his bristly chin. "Tomorrow they'll still seem pretty clear to Neva. She doesn't know Blaine. She'll say, *Don't be a sap, that's the story they cooked up, they're in it together.* So the pressure will be on and Neva will go off like a geyser when she knows I didn't arrest Wynn. You got anything?"

"I know why Nancy Murray was killed."

He leaned forward, his face slack with amazement. "Why the hell?"

"She broke into Doug Graham's office late Thursday night. Probably well past midnight. She climbed in from the alley, got the ring. I imagine she used a little LED flashlight. Narrow beam, piercing—"

Sam was turning, grabbing his phone. He held up a hand for me to wait, barked into the receiver. "Officer"—and I knew he spoke to an investigator at Nancy Murray's apartment—"information received. Stolen ring"—he pulled a folder close, flipped it open—"may be hidden on the premises. Fourteen-karat-gold band studded with rubies. Five-point-seven-carat multifaceted diamond. The ring will be well hidden. Check the usual places, flour and sugar canisters, bars of soap, box of detergent, toes of shoes, maybe even at the bottom of a jewel box with costume jewelry, or tucked in a lingerie drawer, poked down in the mayo in the fridge. Find the ring."

He clicked off, swung to face me, eyes gleaming.

"Nancy tried to set the stage for the robbery to look like a break-in. But she probably decided to leave by the door, not crawl back through the window. Even if she had the flash on when she opened the door, if she saw light from Wynn's office, she'd click off her flashlight." I pictured Nancy Murray standing just inside Graham's office, her hand clutching the doorknob, too panicked to move, not daring to make a noise.

Again Sam held up his hand, turned to the phone, punched. "Officer, make sure prints are taken from the interior doorknob of Graham's office." He clicked off, swung around to face me.

I nodded approval. "Nancy must have been bewildered. Why was someone in Megan's office that late at night? Of course, she had no idea that Doug Graham was dead. So she watched and then someone came out of Megan's office and it wasn't Megan, which must have been even more bewildering."

Sam's big head nodded. "Whoever came out of Megan's office had to walk right past Graham's office to get to the back door. That person had to have a flashlight, so Murray saw a face. The back door opened, closed. Murray probably waited at least five minutes. She crept into the hall and to the back door and opened it. That brings us to tonight. Did she try blackmail?"

"I don't think so. Instead, when the gun was found in Megan's desk, Nancy's reaction alerted the murderer."

The two had looked at each other. Jimmy and I both saw that exchange of glances.

Sam pounced. "That cuts the possibilities to someone present in the office Friday morning." He ticked them off, one by one: "Brewster Layton, Lou Raymond, Anita Davis, Geraldine Jackson, Sharon King. It eliminates Rhoda Graham and Keith Porter."

"Exactly." Slowly but surely I was aiming Sam in the right direction.

He got his stubborn look. "You said Murray was scared when you talked to her this morning. If she knew who killed Graham, why did she let the killer in her apartment?"

"This morning Nancy knew the killer planted the gun, but the killer realized Nancy took the ring. Of course, Nancy was scared. But when the killer knocked on her door and said something like *Do you want the police to get a tip about the ring? If you claim you saw me, I'll say that's crazy, obviously an effort to pretend you didn't also leave the gun. Let me in and we'll work everything out.* Nancy felt she had no choice. They talked for a few minutes. The killer reassured Nancy. *Nothing to fear from me. Let's both forget last night ever happened.* The killer gets up to leave. Nancy's relieved. She walks toward the door, a little ahead of the killer. The killer strikes. After Nancy falls, the killer calls Megan, whispers, hangs up, then is out the door."

Sam again rubbed his knuckles against his chin. "Why didn't the killer hunt for the ring?"

"How long would it take—will it take—to find the ring? You can bet it isn't resting in that red plush case on top of the bedroom dresser. Sure, that would have been one choice. Find the ring, then no one would have had any idea why Murray was killed. The murderer is likely counting on the fact that no one is looking for the ring in Nancy's apartment. Besides, the murderer knows the text on Graham's cell phone set up Megan as suspect-in-chief. It was more important to tie Megan to the new murder than to worry about the ring."

Sam's phone rang. He grabbed the receiver. "Cobb." He listened, laughed. "Worth a wet hand. Thanks." He hung up, turned to me. "Smart kid. New officer. Found the ring taped to the bottom of the plunger in the toilet tank." He gave me a respectful nod. "What made you think Murray had the ring?"

My answer was sober. "She's dead. Why did she have to die? It could only be because she knew who the murderer was, and that's when I knew she'd been at the office last night. If she was at the office, she could have seen the person putting the gun in Megan's desk."

He tilted back a little in his chair. "A pretty nice scenario. But the mayor's going to push to arrest Wynn, especially since she showed up at the second murder."

"We'll arrest the killer before the mayor erupts." I was confident.

One grizzled black brow rose. "That's about as likely as me bowling a perfect strike tomorrow night. Saturday night's my bowling night. I'll cancel. It's going to take twenty-four/seven police legwork and even then we may not be any closer to a solution."

"Don't cancel. If all goes well, we'll have the answers by tomorrow afternoon." I could tell Sam I knew the identity of the murderer, but it would work out much better if he received confirmation the old-fashioned way, a rock-hard identification that couldn't be explained away. Moreover, I needed time between now and then to line up my ducks, as Bobby Mac used to say when he was courting investors for a well.

Sam was willing to follow my lead. Now, to give him the final push in the right direction. As Mama always said, "If a man thinks it's his idea, he'll fight to the death for it." "Tell me about the sock."

"The homemade blackjack?"

I nodded.

He was dismissive. "Like they say in the TV shows, *Move along, nothing to see here*. It was a man's black dress sock."

"I wonder if the sock was new?" It was as if the idea had just occurred to me.

"New?" His eyes narrowed. "I suppose a pretty savvy killer might worry about a residue of detergent. People wash socks, fold them up, toss them in a drawer. There might even be traces of DNA if the sock was handled after washing. I'll have the lab check. They can probably determine whether it had ever been washed."

My voice was diffident. "I don't suppose there was a brand name."

"Same brand I buy at Walmart."

"I wonder if they carry that brand at Target?"

Without answering, he heaved to his feet, walked to his desk, sat in his swivel chair. He swung to his computer, clicked, clicked, clicked.

I followed, perched on the edge of his desk.

He looked at me. "Walmart only." Now he was intrigued. "The killer," he said, thinking out loud, "didn't know until the gun was found in the office that anyone had any idea who put it there. When the murderer realized Murray knew, Murray had to die. But how?" He flexed his big hands. "What to use for a weapon? The gun was in police custody. We ran a check. It was stolen a couple of years ago, probably picked up at a garage sale or flea market. Anyway, here's the killer on Friday afternoon, determined to silence Murray. How? What could be bought and handled so that no fingerprints would ever show? A blunt instrument? How about dirt in a sock?" His voice oozed satisfaction. Then he frowned. "Why not go to a drawer and pick out a sock?" He was thinking out loud. "A man's dress sock. None of the women in the office have husbands. Anita Davis was widowed six years ago. Sharon King never married. Geraldine Davis is a three-time loser. Lou Raymond was widowed two years ago. Now, Brewster Layton—"

I was gentle. "There are socks and then there are socks. I doubt if Brewster Layton has ever walked into Walmart."

Sam's smile was grim. "Not unless it was yesterday afternoon. But he wouldn't use one of his own socks. For all I know they're imported from Italy. So, the killer needs a new sock. That means"— and now he was excited—"between the time everyone left the office yesterday and the murderer showed up at Murray's door, the murderer went to Walmart." He turned back to his monitor, clicked.

I slid off the desk, came up behind him to look over his shoulder. E-mail to Detectives Don Smith and Judy Weitz: *Get mug shots Brewster Layton, Anita Davis, Sharon King, Lou Raymond, Geraldine Jackson. Show photos to all cashiers, stockers, salesclerks, and greeters on duty at Walmart yesterday between noon and eight p.m. Proving any one of them was there will be a leg up. Any connection to the menswear department and men's socks would be gravy on the potatoes.*

I touched his shoulder. "Sam, that's brilliant."

He looked up, made an attempt at modesty. "Well, you got me to thinking about socks."

"Oh, but you figured out what must have happened."

He pumped his right fist. "This may make all the difference. Neva will have to listen to me. I may break the case all by myself. I can't wait to tell her."

Mama was right again. I smiled at him admiringly. "I can't wait to find out what you discover." I felt much like a cat seated by a bowl of cream. "I'll meet you here at three tomorrow afternoon."

I disappeared.

Chapter 15

Does anything smell better in the early morning than bacon cooking and coffee brewing? I waited in a booth with a large cup of coffee cradled in my hands. Lulu's bustles on Saturday mornings. Jimmy's designation of my favorite cafe as Geezer City had a basis in truth. Many breakfast customers were middle-aged to older men who clearly knew each other well. Hearty bursts of laughter punctuated the rumble of male voices resonant as stampeding elephants.

I was also pleased by the richness of my print jacket in lightweight linen, circlets of gold and silver against a creamy background. My slacks, I gazed down in approval, were a matching gold. My gold strap sandals were out of sight but quite perfect, thank you.

Jimmy slid into the booth and sat opposite me. He was Tahiti cool in a palm tree–splashed shirt and white trousers. "Pretty exciting at the *Gazette* last night. They'll be talking about the Phantom of the Newsroom for decades. I never thought I'd see Joan Crandall, my favorite jaded broad, with eyes like saucers and her hair practically standing on end."

My tone was reproving. "Jimmy."

He turned his slender hands palm up. "I had no choice. See"— and now he was earnest—"I got the stuff you wanted, chapter and verse." He pulled a sheet of paper from his pocket and slid it across the table. "Kind of an interesting chronology. But I thought the place was deserted. Joan's computer was still on but sometimes she likes to leave it running. The city editor would snarl about security, and Joan would clap her hands on her hips and ask who did he think was going to get into her files overnight—pixies or unicorns?—and if she had her choice she'd go with unicorns. Anyway, I got to work at her computer and I kind of like being there, you know what I mean?"

I did. Yes, indeed.

He smoothed his silk shirt. "I always wanted to go to the South Seas. So I was in the newsroom, just like I used to be. I even turned on the ceiling fans. Always kept me cool. I got what I needed and clicked Print and pushed back Joan's chair. I went over to the big printer in the corner, and I'm just scooping up the sheets when Joan yells out, she's got that raspy voice like a file against metal, 'Hey, who are you?'

"If I turned around, she'd know it was me. I disappeared. I still had the sheets in my hand. I wasn't going to leave those behind. There wasn't anything I could do about the file on the computer. I intended to delete it. Anyway, I'll bet Joanie's been up half the night trying to figure out what's what. I went up to the ceiling. Joan was standing in the middle of the newsroom watching the papers go overhead. She turned the color of my aunt's Siamese. I made it out to the hall. I was downstairs in a jiffy. It set off the alarm when I unlocked the front door. But"—and he was proud—"here's what you asked for."

The dark-haired waitress, thin, harried, and efficient, stopped at our booth. Jimmy ordered chocolate chip waffles with whipped cream and cherries, link sausage, and coffee. I opted for sausage, scrambled eggs verde, and grits. Coffee, of course.

He pointed at the sheets in front of me. "How can you use that?"

"This afternoon I'll give the dates to Sam Cobb. By then we may really be on the killer's trail." I brought him up to date on Walmart and mug shots. "There's one more thing that could make a huge difference. Do you think you can get Ginny Morse to talk?"

"I never met a woman I couldn't persuade." He spoke as a reporter noting an undisputed fact.

His confidence boosted mine. He could provide the last piece of real evidence. I sketched out what I hoped he could discover. "See what you can do. I'll meet you at the end of the pier at two thirty."

"Sounds hot and hotter. How about meeting at the picnic area under the big sycamore?"

"Excellent choice."

"Here come my waffl— Uh-oh." He was gone.

I turned to see Sam Cobb, in a rumpled blue suit. He wended his way around a clump of men and two tables, came up to the booth. "I could have sworn I saw somebody sitting with you."

"Sometimes"—my smile was bright—"we don't see what we don't see."

"May I join you?" He was already sliding in. "Young fellow," he said pleasantly. "He looked a lot like a reporter on the *Gazette*. He drowned last summer."

"May he rest in peace," I murmured.

Sam shot me a wry look. "I don't know that resting would suit him."

The waitress scarcely gave him a glance as she slapped down plates and coffee mugs, asked generally, "Anything else you need?"

Sam looked at the mound of whipped cream, studded with cherries and extra chocolate chips. "This should take care of me."

She was gone, hurrying to pick up the next order.

Sam studied the plate. "Claire put me on a diet. Says I need to lose twenty pounds. But it would've been bad manners to send the plate back, right? Kind of like not picking up pennies from Heaven." He spooned a scoop of the topping. "The whipped cream was made fresh this morning. Can't beat Lulu's."

I was well into my grits. "Heavenly," I agreed.

He added Lulu's homemade unsalted butter to a corner of his waffle. "I needed Lulu's this morning. Had a pretty late night. I was just about home when I got a call from the *Gazette*. I went straight there. Joan Crandall looked like she'd been to a séance, and it turned out not to be a joke. What really spooked her"—his gaze was questioning—"was finding a file open on her computer, a file she hadn't created. That and watching a sheet of paper propel itself along the ceiling and out the door. She said when she first came into the newsroom she thought she saw someone standing by the printer. She knew she was alone in the building except for the watchman, and he's almost seventy. She said she would have sworn she was seeing Jimmy Taylor, the young fellow I told you about. She called out and he was gone. Then this paper skimmed along up near the ceiling and out the newsroom door. She said she raced downstairs and the alarm was going off. When the dust settled, no one was found, and she said she wasn't about to tell the night watchman what she'd seen. By this time she's pretty frazzled but she goes up to her computer and finds the file. The minute she read it, she knew there was a connection to the murders, so she printed out a copy for me." He slipped his hand inside his suit jacket, pulled out a folded sheet, opened it, then reached out. His big hand closed over the sheet lying in front of my plate. He held the sheets side by side, read aloud:

October 17, 2013—Death notice for Marie Denise Layton, 58, wife of Brewster Layton

May 14, 2014—Lisbeth Carew assumes leadership of Black Gold Oil Company because of the illness of her husband, Edward Carew

September 18, 2014—Divorce granted between Rhoda Jones Graham and Douglas Warren Graham

October 17, 2014—Goddard senior Alison Terry killed in hit-and-run accident on Country Club Drive

October 20, 2014—Collision between Brewster Layton and Doug Graham on Country Club Drive

November 6, 2014—Death notice for Edward Chambers
Carew, 62

April 22, 2015—Death notice for Julie Marie Layton,
12, daughter of Brewster Layton and the late Marie
Denise Layton

July 23, 2015—Doug Graham shot to death

Sam looked at me quizzically. "I could wonder about the rumpus at the *Gazette*. Or mention that your sheet and mine are identical. But let's cut to the chase."

The old familiar dictum from famed silent film director Hal Roach, Sr., was still good advice.

I was equally crisp. "I needed the dates to be sure I was on the right track. Now I know what questions to ask. Detective Loy will report this afternoon at three. Oh, Sam, look behind you. I think I see——"

Lulu's was at the height of the morning crush, voices, laughter, every chair taken, people absorbed in breakfast and conversation. As Sam's head turned, I disappeared. I didn't think he'd mind picking up the check.

∽

The partially knitted raspberry afghan was still draped on the small sofa. Beyond the closed door, there was the sound of women's voices, the ringing of a phone, footsteps in the hall.

The knob turned. Rhoda Graham stepped inside, closed the door, looked at me with no warmth. She looked shrunken this morning, her long face drawn with fatigue, her slender shoulders bowed. Her dark hair with its distinctive silver streak was pulled back into a knot, emphasizing the thinness of her face.

I stood by the sofa. I was sure my turquoise wrap blouse, turquoise skirt with a shell print, and white leather slides with turquoise beaded straps spoke of summer and cheer. Though brisk, I made my voice warm. "I appreciate your willingness to speak with me."

Her dark eyes were cold. "Do I have a choice?"

"Absolutely. I am pleased to inform you that we have made great progress in solving the crimes—"

"Crimes?"

"Were you aware that the firm's paralegal, Nancy Murray, was murdered last night?"

Her eyes widened. Her lips parted. "Nancy killed?"

"The news was on TV this morning." I hadn't seen TV but I was quite sure this was true. "I can report to you that the search for her murderer and your former husband's murderer is now confined to firm members and staff."

"What happened to Nancy?" Her tone was hollow.

"She was bludgeoned to death in her apartment last night."

"Nancy . . ." She took a deep breath. "Someone in the office?" Her face creased in a puzzled frown. "Then why are you here?"

"You can provide information we need to know about your husband."

"I don't want to talk about Doug." Her tone was stiff.

"Unless you help us, Megan Wynn will be arrested for his murder and for the murder of Nancy Murray."

"That's absurd." Her retort was quick, definite, outraged. "I've known Nancy since she was a little girl. Her parents died in an accident and she came here and lived with her uncle. He passed away last year. Megan would have had no reason, no reason at all—"

"Right now all the evidence points to her. But we think your husband may have been having an affair with someone at the law—"

"Not Megan."

"Definitely not. But only you can tell us what happened with your husband before your divorce."

Silence hung between us.

I spoke slowly, emphatically. "Unless you help me, Megan Wynn will be arrested."

She walked to the small sofa, sank down, clutched the half-finished afghan. Her face remote, she looked at me with somber eyes. "What do you want to know?"

⁂

Shoppers thronged Walmart. I hovered above the aisles. The smell of fresh popcorn mingled with the scent of cologne. Customers clogged the checkout lines. A stressed clerk at checkout 5 tapped a speaker. "All checkers report to the front."

The heavyset woman at the register behind her gave a huff. "Lots of luck, honey. Something's going on. Chuck has half the checkers back in the break room and Agnes told me they'd called in everybody who worked yesterday from noon to eight, checkers, clerks, stockers, greeters, but I sure don't see them up here helping us."

I raced to the rear of the store, dairy cases to my right, camping equipment to the left. I passed a counter in a center hallway. It took only a moment to find the break room behind a door marked *Staff*

Only. All the chairs around a long table were taken. Another dozen people clustered at the end of the room.

Sam stood next to a portable whiteboard. Photographs were taped in alphabetical order: Anita Davis, Geraldine Jackson, Sharon King, Brewster Layton, Lou Raymond, Blaine Smith, Megan Wynn.

Blaine's photo on the whiteboard surprised me. But, of course, he had been present yesterday morning in the office. Also, Sam would avoid having the photograph of only one man.

Sam held a pointer in one beefy hand. ". . . carefully study these pictures. We believe one of these persons was present in your store yesterday between noon and eight p.m. If anyone recognizes—"

"Oh." A woman with cornflower blue eyes blinked several times. She lifted a thin hand and pointed. "I was on register one. It was about two thirty and I was going on break next."

A stocky woman with brassy hair in tight ringlets strode to the whiteboard. "It was so weird." She tapped a photograph. "That one was in menswear and used the corner of a Kleenex to pick up a package of socks."

༄

Jimmy's choice of the picnic area at White Deer Park was inspired. I sat on a table and squinted at the pier, starkly white and blazing hot in the afternoon sun. "Jimmy?"

The table was wooden and old. It creaked as he settled beside me. "Beautiful evening in Florence." He sounded mellow.

"Did you talk to Ginny Morse?" Sam had an identification from two Walmart employees, but I hoped Ginny Morse could add flesh to the bones.

"It took me a while to find her. She was shopping in Florence. The housekeeper told me she was visiting the linen shops. I found her in a boutique trying to decide between linen and damask. She asked my opinion. I guess stuffed shirt was on the golf course or maybe drinking wine. I pointed at one and she said, 'Of course. The damask is truly elegant.' I carried her parcel for her and we stopped at a trattoria for some vino. That lady likes—"

"Jimmy, did she *know* anything?"

"She wasn't going to admit anything, black or white or up or down. She said it was her policy to live and let live. I told her I wasn't the bed police, but she better understand that Megan Wynn was going to jail unless the Adelaide police discovered whether Graham was involved with somebody in the office. When she realized I was serious"—his voice was grim—"she got serious, too."

"Jimmy"—if he had been near enough I would have grabbed his shoulders and shaken him—"what did she say?"

"Chapter and verse. She jogs . . ."

I listened and then I smiled. If there is ever a true truism in a small town, it is this little phrase: *Someone will see you.*

⁓

I knew Jimmy was lounging comfortably on a corner of Sam's desk. He had agreed to remain unseen. He'd grinned, said, *Think two of us would spook him?* I doubted Sam would be bothered. After the excitement at the *Gazette* last night, he likely was quite certain of my unseen friend. My aim was to stave off the arrival of the Rescue Express until Megan was in the clear. Wiggins tolerated my appearing because he understood Sam preferred a presence with a voice, but Jimmy in his South Seas sport shirt and white slacks would distress Wiggins.

Sam hunched at his desk. A photo rested next to the two sheets of paper Sam had studied at Lulu's this morning. Sam drummed the fingers of his right hand on the desktop, flicked an impatient glance at the wall clock. It read ten minutes after three.

"I'm only a few minutes late, Sam." I appeared again in my turquoise blouse and skirt, brushed back a red curl stirred by the hot breeze off the lake, settled in the straight wooden chair facing him.

He tapped the photo. "I was going to give you five more minutes before I put out a pickup call."

As Mama always said, "When a man isn't headed in the right direction, help him change his mind of his own accord."

"That would be excellent. Or, as I've heard you say in the past"—this was creative license but I was sure Sam was a hunter and it is something he might well have said—"*Sometimes it's best to flush a bird without warning.* The murderer is unaware of what you know. There are more facts that will come as a terrible shock." I told Sam what Rhoda Grant revealed. He made quick notes. "And the very nice young man from the consulate in Florence spoke again with Ginny Morse."

Sam raised an eyebrow. "The very nice young man from the consulate in Florence?"

"Such a help," I murmured.

"You think Morse will give us a statement?"

"She understands Megan Wynn is in danger of arrest."

He nodded, clicked a button on his intercom. "Alma, get the cell number for Ginny Morse. ASAP."

"If the murderer is confronted without warning"—my tone was diffident—"the effect might be remarkable."

His eyes gleamed. He slammed a broad hand down on the desktop. "Yeah. No warning. Better not put out a pickup call. Get 'em all together." He was muttering to himself. "That's what I'll do. We'll contact them, inform them of Nancy Murray's murder, ask them to come to the law office at four o'clock."

He was now a man with a plan. His plan. Mama was right again.

⌒

The conference room at Layton, Graham, Morse and Morse also served as a law library. Large law books filled three floor-to-ceiling bookshelves. Four comfortable leather chairs sat on either side of a long oak table. Matching chairs were at either end. No doubt the room had often been witness to human drama, divorces, quarrelsome depositions, intense settlement conferences, the reading of wills. But perhaps Death had never before felt so near.

Sam Cobb, his large face impassive, stood behind an end chair. His navy blue suit jacket sagged but his heft and bulk were impressive. A somber Brewster Layton cupped his goatee in his right hand and stared at Sam. Lou Raymond's generous mouth puckered in uncertainty. Anita Jackson's plump face looked stricken and she held tight to the arms of her chair. Sharon King was pale and drawn, her lips pressed together, but her light brown hair was neatly brushed, her white blouse crisp, and her lime green linen slacks wrinkle free. Geraldine Jackson watched Sam, her gaze speculative. Her golden curls were loose and flowing today, which emphasized a face that held a road map of her past, late nights, men, bars, loneliness, and yearning. In contrast, Megan Wynn's face was young and open, but tight lines of anxiety reflected her uncertainty. She had to wonder whether she was truly free of suspicion or whether Sam Cobb had given that impression while continuing to pursue her. Blaine Smith sat next to Megan. He might have been a guard dog, watching out for his person. He was alert, ready to spring to her defense.

Sam glanced at Detective Judy Weitz, who sat at his left.

Judy reached out a firm hand and flicked on the recorder in front of her.

Sam cleared his throat. "Nancy Murray knew the identity of Doug Graham's killer. She knew because she broke into Graham's office Thursday night to steal the diamond ring."

There were sudden indrawn breaths, a murmur from the onlookers.

Sam spoke as if he had been there in the late-night hours. "As Nancy was leaving, she saw someone walk out of Megan Wynn's office. Murray remained quiet. The departing figure didn't see her. The next morning Murray understood that she had seen Doug Graham's murderer leave Megan Wynn's office after placing the murder weapon in Megan's desk. Unfortunately for Nancy Murray, the murderer realized Nancy knew and posed a danger. That's why Murray was struck down. But the motive that matters is the motive that led to Doug Graham's murder."

He folded his arms. "For that, we have to understand Doug Graham, who he was, how he treated others, what he valued. He grew up in Adelaide as a rich man's son until his father's dairy went bankrupt. One day he had everything, the next he was working at McDonald's. He took out student loans to get his undergraduate degree, more loans for law school. He married while he was in law school. Two children came. He worked long hours, always determined to get money, have money, spend money. Marriages succeed or fail for many different reasons. Sometimes a woman or man realizes a partner isn't someone they admire or respect. To Doug Graham, money and position were all that mattered. There wasn't time to go to sporting events or school programs, always work. There was the hunger for a big house, fine clothes, fancy office. The Graham marriage was in cold storage for the last few years. Rhoda Graham suspected her husband was having an affair, but she kept the marriage going to keep the family together. Doug Graham had seemed content with that status. Rhoda assumed Doug wasn't interested in marrying the other woman."

I watched a particular face. There was no change in expression.

Sam picked up the tempo. "Everything changed in May of 2014. On May 14, 2014, Lisbeth Carew announced the illness of her husband, Edward. Doug Graham had handled several matters for the Black Gold Oil Company and for Edward Carew. In late May, Doug asked Rhoda for a divorce. She agreed. The divorce was granted in September 2014. It's interesting to note that Doug made no move to marry his lover." Sam looked at Brewster Layton. "Your law firm has a well-known ironclad rule: No sexual dalliance between partners and employees."

Abruptly the room was utterly still. Lou Raymond looked toward Geraldine Jackson, jerked her gaze away.

Geraldine didn't miss the glance. Her face flushed. "That's a crock. I knew his kind. Silver tongue and a lying heart. I may have married a bunch of losers but they meant what they said." A bark of laughter. "At the time. They just never had staying power."

There were other covert glances at Geraldine. Brewster Layton's gaze narrowed. Anita Davis's lips parted in shock. Sharon King's lips tightened in distaste. Megan shook her head in disbelief. Blaine looked curious.

Geraldine heaved to her feet. "You can all go straight to hell. Like I said, I always knew Doug was a jerk. I never gave him the time of day—and don't think he didn't try."

"Sit down." Sam's deep voice was commanding.

Geraldine was breathing fast, but she slowly sank into the chair, her face flushed.

Sam held up a big hand. "Let me finish. When he was divorced, Graham persuaded the woman to keep quiet. Perhaps he said, *You can look for another job and then we'll wait a year. Everything will work out.* That wasn't the true reason. He got a divorce because Edward Carew was terminally ill and Lisbeth Carew was turning to him, finding support. He knew what he wanted. The Carew millions. That brings us to Thursday morning. Jack Sherman grabbed the velvet case from Graham's desk, held up the ring for everyone to see. Now everyone knew, including the woman who thought she was loved, but discovered she'd been betrayed. At some point in the morning, she accused him. He couldn't deny the ring, but he thought he could persuade her. Perhaps he thought she might share his greed. The Carew millions. They could meet as they always had. Think of the clothes and trips. She didn't answer, turned away. He knew he had to persuade her. He tried several different drafts of a note, finally composed one. She received the note. Perhaps she told him she'd talk to him tomorrow. But she had already made up her—"

"Who?" Brewster Layton's voice was steely with anger.

Sam nodded at Judy Weitz. "Play the recording from Virginia Morse."

The quality was scratchy, a cell phone connection in Italy. Ginny Morse spoke somberly. "This is Virginia Morse. I'm a long-distance runner. I train in early morning on the roads around Adelaide. I often run through White Deer Park, make a four-mile circle and end up coming back through the park on Archer Street. About three years ago I saw a garage door lift and recognized Doug Graham's car. I slowed down to be sure. He never noticed me. It happened four or five more times—"

A chair scooted back. Sharon King was on her feet, eyes staring, face parchment-white, hands held up before her as if warding off an attack. "That's a lie. It's all a lie—"

Detective Smith was standing by the door. He pulled it open, and a stocky woman with brassy hair edged inside.

Sam looked toward her. "Can you point out the woman who used a Kleenex to pick up a package of socks in the Walmart menswear department yesterday afternoon?"

The stocky woman, breathing rapidly, looked around the room. Her glance slid past matronly Lou Raymond, wide-eyed Anita Davis, red-faced Geraldine Jackson, tense Megan Wynn.

Her light eyes glittered. She lifted a broad hand and a stubby finger pointed.

Sharon King's delicate features twisted in despair. She took one step back, another.

Sam strode close to Sharon, looked down. "Doug Graham lied to you, didn't he?"

Tears trickled down Sharon's thin cheeks. "He told me he loved me."

Chapter 16

Jimmy and I followed Megan and Blaine to her apartment. Blaine petted the calico cat while Megan changed clothes. She came into the living room in a white top and pale blue linen shorts and matching blue flip-flops.

Blaine came to his feet and beamed. "I promised you a steak. I have a little patch of garden and I just harvested some corn. We'll have filets and corn on the cob and lift a glass of champagne to celebrate the launch of Smith and Wynn, the best attorneys-at-law in Pontotoc County."

She looked up with a tremulous smile. "I'd love to." There was no doubting her delight. Then she said hesitantly, "Do you mind if I stay with Mr. Layton until he finds someone to take Doug's place?"

"I wish you could be at our office"—he spoke with great proprietary pride—"tomorrow, but I know you want to help them out." They were hand in hand as the door shut behind them, taking with them eagerness and excitement and optimism.

"Want to bet he has a chef hat and apron?" Jimmy's tone was sardonic. "Sure he does. He's a dweeb. But"—reluctantly—"I have to like the guy. What do you want to bet he was an Eagle Scout?"

I stayed mum.

"I never made it past Tenderfoot. I didn't like chiggers. But you know what"—there was acceptance in his voice—"Megan will be okay."

"And now . . ." My tone was gentle. I was looking toward the corner of Megan's living room and the golden stairs curving into brilliance. I knew Jimmy was looking, too.

"Yeah." Suddenly he was upbeat. "I'll be up there in a sec. But first I want Megan to know it's all right. I'm going over to his place."

Jimmy was gone. So were the golden stairs.

I reached Blaine Smith's old-fashioned bungalow. There was no car in the drive. I circled the house. A gas grill sat near the back steps. Several wicker chairs looked inviting in the shade of a sycamore. His garden filled a good third of the small backyard. A stockade fence enclosed the yard.

Car doors slammed. Blaine's voice boomed. Megan's husky tone was excited, cheerful.

Was Jimmy inside the house?

I was in the living room as the front door opened.

". . . and I'll make the salad."

I had no sense Jimmy was near. I returned to the patio. The back door opened and Blaine hurried down the steps to the grill and lifted the lid, turned on the flame. In no time at all, he stood at the grill, tending to sizzling steaks.

Megan brought a tray with two slightly frosted tall glasses. "I found lemons and made some lemonade. We'll save our champagne for dessert. The table's all set."

Blaine looked over his shoulder, grinned. "We make a good team. The steaks are—"

Golden stairs rose near the sycamore, bright and shining, up and up.

Where was Jimmy?

Absorbed in each other, neither Blaine nor Megan saw the back door open for an instant. A small sack was lifted, taken inside, the door closed.

I hurried inside.

A rustic planked table was set for two in a small alcove near the kitchen.

The sack moved through the air, opened a few inches above a blue pottery plate. A Dove chocolate raspberry bar slowly descended, was placed directly in front of the plate. The sack moved across the table, opened again. A second bar was placed ever so precisely in front of the opposite plate.

"Jimmy"—there was a catch in my voice—"that's very sweet."

"Do you think Megan will understand?" His voice was anxious.

"She will understand perfectly."

The golden stairs rose in the corner of the room.

And then they were gone.

༄

The Rescue Express rocketed through the star-spangled sky, the whistle deep and commanding. I held to the railing of the caboose, welcomed the thrum of wheels on steel rails.

Wiggins's reddish brown hair sprigged from beneath the rim of his stiff cap. He patted my shoulder and harrumphed, always a means of pretending he wasn't touched. "Nice young man."

"Very nice." My voice was soft.

"Rather a coup on your part, Bailey Ruth. Although there were several instances when you were perhaps too much *in* the world. . . ."

I listened respectfully, but I was thinking of Jimmy as he took the golden steps two at a time on his way to the next great adventure.

5-26-17
26.00